I AM

Matthew Hubbard

To Barbara,
Thank you for reading!

Matthew
Hubbard

MP

I AM by Matthew Hubbard
Copyright © 2014 by Matthew Hubbard
Cover design by Zach Patton

Printed in the United States of America

First Edition, 2014

ISBN-13: 978-0692345085

ISBN-10: 0692345086

MHP

www.matthewdalehubbard.com

also by Matthew Hubbard

DROWNING

This book is dedicated to anyone who ever said I was not good enough. Because I am, I am, I am.

I was nineteen years old.
I was in my freshman year of college.
I was enthralled by the future.
I was no longer a virgin.

I was seventeen years old.
I was in my junior year of high school.
I was as clueless to who I was, just like everybody else.
I was kissed for the first time.

I was ten years old.
I was in my fourth year of elementary school.
I was excited to watch cartoons every afternoon.
I was sexually molested.

This is my story.

It is not the story of who I was.
It is the story of who **I am**.

I am persona non grata.

There is a haunting portrait of me hanging in our hallway. I was around six years old, and I'm sitting in a school desk. My arms are neatly folded in a pose. My hands are chubby little things with fingers haphazardly laced together in an embrace. No, I'm not smiling but grimacing rather. The photographer snapped the photo right when my mother stepped outside of the studio room. I didn't want her to go. I was scared she would leave me. Just like a child who gets lost in a grocery store.

That look has followed me throughout my childhood. It has always lurked in the shadows, surfacing when I least expected it. Just when I'd thought I was free from the fear in those little boy's eyes, the unexpected made itself known in the overly ornate mirror hanging in the living room. All I could focus on was *that* haunted look in my reflection as I slowly suffocated from lack of living.

It felt like an eternity rather than a mere four weeks since I donned the peculiarly shaped hat (mortarboard, I think they're called) along with the hideous gown that made me look like a singer in a church choir. I sat on a hard, metal chair for entirely way too long while the dean stumbled over the names of my fellow graduates (amid the gratuitous roars of "Hallelujah" from parents). I scampered across the stage when my name was called forth, stopping to shake hands with the man I had never once met during the four years spent in his esteemed institution, and then I took home the prize for all the hard work and countless hours of test preparation. Literally.

Yes, I graduated from college. Yes, I reached the goal I had set for myself. No, I did not go on to live happily ever after in the twisted fairytale of adulthood my professors had driven into my head. All the countless discussions in my classes had always revolved around the surefire promise of a job upon graduation. It had always been the positive, the guarantee of employment. Professors should be impartial and tell their students they won't always succeed, not that I'm being pessimistic. I firmly believe in rationalization. There's too much irrationality in life to be any other way.

I had to move back home, back under my parents' roof with my three younger siblings. It was the epitome of taking one step forward only to take two steps back.

Limbo.

There was no other way to describe it. I wasn't a child, yet I wasn't a functioning adult. I was caught in the middle, the in-between. It felt like some higher being pressed the pause button on the remote control of my life without having neither the decency nor the common courtesy to move his (or her) finger over three minuscule centimeters and at least press the button for slow motion.

It was in this movie still of a life I found myself sitting, watching my reflection while a Wednesday stretched into the evening hours. I could hear one of the aforementioned siblings out in the front yard running around and screaming like a crazed baboon. The enticing promise of summer vacation permeated the atmosphere, and my kid sister was reveling in it. She would be free in two days, and then the normal quietness of my day-to-day routine would be no more. Early onset migraine aches made themselves known upon this revelation. My damnedest was going to be tried to not have babysitting responsibilities.

The lack of affection for my own blood wasn't the case. I loved them as much as any older brother could.

However, the age gap prevented us from being as close as those Hollywood portrayals of sibling love.

Coming in at the closest to my age was Raleigh, and she was seventeen (we lived in completely different worlds). Next was Jackson, who was fifteen (same rules applied). Memphis, nine, was the youngest (acting like a crazed baboon was quite common in whatever world she lived in).

Yes, my parents named their offspring after cities. I didn't know why. Maybe there was some unfathomable meaning to it or maybe it was where we were conceived. Like I said, I didn't know and I didn't want to know. I was me—just me. I wasn't entirely sure what that meant, but I was trying my best to define it.

The reasoning behind my parents' actions was a mystery. However, I did know that life wasn't measured by the reasoning behind your actions or the choices you were faced with or the decisions you made based on those choices. To me, life was measured on whether you followed through with whatever you had decided to do. Were you able to walk the walk after talking the talk? All that mattered was whether or not you believed in yourself enough to follow through. Therefore, I would make my fourth trip to the grocery store for my mother tomorrow because that's what I did. I followed through.

The phrase "I feel like a stranger in my own home" came to mind as I waited in the living room while supper was being cooked. Raleigh could be heard through her bedroom door as she talked ninety miles-per-hour on the phone. Jackson was hidden away, and the sound of a spaceship's lasers echoed off the hardwood floor of the hallway. The baboon was still out in the front yard, making an awful lot of racket.

The 4 o'clock news program was wrapping up, and the weather girl made her final appearance to discuss the forecast. Her smile never faltered as she delivered the catastrophic update that it was supposed to rain this weekend. The official start of summer vacation for high school kids in the area would be dampened. Poetic irony was hilarious when it didn't have any effect on you.

Right on schedule, my dad arrived home from his management job at the electrical power plant. Supper was served based on his schedule. Like clockwork, my mom beckoned everyone to the dining room table.

Sure, we were a family, but we weren't what people were led to believe. We had money, but we weren't loaded. We held some family values, but they weren't held *that* high. Sometimes, people forgot my parents had four children. I was that "Oh, yeah..." child who was often overlooked and left out.

It wasn't because we looked nothing alike though. We each came with a variation of brown hair and green eyes. It was more so the fact my mother's picture perfect family was only perfect if I was cropped out of the photo. I blamed the church and Southern Baptist hypocrisy for their inane ability of conscious repression.

"But what would people think?" my mom said patronizingly, and I looked up from my plate. It was her go-to objection every single time something came up. She called it being concerned, and I called it like I saw it. A cop out.

"Who cares what people think?" Raleigh had to keep herself from shrieking. I could see her hands gripping the edge of her seat as she tried to control herself. "It's just a party."

My dad started to speak, but my mom cut him off. "A lot of bad things have happened *just* because of a party," she said indignantly. "Ain't that right, Troy?"

God, it was the same stunt she played when I was in high school. She would eventually let her to go to this supposed party. All the talk of opposition was just another coping mechanism so she wouldn't feel like a bad parent. Go figure.

"Charlotte, I don't see why we shouldn't—"

"Only on one condition, Troy," she interjected, and then turned to face Raleigh. "Your brother goes with you as a chaperone."

My dad turned his head downward and ate without so much as another word while everyone else looked toward Jackson. Hell, I even looked at him. Surely, she didn't mean me, did she? I was rarely brought up in the dinner conversation much less subjected to the responsibilities of being an older brother. Memphis, the baboon, looked skeptically from Jackson to me. She already knew where things were headed.

"If you really want to go," she added, "you are going to have to ask Phoenix if he will go with you."

Who saw that one coming? Not me, that's who. Raleigh and I aren't even close, not anymore. I don't think I've said more than a few words to her at a time since I had come home. She had been thirteen when I went off to college, and we missed out on bonding in those crucial years of teenagedom. Like she was going to be all "Hey big bro, will you take me to this party so Mom won't have a cow? Please? Pretty please?" Raleigh would either **(A)** not go to the party, or **(B)** sneak out…and probably get caught.

For the remainder of dinner, I sat there with perplexing thoughts as to why my mom would bring me into the confrontation. She probably wanted to give herself ease of mind but was covering it up with her want for me to feel included in the family. That was so *like* her. I looked over at my dad. He let out a sigh and looked up from his plate with a vacant expression. Our eyes met. He nodded his head and smiled a fake smile of reassurance, giving me a look that said, "You're the responsible one."

Can I just say what the fuck? Since when was I held in such high regards that they would feel safe with me in charge? Why were they ignoring the past and pretending as though I was Perfect Son No. 1?

Raleigh didn't so much as look at me with curiosity to see if I would agree to their conditions. I picked at my food, slowly disappearing back into the invisibility to which I had grown accustomed. I finished my meal without contributing to any further conversation and went upstairs, leaving the subject behind all together.

As my tired and weary feet carried me down the hallway, I bypassed my picture with the haunting look. That little boy's eyes bore into mine as the last memory of happiness from my childhood floated to the front of my mind. My mother and I were at the court house in town. She'd been in the process of renewing her driver's license when the clerk asked her if she wanted to be an organ donor. Before she could answer, I had started crying. "But momma," I had whimpered, "if you give your eyes away when you die, how will you see Jesus when you get to Heaven?" My mother had gotten down on one knee, given me one of those warm hugs that made everything better, and whispered into my ear the three magic words that made me feel loved, the words whose meaning have long since been forgotten.

How I have longed for that comfort, for everything to be better, for the way those words had felt against my ear. That was all I could think about as I slipped inside my room. The door closed with finality, shutting me off from the rest of them. If only it were that simple. It was as though my family was stuck in a verse of a song. The tension has been building and escalating in anticipation for the chorus, the breaking point, but it has yet to arrive with that harmonious symphony of everything coming together.

I had halfheartedly expected my parents to carry on in the same oblivious way as they'd had before I left for college, but the other half of my expectations wanted something...more. Maybe I hoped they would've surprised me by caring. Maybe they would look me in the eye and know—they would just *know* the things that I wanted to say, the things I was too afraid to say. Maybe they would be the parents I wished they were.

Instead, they have acted as if nothing had happened. How could they disregard the unspoken actualities that were always lurking in the corners of their perfect home? There was no way they could continue to pretend *it* didn't happen.

Ten years old. That's how old I was. I was a fourth grader at the local elementary school. It was amazing what trivial details I could remember from *that* day. We were adding fractions in math, and I completely sucked at it. Recess that day had been the most epic game of tag the school had ever seen, or so my classmates and I thought. If I thought really hard, I could still smell the playground combination of dirt and cookies.

Priorities didn't matter to me then. All I wanted to do was go home and watch cartoons. The homework assignment of fractions was of the purest evil imaginable, and it was the last thing on my mind. The bell sounded, declaring the school day to be over. I was a big boy, and big boys were allowed to walk home by themselves.

When I closed my eyes, I could still see the images burned into my mind. I had just passed the church, trying not to run down the sidewalk. "Running isn't what polite little boys do," my mother had scolded me time and time again. That was where my memory went fuzzy. Like someone pressed fast forward and all I could see were glimpses as the scene changed.

It had been a child's word against an adult's, and it didn't hold much power. At first, they claimed to believe me despite the circumstances—that was the word they used. Apparently, the "circumstances" hadn't added up or made sense. It was all played off as a misunderstanding and was kept quiet on the fact that I had *imagined* it, that I had *thought* it had happened.

It had been pretty fucked up parenting on their part. I hadn't imagined anything or needed to keep quiet about it. What I'd needed was to talk to someone. What I'd needed was someone to believe me, to just have faith in me. What I'd needed was someone to explain why it'd happened to me, to help me deal with being sexually molested.

Was it normal that a teenage boy couldn't masturbate without an avalanche of guilt tumbling down on top of him? Was it normal for one to have anxiety attacks when they found themselves in a sexual encounter? Was it normal for the fear of intimacy to hover above one's head like a storm cloud? I had been too scared to ask. It was like when the longer you keep quiet about something the harder it was to form the words in your mouth. I still didn't know, and I was still scared to ask.

Maybe things should just stay where they were—in the past.

I am shopping at Subterfuge Grocery.

Small town life was nothing like it was rumored to be. Sure, the eternal optimists tried to sugarcoat the fact that their lives were as boring as everyone else's by labeling the monotonous and the mundane with "small town charm," but that was like slapping lipstick on a pig and calling it a beauty queen. It was the same damn thing, the same damn people, and the same damn life around every same damn corner. Nothing was what it seemed. Nothing was what people made it out to be. Ever. Sulfur Springs was no different from any other small town in Alabama.

Sometimes, you got stuck behind a godforsaken tractor driving down the road at a mind-numbingly slow crawl of speed. You were just itching to pass the dumbass redneck. The steering wheel was gripped tightly as you veered across the median to see if you could, but you couldn't. It was always the same damn thing: either a car was coming or there was a curve up ahead and you couldn't tell if it was safe.

I was pretty sure some wiseass would say to count my blessings and take the time to enjoy the scenery. Easier said than done. The blessings were few and far between. Sure, the scenery was nice to look at, but the fumes from the tractor were enough to make you sicker than a dog. There were drawbacks to everything in life. Don't let anyone tell you any different.

The prayers I had been muttering under my breath were answered as I waited at a four-way stop. The tractor turned to the right. Halle-frickin'-lujah. Let heaven and nature sing. Kiss my ass. Blah, blah, blah.

The sudden knock on the driver's side window startled me, and I jumped sky high. An exuberant boy with frizzed red hair and a mouthful of braces smiled from ear to ear, motioning for me to power down the window. Right. Like that was going to happen.

He held up a box of doughnuts with "JESUS LOVES YOU" scrawled across the top in loopy cursive and questioningly nodded his head toward it. The last thing I wanted was to buy holy dough from someone I didn't know. He didn't even look all that trustworthy. I mean, it could be some kind of drug peddling scheme artfully disguised as a church fund raiser. I wouldn't put it past this shithole of a town. No, thanks.

Slowly and steadily, I reached and turned the radio up louder as he opened his mouth to speak. There was a good guess as to what he was going to say—probably some lame excuse explaining why he "needed" the money. Ignorance was bliss, so I blissfully ignored him and drove through the four-way with an apathetic foot of lead.

There wasn't any time to waste. Today was Thursday, and a grocery shopping trip was underway just like all prior Thursdays. What at first had started as a random visit had fallen into a routine due to the sheer simplicity of a simple-minded thrill. And so, the weekly torture was set to commence as I wheeled into the parking lot right at the usual time.

Miles stretched between the car and the automatic doors. The fiery sun bore down on the back of my neck as my feet followed the familiar path across the asphalt. A hazy heat distorted the air with its vertigo-inducing wave, and it looked as though the store front was melting. If only.

Timid footsteps led through the deceptive haze and across the barrier of the motion detector. A cool, conditioned gust swept hair out of my face as the doors effortlessly glided open. Deep breaths rattled through my lungs as I crossed over the threshold into something far more terrifying than any circle of any Hell ever imagined.

As I reached for a buggy, I noticed some of the store usuals living up to their name: the teenage cashier and bag boy were working their usual shift, and the old church ladies were taking their usual sweet time in the produce section just inside the doorway. Great.

Quickly, I pulled the more-so-wadded-than-folded list from my pocket and set off through the sea of clucking hens. I knew what was coming. It was expected. The lady who resembled an anti-loving grandmother, or Old Bitch No. 1 as I liked to call her, looked me over from head to toe. Her eyes were tiny buoys lost in a sea of wrinkles. Her saggy jawline quivered as she pursed her lips and asked, "Aren't you Ruth's boy?"

"I'm afraid not," I lied with a laugh on the inside. "I'm Wilma's son."

Last week I had told her my mother's name was Ruth, but she still proceeded to nod her head and buy what I was selling. Deceiving her was a little game I liked to play, and it was as easy as it had been when I first moved back. Besides, the old broad had it coming. She deserved a little befuddlement for the misery she'd caused me during elementary school.

A satisfactory smile stretched across my face as I pushed the buggy past the clucking church ladies and checked the list. The usual combination of vegetables and salad counterparts soon filled one of the conveniently placed bags that felt like it was made of material from another planet, and then it was time for Lisa in the meat section.

Lisa the Meat Specialist acquired the nickname for two reasons: **(1)** the most obvious being that she was a butcher, and **(2)** she sold dildos out of the trunk of her car. Times must be hard (no pun intended) if Lisa the Meat Specialist had to work two jobs in order to survive. Her business dealings on the side were not something most people knew about unless they were in the market for a good, self-pleasuring time, but I knew. No, I wasn't a loyal customer of the junk in Lisa's trunk. I just paid attention to the world around me.

"The usual?" she asked from across the counter with the smile of someone reveling in living a double life. Little did Lisa know that I was on to her, that I saw through her gimmick of a day job.

"Yes, ma'am," I said, returning her smile with an all-knowing edge.

None the wiser, she handed over the cuts of meat I had always bought and wished for me to have a good day. I wanted to reply and wish for her to have a *good* night, but I stopped myself. No matter the double entendre nature, social niceties would lead to socializing.

Working my way through the list, I wandered up and down the aisles on auto-pilot. Like it took *that* much brain power to follow instructions, no matter how hastily scribbled they were. Medial tasks were just another part of my life.

The usual people were sighted doing their usual routine of getting their usual groceries on a usual Thursday. There was the Holiness woman with the big ass bun on her head, the bored stock boy shelving canned food in a sluggish pace, and the indecisive old fart who always blocked the aisle as he analyzed different products with too much detail. The sad part was I had become one of them. I had slipped in a puddle of the usual. I had fallen out of the usual tree and hit every damn usual branch on the way down. I had lain down with the usual dogs and caught those proverbial fleas of usualness.

Then, there was unusual. The buggy wheels squeaked, squeaked, squeaked around the end cap and into the next aisle. There she stood, an element of change. I was the deer, and she the headlights. The bleached hair was a little too bleached. The tanned skin was a little too tanned. The tiny bikini top was a little too tiny.

I stopped abruptly, unsure of what to do. Who the hell was she? Better yet, why the hell was she in *my* grocery store? I wanted to go over to her and tell her that she wasn't supposed to be here, that she was not part of the routine.

She looked over her shoulder, her hair cascading down her back. Realizing my mouth was agape like some lowlife barbarian, I attempted to be nonchalant as I gripped the buggy handle until my knuckles turned white.

Eye contact was made, and she winked. She fucking winked and gave a "come and get me" grin. I mean, who does that to a complete stranger? Not me, that's who. After a dry swallowed gulp and fervent footsteps, my clenched fists loosened their grip.

The system had been thrown off balance by her, The Variant. The usual wasn't usual anymore, which was exactly what I wanted. I should be thankful, but change and I had our differences (i.e. I never got what I wanted or what I expected). Thanks for nothing, inevitable warrior of fate.

Composure fully reasserted itself, and focus zeroed in on finishing the list. Bread and cokes. Check and check.

As usual, there was only one cashier lane open. As usual, there were a good five people already waiting in line. As usual, I had to wait. Five minutes. Ten minutes. I begged yet again for someone to shoot me and end the misery.

Have you ever had one of those out-of-body experiences where you were there but you weren't all at the same time? I bet anything that the guy who had studied that theology got firsthand experience by waiting in line at a grocery store because...I was there, but then again I wasn't. I blinked, and the next thing I knew I was saddling the conveyor belt with the usual.

Beep. Beep. Beep.

The cashier dragged the canned food across the scanner in such a mind-numbingly slow pace my eye tensed in preparation to twitch. Her "MY NAME IS..." tag still declared her to be Rhiannon. That hadn't changed. She haphazardly slid the items down to be bagged, but the bag boy wasn't at his station. Through the storefront windows, he could be seen helping Old Bitch No. 1 carry groceries to her car. My patience was being put to the test.

"It sure has been a hot one," she said in an attempt to make small talk as she tossed a package of ground beef onto the accumulating pile. Like I cared enough about wanting to make acquaintances. I hate small talk. It was pointless and awkward. The thought of having to part my lips, inhale to speak, and then actually carry through with speaking depressed me.

The right side of my face pinched up in what I hoped resembled a polite smile while my head nodded once in agreement. She didn't catch my anti-social drift and kept right on with the chatter. Her brunette ponytail bounced animatedly as she kept adding to the pile of the yet to be bagged groceries.

She continued to sputter words to keep the conversation going. It was as it had been every week: she tried to strike up conversation, she parted those overly glossed lips in a coy smile, she dropped irrelevant tidbits about herself, and I did nothing. This weekly occurrence had become a tradition, something I could rely on to happen like clockwork. Why ruin it with a gesture of camaraderie against the summer heat?

The food continued to pile up as the incessant beep, beep, beep echoed between the words gushing forth from her mouth like a geyser erupting. A dull ache tinged around my temples and my palms grew sweaty. I closed my eyes and tried to focus on the meticulous drone of the AC filling the air with its bittersweet odor of coolness. Breathing deep, steady breaths, I peeked out from under an eyelid. Where was the damn bag boy?

A spasm shot through my right hand. I wanted to just reach out and bag everything myself, to stop the heap from growing into an epic proportion; however, hesitation stopped me. It was the bag boy's job to bag the goddamned groceries, not mine. He should be entitled to do what he was hired to do. My fingers impatiently tapped against my thigh as I waited.

Finally, the whir of automatic doors sounded as they glided to an open. I let out an audible sigh as the boy came galloping inside like a dog returning from fetching a stick. I looked at him pointedly, and then I cut my eyes to the Himalayan mountain range awaiting his expertise. He gave a goofy grin that promised all was right in the world and murmured an incoherent form of greeting before he began doing what he should've already done.

"Now, is this going to be cash or credit?" she asked, drawing my attention back to her. Those sticky, shiny lips turned up to reveal a saccharine smile of bleached whiteness. Like she didn't already know. I had the bank card already out and waiting to be violated by the reader.

Her question didn't deserve an answer. I took the card and swiped it, holding my breath. Effortlessly, it slipped through the slot with a reverberating click akin to a lock locking. No scream. No cry of outrage from the checking account. The screen blazed to life with those reliable words as it had always done:

ENTER YOUR SECRET CODE.

It was this moment right here that kept me coming back to this stupid, fucking grocery store. I felt like a secret agent disposed in covert affairs. I felt like a spy bound in a clandestine battle for superior intelligence. I felt like an alternate life washed over me as I keyed in my code.

Call me whatever you will, just don't blow my cover. I was an espionage provocateur. Did I accept my mission? Yes. I pressed the enter key. "Here you go," the civilian said, holding out the receipt. Into my hands, I took the most fragile, detailed instructions. Civilian No. 2 had unknowingly laden what looked like your average buggy with bags of supplies. Keeping up appearances, I pushed ahead to the next phase of my assignment.

The whir of the gliding doors was the last thing I heard before the bubble of bittersweet AC burst. A rush of heat straight from the devil's armpit smacked me in the face. I crossed the threshold and stepped out into the humid, summer day. I didn't look back. I knew everything would still be there next week. I could count on it.

I am cast as the lead in Celibacy & the Suburbs.

"Phoenix!"

The screech of my mom's voice was as disheartening as the sound of a clock's alarm. Through an eye glued shut by sleep, my room tilted sideways. Arms and legs were both slow and unaware of the fact my brain was awake. They both refused to answer the urge to move.

A loud knock sounded on the door, and then it opened. My mom popped her head inside with perkiness. "Hun, are you awake?" she asked sweetly, which was always foreboding. I responded with an incoherent grunt. "Could you do me a favor?"

Could was the key word. *Would* would've been better suited. I lay there with my eyes closed, mulling over the answer to her question. I gave a half-grunt, half-groan reply.

"Would you pick your brother and sisters up from school for me?" She continued before I could answer. Spans of silence seemed to make her antsy, and she filled the void with her own voice. "I don't want them to have to walk home in the rain."

Karma went by many pseudonyms, and Poetic Irony was one of them. Regardless of the fact, it was still a bitch. It took all the energy I could gather from the depths of my still sleepy soul to open my mouth and agree to do her biding. Why? I didn't know.

It was almost noon. Leave it to my mom to wait until the last minute to ask me to do her a favor, thus pushing me straight out of bed and through the door into the rain with nothing more than gym shorts and a tank top. The disarray of bedhead was the cherry on top of the shitty morning sundae. Correction: karma was a *fucking* bitch.

The rain pitter-pattered against the top of the SUV as I drove through town. Don't let the fancy gas-guzzler fool you. My parents bought it for me back when their definition of "keeping up appearances" differed greatly from the present day interpretation of being conservative and eco-friendly. It had been their way of "making up" for the past. Whatever.

The pitter-patter was hypnotizing, and it lulled me into a semiconscious state of thought. My life had been enjoyable when I *actually* had one. I had friends (well, they were more so acquaintances) and was always on the go. I'd always had plans.

The me I used to be: I took a hell of a lot of shots in five minutes and mooned everyone before collapsing into the bathtub in a fit of laughter (that night was a blacked-out blur), I performed a horrendous rendition of a country song at a karaoke bar (completely sober none the less), I participated in No Shave November (I discovered I looked good with facial hair), I even got stoned (for the first time) with four complete strangers.

A month ago, my life had been somewhat eventful. Things weren't always good or the best, but at least I had a reason to get up in the morning. 4 weeks/28 days/672 hours later, I was waiting in the pouring down rain like some damn chauffeur. My life painstakingly changed from being a fancy-schmancy television dramedy that was broadcasted nationwide into a knock-off called *Celibacy & the Suburbs*, which aired on the local channels in the dead hours after midnight. True story.

Right on cue, the sickly sweet smell of summer rain filled my nose as the drivees requiring my chauffeuring services yanked the doors open in their haste to take cover from the cats and dogs falling from the sky. Jackson decided to ride shotgun, while Memphis and Raleigh clambered in the back. However, there was an unforeseen plot twist. Dun-dun-dun. The too bleached, too tanned Variant slid into the backseat. Of course, it would be none other than her.

"Terri needs a ride home," Raleigh said without looking at me. She knew I would go along. Like I was going to tell her friend to kindly exit the vehicle, that there was no room for her variance?

A shoulder shrug got the point across that I didn't care. Raleigh started chattering mindlessly with Terri the Variant as I pulled out of the school parking lot. Jackson was silent, staring contemplatively out the window. Memphis met my gaze through the rearview mirror and rolled her eyes, jabbing a thumb toward the chatterboxes. She understood me more than anyone.

Raleigh told Terri to shut up, and then there was the hiss of enthusiastic whispers. A little, dainty "humph" of a throat being cleared cut a path through the silence. "Sooooo," Terri said loudly with a strong twang as if she were about to whip out a banjo and sing a ballad.

"Terri, this is Phoenix," Raleigh said in a monotone, not wanting to play along.

And so, the scene unfolded…

the shot fades in on a rainy day
*SUV driving down the street *
switch to the interior of the SUV
Variant: I didn't know there was an older brother.
Little Sister: He's been away at college.

26

Variant: Ohhhhh! He's a college man.

Little Sister: Whatever

—older brother fails to comment—

Variant: Single?

[shoots a scrutinizing stare to the driver's seat]

Little Sister: More than likely.

—older brother fails to comment—

Variant: Invite him to the party.

Little Sister: Shut up—

Variant: C'mon Ral! I think he should.

Little Sister: Whatever.

[rolls eyes]

—older brother fails to comment—

tense silence settles around the passengers

SUV slows to a stop

Variant: I'll talk to ya later.

Little Sister: See ya.

Variant: Thanks for the ride.

—older brother fails to comment—

cue foreshowing music

end scene

As soon as the SUV rolled into the driveway, they bolted quick, fast, and in a hurry. I was left sitting there alone. Like always. If not for the radio playing the same damn song they had every hour on the hour, I would've stayed in my seat and enjoyed the isolation. It wasn't like I had anything else better to do, but I went inside anyway.

Through the rain, through the front door, across the living room, and up the stairs I went. It was Friday, and it was the start of summer vacation. Neither of those two facts meant anything to me. Not anymore. Fridays had lost their air of specialness a long time ago, and summer vacation no longer applied to an ex-student.

Figuring I should at least attempt something productive besides the usual moping around and reading a book type of scene in which I usually starred, I decided to further my quest for employment. As easy as 1-2-3, the laptop was powered on with the internet browser launched. If only the job market was as simple. And life wasn't so boring.

I searched the most frequented job sites, and then I searched the less frequented job sites. I even did repeat searches in naïve hopes something might've been overlooked. Overwhelming feelings of inadequacy slowly sank their teeth into their favorite meal—my ego. A mumble of "hell fire" slipped out (which sounded more like "hell far" due to an accent that only thickened when fueled by agitation).

With a click, the millionth job application loaded onto the screen. It was funny how your list of expectations as to what form of employment you wanted drastically changed as time progressed (sarcasm). It was a little something called desperation, and it smelled like a dream dried-up in the sun.

College was beginning to feel like it had been a waste of time and money. Four years spent toward a degree in English Language Arts...for what? Not a damn thing. Pacification blurred with satisfaction in regards to working at a fucking department store. Life had a dry sense of humor like that.

With a final click, my soul died a little. I stood a chance of getting a lame-ass retail job. Softly, I closed the laptop. I couldn't bear the potential humiliation any longer than what I had.

The timid knock on the door was welcomed. Anything for the chance of distraction, for a change of scenery.

begin scene
little sister shyly enters her older brother's room
Little Sister: Um...hi.
Big Brother: Hi.
Little Sister: So...how's it going?
Big Brother: Fine.
Little Sister: Good...that's good.
Big Brother: Was there anything in particular you wanted? [looks pointedly at her]
Little Sister: No...I just wanted to say, um, thanks for taking her home.

[avoids his gaze]

Big Brother: Ok.

[shrugs shoulders]

Little Sister: Seriously, she wants you to come to the party tomorrow.

[turns from him]

Big Brother: Oh?

Little Sister: Yup.

awkward silence

Little Sister: So…will you go?

Big Brother: Do you want me to go?

Little Sister: I mean…if you want to.

Big Brother: I'll think about it.

cue sappy music

close up of little sister biting her lip

Little Sister: Please?

Big Brother: I guess…I guess I could.

[knits eyebrows together in thought]

Little Sister: Ok.

[looks relieved]

Big Brother: Ok.

Little sister exits the room

Close up of the puzzled look on the older brother's face

fade out

Voiceover announcer: Tune in next week to see what sorts of remotely uninteresting things will happen on an

all new, all boring episode of Celibacy and the Suburbs! Check your local listings!
roll credits

Despite the brevity, it had been the first time in a long time my sister and I had actually carried on a conversation. A touch of sadness settled over me. It was my fault that we weren't close anymore. I was to blame for the distance that had grown between us, all of us.

A dog's barking shifted attention from the bedroom door to the window, and I peered out into the world. The elderly lady next door ambled down the steps of her back porch. A smile was at home on her weathered face as the dog excitedly danced around with a stick in its mouth. The dog was new. It had to be. I would've remembered otherwise.

Of all things I remembered about living in this house, the most prominent was the jealous twinge I had always felt toward my brother and sisters. They grew up in this house, but not me. Back when I was the experimental child and there was only three in our family, we lived elsewhere. I had a different room, a different window, a different view of the world.

Not that it mattered, but part of me wished I had that one view as they'd had. They could look out their window as they had always done and know what would be there. The perception of place and time was tied to that view. Childhood memories were related to that one, specific view. Mine were not.

It felt like a part of me was missing, like a part of me was still a child looking out his bedroom window in a house where I didn't live, in a house where nobody was home. I was separate from those childhood memories. I was living in two different times. I was living with two different views of the world.

Change was always prevalent, always happening with or without your consent. I would have to adjust to it just like I was going to have to adjust to the dog's presence outside my bedroom window. As much as I despised change, I couldn't help but to appreciate it. Change was life's way of presenting an opportunity to start over, to let things go. You just had to be willing to meet it halfway.

I am a social pariah.

I was lost in a sea of raging hormones, and I was getting seasick. High school kids were so stupid in thinking that getting a bunch of people together, tapping a keg, and having loud music made for a *real* party. Sure, the same viable key ingredients were called for, but it wasn't the same. Partying for the sake of partying just went to show how old they were.

These wannabes didn't know the definition of the word. They would not fully grasp what it meant to "party" until they were beyond stressed out from the piles of accumulating homework, studying for tests, and (insert any fundamental college requirement here). Don't get me wrong. There were those exceptions of collegiate students who party non-stop, but they didn't matter. More than likely, they'd never amount to anything unless their parents had connections or if they knew how to kiss a hell of a lot of ass.

Yeah, people always wanted you to believe they got as far as they did solely on merit alone, but I bet their lips have grazed more ass cheeks than you'd think. Wasn't it a shame how far you climbed on that ladder of success was directly proportional to how much *derrière* you were willing to kiss? I should've puckered up more often.

Half of these kids were plastered and making complete fools out of themselves. Ten bucks said most of these drunken idiots would be hung over and sitting on the last pew in church come tomorrow morning. What a nice batch of hypocrites this generation was.

Raleigh had ditched me as soon as she'd stepped foot out of the car. As much as I would've liked to return the favor, I couldn't bring myself to do it. Instead, I blossomed into a flower and perched upon the wall in a dark corner of a stranger's living room.

My roots planted me into place as I watched the train wreck unfold. Raleigh was nowhere to be found, and part of me was worried about her drinking underage. Like I was going to stop her if I saw her. It'd be the pot not only calling the kettle black but also pointing out they both held water, were used to heat things up, etcetera.

I've been drunk more times than I could remember. I've woken up with bite marks, bruises, and carpet burns. More blacked-out blurs took up residence in my memory than actual memories. The two day stretch most people referred to as the weekend was a black hole reoccurring every five days.

With the past aside, I sure as hell wasn't going to partake in the festivities. My body had come to appreciate my having full control over it, especially in this hell hole infused with country music. Watching was almost as fun as participating, and memories were included.

My eardrums were .0295 seconds away from slaughtering my brain if they had to put up with the dull roar any longer. The strobe light flashes of a camera were forcing my retinas into cahoots with my ears. If I didn't leave soon, there'd be a catastrophic, self-induced meltdown of epic proportions.

The camera happy photographer was documenting every elicit detail of the party. So many people were not only throwing up deuces but also doing duckface that I felt like I was on a damn farm. E-I-E-I-O...with a duckface here and a duckface there. Here a duckface. There a duckface. Everywhere a dumbass. I mean, did they even realize how incredibly stupid they looked? What a bunch of pathetic wannabes.

I was squeezing past people and trying to keep the body contact to a minimal at best when a heavily intoxicated Terri the Variant grasped onto my forearm in an attempt to get my attention. Like her shouting my name wasn't enough to cause a scene. Her breath could've peeled the paint off the walls, and it nauseated me to no end. That combined with the sickening headache waged by my two allied senses was enough to put me on edge.

"Ohmigawd," she said with a burp, and I involuntarily flinched with repulsion. "Youuuu are soooo dadguuuum cuuuute." Her words were drunken thoughts, and I wasn't about to buy into them.

Two out of five senses were in rebellion. The remaining three were drastically close to throwing in the towel. My tolerance level was just shy of its maximum. I loosened her grip on my arm and made an effort to move around her.

"Dance wiff me," she slurred as she grabbed at me, attempting to do a two-step that looked more like a trip-stumble.

The flashes, the blaring music, the smell of rancid breath, everything was all too much. All I wanted was to breathe some fresh air and clear my head. Was that too much to ask for?

Terri the Variant imposed her ways of variance once again as she groped me. She fucking groped at my crotch. Hell no. I couldn't...I couldn't handle unexpected touching. I just couldn't. It was like this personal space issue I had or something.

The harsh, intrusive flash of a camera went off in my face. I shielded my eyes and pushed my way through the crowed. It felt like an elephant was sitting on my chest. I had to get out of there before my lungs were crushed underneath its massive weight.

In the blink of an eye, I was outside and the kitchen door was swinging shut. A sudden intake of cool, night air cleared my head. Hostile senses receded from the frontline, leaving a minuscule migraine in their wake.

"Who goes there?" A male voice called out from the backyard. "Friend or foe?"

Squinting didn't do a lick of good. It was too dark to make anything out. A brief snippet of incoherent music echoed into the night, and then the kitchen door slammed shut again.

"Lookie here," said a familiar girl's voice. "It's Mr. T."

Mr. T? What the hell? Everything was happening so fast. Like the momentum from the party had swelled and spewed and burst forth, leaking into the summer night. She walked right by me and into the darkened backyard. Temptation ordered me to follow, but rationalization issued caution.

"Well, I'll be damned if it isn't!" exclaimed the guy's voice.

"Don't stand there looking like a fucktard," the girl said. "Come on if you're coming."

Seemed like a foolproof invitation to me, and I foolishly followed her. It was the first time in a long time that curiosity had gotten the better of me. Her footsteps led me to a table underneath a massive tree from where the male voice had emanated.

The sight of the girl and boy together jogged my memory. *You're the cashier girl and you're the bag boy*, I said in my head with that "aha!" moment of finally putting everything into perspective and having it make sense. I must've said it aloud without realizing it because they looked at me as if I had a few screws lose or some shit.

"And, you're Thursday's usual," the bag boy said with this tone of pretension. "Always there like clockwork. Seldom friendly. Never lets me do my job and help take the groceries to the car."

Flabbergasted. That was the most suitable adjective for how I felt. Completely flabbergasted. This guy was always smiling with that "everything's going be A-OK" attitude, but evidently that had been a façade.

"Dude, would it kill you to be, like, I don't know…polite every once in a while?" the girl asked with sarcasm.

My thoughts had bypassed the proverbial filter and darted to my tongue as I experienced word vomit of the tactless kind. "You know you could speed up the checkout line a little. You're as slow as Christmas," I blurted, and then I turned toward him. "As for you, would it kill you to, I don't know, actually do your job instead of dicking around?"

Emotions flitted across their faces. I was prepared for the worst, but the bag boy's face broke into a grin. He let out a loud crack of laughter that shook the night, and the girl followed suit with a trill of disbelief and intrigue.

"You're all right, Mr. T," he said, shaking his head from side to side. "Have a seat."

Not the response I had been expecting, that was for sure. Tentatively, I eased into an opposite seat and tried to make sense of the two abnormal human beings in front of me. I never really paid attention to them in general. All I had seen was their uniform. The girl was pretty. Much prettier than my previous assessment of a brunette with shiny lip gloss. Her dark eyes seemed to match her hair like the perfect accessory to complete an outfit. I couldn't picture the usual "fetching dog" attribute for the bag boy anymore, not after he shattered my perception of him. Even when sitting down, he looked tall. He was her opposite, the yin to her yang. His hair was lighter as well as his eyes.

"I'm Ackerley Dean," He introduced, motioning to himself, "and this is Rhi Moreno. Who might you be?"

"Phoenix."

39

"What a peculiar name." Ackerley looked down the bridge of his nose.

Funny thing was that I could have said the same damn thing to him, but I had something most people referred to as manners.

"What's your story, kid?" he asked.

"What?" I rolled the word "kid" around in my mouth with bitterness.

"Did you just move here?" Rhi asked. She laced her hands together and leaned forward on the edge of her seat as though she were conducting an interview with the new kid in town. Hilarious.

"I moved here about a month ago," I answered, throwing caution to the wind.

"What brings you to this little soirée of Sulfur Springs' crème de la crème?" He rested his elbow on the table in a bored, nonchalant gesture.

"How do you know Norm the Storm?" She arched her eyebrows, punctuating the question with skepticism.

"Who?"

"This is Norm's house. He's the quarterback of the football team, which is why he is called 'The Storm' — "

"I don't know why they call him that," Ackerley cut her off. "He's nothing more than a little drizzle."

"He thinks he's hot shit." She tilted her had back and forced a short-lived laugh. "In fact, he's nothing but a cold turd on a piece of white bread."

Ackerley's lip curled with disgust, and his eyelids fluttered as he cocked his head to look at her. "Seriously, Rhi? Seriously? I think I could have gone my entire life without hearing that."

"Hey, it's something my grandma always says." She shrugged her shoulders.

There was a moment of silence as words went unspoken between the two of them. Their "hey, we're cool so let's speak in witty phrases" felt like overkill. Why did they have to try so hard? Seizing the perfect opportunity to shift the focus off of me, I decided to call them out.

"If you both despise this guy, then why the hell are you here?" I'd like to see them try to navigate that answer with clever witticism.

"Oh, we have our reasons," he said as a mischievous smile played on his lips.

Rhi held up the camera as if it were the Holy Grail. She cut her eyes toward me and winked. "We most certainly do have our reasons. If it wasn't for the sweet, sweet taste of vengeance, then we sure as hell wouldn't be here."

"I, for one, would much rather watch grass grow. I've seen writing on bathroom stalls with more depth than all of those vapid dimwits combined." He waved a hand toward the house. "Speaking of which, did you get the goods?" he asked, raising his eyebrows as he nodded at the camera.

"You bet your sweet ass I did."

"Excellent." He rubbed his hands together like a mad scientist. Any second now, I was expecting him to yell for Igor to throw the switch.

"It's only day one, and we're already off to a good start." She smiled smugly, standing up and grabbing the camera off the table with delicacy.

Ackerley took her lead and rose from his chair. More unspoken words drifted between the two of them, and then they both suddenly cocked their heads and looked at me. Their precise timing was kind of creepy, not going to lie.

"Sorry to leave you hanging, new kid," she began, "but my business associate and I have important items on our agenda to take care of."

"It has been real, and it has been fun," he said.

"But it hasn't been real fun."

"We're off like a prom dress."

With that being said, Ackerley turned on his heels and set off across the yard as Rhi followed him. I watched them go as I tried to process the oddity that I'd just witnessed. Sure, they spoke in cinematic phrases, but somehow it worked. It felt natural for them to do so.

Maybe they were the type of people that television characters were based on.

Right before they rounded the corner of the house, Ackerley turned over his shoulder and hollered, "See ya Thursday, Mr. T."

They vanished as though they were figments of my imagination. Like I had imagined the whole odd scene in my head. Trust me, I wouldn't put it past myself. Either those were two of the most interesting people I've met in long time or I didn't get out much. It could very well be the latter.

I am looking at the world through a kaleidoscope.

Mondays are the most despised day of the week. If you were feeling down, then you had a case of the "Mondays." If you were grumpy and in a mood most foul, the blame went on Monday. If you only lived for the weekends, then Monday was the cause of your social life's demise.

Today was different. Maybe it was the thrill of summer vacation filling the air with its excitement. Maybe it was the reason why I was dressed in khakis, a button-up shirt, and those stretchy socks that were always cool to the touch when you put them on but hot and sticky when you took them off.

Getting dressed up had its perks. Being all professional looking was a vacation from the sweats and a t-shirt style that had become my wardrobe of choice. I felt...pretty damn good about myself.

Everything was brighter and not so disheartening on days such as these. The sunshine was welcoming and friendly, and you paused to let it warm your face before getting into the car. The same song that the radio played repeatedly didn't annoy the hell out of you; in fact, you found yourself singing along. Traffic wasn't as nightmarish as anticipated, and you took the time to be courteous by letting someone pull out in front of you. The past stayed in the past, becoming separate from the present. You saw the world through a different perspective. It was like you were looking at the world through a kaleidoscope.

No case of the "Mondays" here. I was practically whistlin' Dixie as I took the stairs two at a time. Being all chipper and sprightly felt kind of nice. The intimidating, brooding expression usually in place seemed to lessen as I pushed through the glass doors into the air conditioned building, but then the receptionist snidely asked how she may assist me in such a way that suggested she wouldn't so much as piss on me if I were on fire.

"I'm here for the job interview," I said, pronouncing each word with precision. After all, I was proud of potentially having a job.

"You and four other people," she retorted in a monotone. Clearly, her Monday wasn't as appreciable as mine. It was also quite clear she was a bitch.

I took a seat with the four other job seekers, and then awkward silence made itself known. What were you supposed to say in situations like that? Sure, you could pretend to be nice and smile and comment on the weather. All that small talk was fake as hell. I just didn't see the point in it. We all knew there were basically three possibilities as to what the others were thinking: *I hope one of them screws up* or *I am better qualified for this position* or *I deserve this job more than the next person.*

Sharp clicks of high heels echoed down the hallway, drawing nearer and nearer. The door to the left of the receptionist's desk swung open, and then a lady appeared. She was short, which I guess explained her reasoning for the heels, and she was plump. The fabric of the dress she was wearing was stretched tautly around her midsection, making her to appear plumper altogether (I bet she thought it was flattering, but no). Hair that color wasn't natural. It was cut short in some modern way of styling that she evidently didn't know how to manage. She was trying too hard. What was the point in trying to be something you weren't when the whole world could tell who you were under the disguise?

"I am Ms. Wetherell. Follow me," she ordered, wearing her authority on her sleeve.

Left. Left. Left, right, left. We marched down the hallway, our footsteps syncing with the sharp clicks of

46

her heels. "Due to time restraints, we will be conducting this interview in a group setting," Ms. Wetherell matter-of-factly informed. Like we were in any position to object. She pushed on through a door with an overhead label reading "Conference Room" without pause. We crossed the threshold, leaving behind our freedom. We were now prisoners of unemployment warfare.

A firing squad of colleagues were awaiting us, poised and ready at the will as we were lined up in front of them. Formalities were cast aside in haste as their fingers embraced the triggers without warning. Ready! Aim! Fire! I was the first victim.

Bullet #1: What's your name?
- *Phoenix Harper.*

Bullet #2: Tell us something about yourself?
- *I just graduated college.*

Bullet #3: Why did you apply for this job?
- *I was qualified.*

Bullet #4: Why do you think you'd be the best fit for this job?
- *It's what I went to school for.*

Bullet #5: What are your expectations in relation to the job at hand?
- *To do the job to the best of my capabilities.*

They reloaded as my ego slid to the floor, confidence bleeding out a puddle of esteem. There went the a-typical start of the week I'd been having. How could I have forgotten Mondays were notorious pranksters?

Ready! Aim! Fire! The same questions shot forth again and again, but everything was different. Victims No. 2, 3, 4, and 5 had learned by my example. They were ready with a bulletproof ego. My fellow job-seeking compatriots were just as fake as everybody else. They orchestrated extravagant answers, which put mine to shame. They put too much effort into trying too hard while I lay bleeding on the floor. "Fuck you" was all I had to say to them.

Fuck. You.

I picked myself up, dusted myself off, and licked my wounds. The day wasn't as friendly as previously conceived. The sun cast down an immense heat, causing perspiration to bead up and dampen the back of my head. The air conditioner was on, but it just didn't feel like it was enough. That was the feeling I hated the most. Having something that didn't feel like it was enough sure as hell weighed your spirit down with a leaden weight, anchoring you into place on the outskirts of satisfaction. That was the problem with kaleidoscopes—one twist by the hand of fate caused the whole picture to distort and change right before your very eyes.

The same stupid song that was played on the hour every hour came on (again), and I turned the radio off. I was still sweating like a whore in church, and the air didn't feel very conditioned. The windows powered down, letting in a stifling wave of humidity in the wind. At least it gave a somewhat cooling effect. Small town traffic was more nightmarish than I could've ever imagined, and road rage spread throughout my veins. Taking the side roads was the best remedy for the situation.

Despite the whole town of Sulfur Springs being scenic, the side roads were the scenic route. There were quaint houses, as my mother happily called them, and lush, again my mother's adjective of choice, gardens on every block. The people always tried to achieve a postcard effect, showcasing not only their homes but also their lives to be perfect. In all the years I'd spent growing up in this town nothing had changed at all. It was the same ol' shit with fake people carrying on their fake lives with fake intentions.

The same block of houses. The same church. The same sidewalk where I tried my best not to run. The same time of day. Déjà vu overpowered me with its familiarity. I slowed to a stop and looked out from the window. It was as though I had come up on a car accident. I didn't want to look, but then I couldn't look away.

It felt like they were someone else's memories instead of mine. It felt like I was looking into the window of a house where no one called home. It felt like a part of me was gone and would never come back.

"What are the odds of me seeing you here?"

The sudden appearance of a voice other than the one in my head caused me to jump. Leaning against the passenger side was someone who I knew but didn't really know. Unable to process a single thought, I stupidly gawked in silence.

"Are you just going to sit there like a knot on a log or are you going to ask if I need a ride to work, Mr. T?"

I didn't even know this Ackerley kid, but he seemed to think we were some kind of quasi-acquaintances. "Uh…yeah. I mean, I guess I can. Do you?" I sputtered. Evidently, being caught off guard made me more charitable.

"Aside from it being hot as balls out, it *is* a nice day," he said contemplatively. "I was planning on walking, but since you asked so nicely…I don't see why I should be impolite and decline your offer."

Ackerley climbed into the passenger seat. He looked different in the daylight. His hair was a cross between brown and blonde, and his eyes were a cross between blue and green. The air of pretentiousness that'd surrounded him the other night was gone. Maybe it was the fact his business associate wasn't by his side, feeding his use of clichéd euphemisms.

"Um, thanks for the lift," he said, losing his demeanor. "I had a flat, and my mom and ste—my parents are at work. Ergo, I had no way other than walking."

"No problem." I kept looking straight head, navigating across town to the grocery store.

He sat there for a few moments without so much as a word. He shifted in the seat once, twice, three times before breaking the silence. "Say, why are you all dressed up?"

"Job interview."

My response was clipped, not that I was being unfriendly. I just didn't feel like reliving the events of the brutal execution of my hopes by the firing squad. He said something about being glad he already had a summer job, but I didn't emphasis the point that I was looking for something to last well past the end of his summer vacation.

"What'd you say your name was again?"

"You mean to tell me you just got into a car with a stranger?"

"Listen here, kid. I didn't get in the car with stranger. I *know* your name is Phoenix," he said bluntly, furrowing his eyebrows. Like he didn't like the implication he did something childish. "I was trying to figure out what your last name was without asking you directly. I like to be tactful, thank you very much."

"It's Harper," I replied with a slight grin. Kid? He was in for a rude awakening.

"Any relation to Raleigh Harper?"

"Yes, actually."

"She and I are in the same class," he said. "I hadn't the foggiest idea she had another brother. Let me guess...are you a half-brother or a step-brother or something like that?"

"Or something like that," I said with nonchalance. Time to rain on his parade of superiority. "I'm her older brother." Maybe the facts would sink in.

"Older? Raleigh has an undisclosed older brother?" he asked, turning in his seat. He gave me a scrutinizing stare as though he were trying to find some sort of pretense. "Just how much older are you?"

"I'm twenty-two." I shrugged my shoulders. "You do the math."

"No, you aren't. There's no way you are four years older than me," he said. "Are you?" I replied with a nod of my head. "God, I feel extremely stupid. You let us sit there and treat you like you were the new kid in town. Asshole."

"You're in Raleigh's class. So, that makes you what? Seventeen? Wouldn't that make me five years your senior, kid?"

"I'm not *stupid*. I know how to do simple math. I will only be seventeen for another week, then hello legality," he said indignity as I pulled into the parking lot. "By the way, I'm not a kid."

"Right," I said under by breath as I stopped in front of the store.

"I guess I better go bag groceries for minimum wage." He sighed and rolled his eyes as he opened the door. "Thanks for the ride, Mr. Harper."

"Mister?"

"You're supposed to respect your elders, aren't you? You're practically ancient, so...."

"Who's being the asshole now?"

"That'd be me...." He flashed a mischievous grin. "As always." With that, he closed the door and walked into the grocery store without looking back.

The whole thing was weird. There wasn't any other way to describe it. It was one of those unconceivable events that happen out of the blue. First, there'd been the merciless job interview. Second, the spontaneous socialization. Seriously, I needed to get home before a third unforeseen event decided to wreak its havoc on my life.

I am the running man.

Don't you hate it when people try to tell you what you are thinking? It's like they know exactly the things that are going on inside your head. How could you have forgotten that some people are all-knowing, higher beings with a power of omniscience rivaling the likes of any deity ever imagined? They claim to know the reasoning and motives behind your actions. Like they are full of such all-encompassing wisdom.

NEWS FLASH: The <u>only</u> thing they are full of is **shit.**

How could someone just sit there and patronize you? How could they claim you made something up, that you imagined it? How could a parent tell their child something didn't happen when it did?

Why in the hell would I imagine something like that? Why would I force myself to suffer in silence?

Why would I spend years afraid to talk about it, afraid I would be chastised for the truth—my truth?

If it was all a figment of my imagination, then I would like to know why the dreams still haunted me, causing me to wake up with sweat-soaked sheets tangled around my body. Like the one I'd had last night.

A sharp intake of breath—that was what happened when you awoke with a start. It was all disorienting. You didn't even know what day it was or where you were at. Then, the feeling of relief washed through you as you realized it was all just a dream. It wasn't *just* a dream though, not for me at least.

The alarm clock's bright display notified me it was only 7:43...in the morning. Talk about a rude awakening. There was no way I could go back to sleep even if I wanted to. There was no telling what sorts of horrors my *imagination* would dream up if I did.

Maybe if I lay in bed long enough, time would pass and morning would be long gone. It felt like a sauna with the confines of bedding. Legs twitched, kicking the sheets off my body. Eyes stared, boring a hole into the ceiling. Fingers drummed, tapping the mattress.

I risked a glance. The clock now read 7:45. A moan escaped my lips. It was most definitely going to be one of those days. It still felt like I was burning up. The day hadn't even started yet, and it was already shaping up to be a hot one.

Would a little AC be too much to ask for? Stupid parents and their stupid "energy conserving" ways. I peeled myself off the bed in search for comfort. The window overlooking the backyard gave way as I pushed, sliding open. A light breeze softly caressed my face with its dwindling morning coolness.

The sky was overcast, and it looked much earlier than what it actually was. Everything was calm. The world seemed a lot less intimidating when it felt like you were the only one in it, the only one awake.

I could see over the fence and directly into the neighbor's backyard. The house was sold and bought during my exile into higher education. The fact that I still didn't know who the new owners were bugged me, and I had been trying to figure it out without asking. What was it that kid said? Tactful. Yes, I wanted to maintain tact.

The former owners hadn't taken as nice of care of the property as the current ones. There was one of those large, ornate gazebos with a sprawling patio and a swimming pool. I bet my mom hated it because they had a better backyard. It probably had her itching to find the best landscaping team in Alabama. I wouldn't put it past her.

Splashes drifted in the window. Someone was doing laps in the pool. I glanced over my shoulder. Who in their right mind would be swimming at 7:53 in the morning? Whoever she was, she had just climbed out of the pool. Her hair was dark from the water while her swimsuit was...let's just say she was most certainly female. No doubt about that.

She wrapped a towel around her body and looked up. I quickly ducked, stumbling and falling to the bedroom floor. I wasn't a pervert by any means. That was the last thing I wanted to be accused of. If she had seen me, she probably thought I was getting off by watching her or something. Jesus.

I stayed in the odd position of kneeling with my forehead resting on the hardwood floor, afraid that if I made the slightest move my whereabouts would be made known. An eternity crept passed, and then I sat up. 7:57. Son of a bitch. I had only been awake for no more than fourteen minutes, and I was already in desperate need of finding something to do.

Figuring exercise wasn't such a bad idea, I decided to take a page from the neighbor's book. Maybe it would help to clear my mind. After pulling on a pair of running shorts and an old t-shirt, I rammed my feet into my sneakers without untying them and headed downstairs.

My mom was already awake to no surprise. She was sitting at the kitchen table along with my grandmother. Why in the hell was *she* over? I didn't know. They had notebooks spread out in front of them, and it was clear they were up to something, a.k.a. my definition of "no good."

"You're up early," my mom said cheerfully, looking up from the table. She must've seen the unasked question on my face. "We're planning the big family reunion. You're welcome to help us!"

Family reunion? I would rather pierce my eyelids with a rusty nail than make plans to see my extended family, much less actually see them. "Uh…no. I couldn't sleep so I thought I'd go for a run." I shrugged my shoulders, and then I decided to add a side note. "It's hot as hell upstairs." Hint: lay off the gimmick and turn on some AC.

My grandmother, being the religious zealot that she was, got all sourpussed. "Charlotte, that boy of yours needs to come to church." I just loved the way she talked around me. She never once lifted her eyes in my direction. "Him and that filthy mouth! You and Troy raised him better than to disrespect his elders with such foul language."

I couldn't stand that bitch. I'd show her no respect because she sure as hell didn't deserve any. The way she held herself so highly on a pedestal got all up under my skin more so than usual. Commence the breaking point in 5…4…3…2…1.

"Gee shucks," I interrupted, turning to face her with a smile that suggested I was ever-so-embarrassed by the slip of manners. "By all means, let me rephrase then...heck." A look of satisfaction spread on her old, wrinkled face. Time to knock her off the pedestal from which she reigns. "It's *fucking* hot as heck upstairs."

The sound of the door closing punctuated my words. I hope she had a conniption fit. It served her right. She could kiss my ass for all I cared. I was not about to waste any of my time worrying about her or her feelings or the horse she rode in on. I had better things to do. Like watch grass grow or teach myself a foreign language or (fill in the blank with anything because I didn't give a flying fuck).

At the least the overcast prevented the sun from baking the atmosphere like an oven. It was shy of instant perspiration, but the temperature was sure to rise above and beyond the sweat factor. After a few stretches, my shirt was already damp and sticking to my back.

Around the side yard, through the gate, and down the sidewalk I went. Most of the neighbors were already at work (parents) or still asleep (children). It felt like the world was mine. Each footstep pounded the concrete as I toured the neighborhood.

Welcome to Sulfur Springs!
We hope you enjoy this quaint, little part of town.
The tour itinerary is as follows:

59

8:36 A.M. — On your left, you will see the spacious yard of my neighbor, Mrs. Thomas. <u>Side note:</u> She's widowed, and she recently acquired herself a new dog. She seems to be a nice, old lady. A smile is always on her face as she waves from the rocker on the front porch.

8:39 A.M. — Across the street from Mrs. Thomas, you will notice a rather large house made of the reddest brick. It belongs to the Anderson family. Mr. Anderson is a pharmacist. He and his wife own a drug store in town.
<u>Side note:</u> It's where my best friend during high school lived. I have lost contact.

8:40 A.M. — The house at the intersection of 3rd Street and Dogwood Lane is where I attended the pre-senior party the summer after junior year.

Side note: This is where I attained that proverbial first kiss from one Miss Sasha Travis.

8:42 A.M — Now, we will take a left and proceed down Dogwood Lane.

8:49 A.M. — The house across the way belongs to none other than Lisa "The Meat Specialist" Jacobs.
Side note: She sells pre-packaged fun out of her car trunk. Sorry, cash only. No personal checks.

8:58 A.M. — The house on the right at the intersection of Dogwood Lane and 4th belongs to John and Lola Hughes.
Side note: John spends his days with his fellow Shriners planning for the next parade to drive tiny cars in while Lola saddles up her high horse to ride everywhere she goes. They are my (supposed) grandparents.

9:00 A.M. — Now, we will take another left and proceed down 4th Street.

9:02 A.M. — The house to your immediate left belongs to Martha Gibson. She's a prude, God-fearing church lady and friend to Lola Hughes.
<u>Side note:</u> She is the retired principal of Sulfur Springs Elementary. Her alias was Old Bitch No. 1 (or just Old Bitch if I was in a hurry).

9:10 A.M. — We are now at the house directly behind the Harper property. I'm not quite sure who lives here. Don't report me to the welcoming committee for my lack of tour guidance knowledge.
<u>Side note:</u> Scratch that previous statement. The front door just opened. I know who lives here.

There stood the previously swimsuit-cladded female on the front porch of the house directly behind my backyard. I knew her. Didn't that just beat all? I have seen her approximately five—this morning made six, but I wasn't planning on seeing *that* much of her—times since I made like the prodigal son and returned home.

I knew Sulfur Springs was as small as a small town could get, but what were the odds that she would live behind me? What were the odds that the cashier at the grocery store would be my neighbor? To be quite honest, it pissed me off. Not the fact that she lived there, but the fact I didn't already know. I was rarely oblivious to such minor details.

"Hey asshole!" Rhi called as she took to the stairs. "Do you get off on things like that?"

Damn it to hell. She saw me and thought I was a pervert. "I swear I wasn't watc—"

"Thanks for letting us carry on like dipshits and not telling us who you are."

Wait? What? She was referring to the other night. "You're welcome" was the only thing I could think of to say.

"Smartass," she said, strutting down the sidewalk. If it weren't for the bright smile on her face that contrasted against her tanned skin, it'd be hard to distinguish her sarcasm from intent to harm.

The light caught the red tints of her dark brown hair. As she drew closer, I could see the slightest dusting of freckles across her nose and cheeks that suggested a childish innocence; however, her sailor mouth quickly disproved it. She was a paradox of a conventional yet unconventional girl. She was rather beautiful.

"What are you doing out here?" she asked, coming to a standstill in front of me. "You're hot, by the way."

The seductive way she said it took me by surprise. Making like a goldfish, my mouth opened and closed a few times unsure of what to say. She laughed at the dumbfounded look, and then said, "Literally. You're sweating like a pig."

"I've been running." I gave a half-assed gesture toward myself. Like my shorts and shoes would back up my statement. "I guess this little piggy needs a shower when he goes home." I slipped up. There I was being nice, friendly even. What was happening to me? I didn't need friends. I wasn't planning to stay in this godforsaken town for long.

We stood there for a few moments, looking around the street just for the mere fact of having something to do other than talk. "You're really twenty-two, huh?" she asked, her comical candor fading to curiosity.

"Yep," I answered, wiping at my face with the stretched out collar of the shirt.

She furrowed her eyebrows in concentration as she looked at me. "Shouldn't you be, like I don't know...in college or something?"

"Nope." I scanned the street nonchalantly. This much conversation was beginning to make me feel awkward. "I, uh...I graduated college a few weeks ago."

"Shut the hell up. Did you really?" A grin broke out across her face. She shook her head in disbelief to which I responded with a head nod. "Then why in the hell did you come back here to Bum Fuckin' Egypt?"

"What else was I supposed to do? No job." I looked at her snidely, and then I added, "Yet."

"Aww," she cooed.

The thing I hated more than condescension would have to be patronization. It was infuriating. My temperature was rising right alongside the degrees in Fahrenheit. If she told me not to worry or to hang in there or that everything would be okay, I would...I don't know what I would do, but it wouldn't be very nice.

"Suck it up." She cocked her hip to the side and put a hand at her waist. "Stop being such a whiney, little bitch for cryin' out loud."

What'd I say about paradoxes? I couldn't help but to smile. Rhi's personality was the type that could make you laugh without trying to make you laugh. She had this way about her that practically screamed, "Screw conventionalism!" While she was unintentionally comical, she was also unintentionally intimidating. Her words came out sharp. Like she ate razor blades for breakfast.

A car turned onto the street, and we both looked up. "Finally," she murmured as it slowed to a stop beside us, and then the window powered down. "It's about damn time. Where in the hell have you been, man? My grandma drives faster than you do."

Ackerley took one look at me and covered the side of his face with his hand so I couldn't see his mouth. "Rhi, I think we have a stalker," he said in a stage whisper, jerking his head toward me. He dropped his hand, and a dramatic expression of sincerity spread on his face as he met my gaze. "Gee Mr. Harper, it sure is hot out today, isn't it?"

What was it with these two? They seemed somewhat tolerable when they were apart, but when they got together a migraine wasn't far behind. It was daunting to say the least. Like they were trying too hard to look like they weren't trying hard at all.

"I see you fixed your flat," I said, trying to maintain a stable conversation ground.

"That's what she said," he scoffed.

They both laughed harder than necessary at the lame one-liner. Houston, we had lift-off. I could feel the onset migraine pains, I swear. "On that note, I will be leaving." I turned, and started to walk away.

"Dude," he hollered. "Do you want a ride? I owe you for the other day."

I paused, looking back over my shoulder. "You do know I live right on the other side of the block, don't you?"

"You live behind me?" she asked, tilting her head to the side with a perplexed look.

"Literally."

"Of course he does," he declared, trying to sound like he knew it all along. "That is where his family lives. So...it'd make sense for him to reside there as well, dumbass."

"You're the dumbass, dumbass," she huffed

"Well...later." I didn't know what else to say. I gave them both a noncommittal hand wave and trotted off down the sidewalk.

All I cared about was going home and showering. The temperature was already in the 90's. The sun was blazing down, engulfing me with its rays as though I was a speck in the universe. Like I was a tiny, little ant. It felt like someone was holding a magnifying glass over my head. It felt like all the repressed thoughts I was doing my damnedest to not think about were being magnified—made known and brought into the light. And just like the ant...I was starting to burn.

I am a penny.

Life never ever goes the way you expect it should. It doesn't abide by plans for the future, no matter how precise and clear-cut they may be. It agrees to disagree. That's life... that's what all the people say. Just give a shoulder shrug as a "What can you do?" apathetic gesture.

No offense to all those people and their wise words, but that philosophy fucking blows. I was sick of sitting around and twiddling my thumbs while life made me its bitch. I was sick of not having control of my life. I was sick of being sick. There. I said it. Sue me.

Hitting my head against the wall (repetitively) was starting to look like a safe bet. Some days were better than others, and some were a swirl downward into the black hole of small town life where there wasn't a get-up-and-go thrill. Sitting on a throne of fire and brimstone, "mosey-on-over" was an ironfisted dictator of all attitudes. I hereby decreed from this Thursday forth that Sulfur Springs shall be hailed as my own personal living hell.

And so, I gave myself one final pep talk before I faced the flames. Car keys? Check. Wallet? Check. Grocery list? Check. Dignity? Nowhere to be found.

The bottom step on the staircase creaked underneath my shoe, and my mom requested my appearance in the kitchen by way of hollering my name. "Are you going to run to the store for me today?" she asked, her voice echoing.

She should've already known the answer to that question, but she didn't pay any amount of attention whatsoever. Besides, I was *not* doing it for her. The simplicity of that simple-minded thrill was the only reason I went to that stupid grocery store.

"Of course," I replied as I walked into the kitchen, sarcasm completely going over her head. Raleigh and Memphis were sitting at the bar, but Jackson was nowhere in sight. I guessed he was locked away in his room. Smart kid, that one.

"Raleigh needs to go to town. You don't mind taking her, do you?"

No. No, I couldn't take her. Thursdays were my day, the highlight of the week. There weren't many things I had going for me, but at least Thursdays were reliable. Don't take that away from me.

"If you don't want to, that's fine. She can tag along while I run errands with your grandmother. She could help keep an eye on Memphis." My mom continued to ramble, like always, without giving me the chance to answer. Maybe it was a mother thing. Maybe it was supposed to a buffer a child's immediate thoughts of opposition.

A grimace shaded Raleigh's face. I was hooked, line and sinker. I forfeited the only day of solitude I found enjoyable for the sake of her betterment. Cruel and unusual punishment of that magnitude was bound to cause her mental anguish.

As if it was going to kill her to ride in the same car with me, she dragged her feet and followed me outside. The car door opened and closed without as much as a word to disrupt the lull that had fallen between us. She and the sullen expression on her face took up all the breathing room, and I was beginning to suffocate from the smothering weight of the silence.

Her apparent dislike of me was both saddening and nerve-racking. I felt the need to clear the air. "Where do you need to go?" I asked.

"Anderson's Pharmacy," she answered robotically without looking at me.

"Mom wouldn't let you take her car, would she?" I asked in an attempt to start a conversation. No response. She just kept staring out the window. "Um, you know...if you wanted to, say I don't know, borrow mine...all you have to do is ask."

Consider her attention grabbed. She turned to look at me with an unreadable expression. Her muddy green eyes stared intently at me while I waited for her to say something—anything.

"You can't do that," she scolded, those muddy greens eyes igniting with a fire. "You can't play the big brother now. It's too late."

"Look, I was only—"

"How could you?" she blurted. Her voice went quiet, but her words screamed out in anger. "I thought we were close...I thought we were friends. But no, you abandoned me the first chance you got. No calls. No letters. Nothing. It felt like you had died, fallen off the face of the earth. You only came home a handful of times, only staying long enough to prove you were still alive." She took an intake of breath, her nostrils flaring. "You ran away and never looked back. It's too late. As far as I'm concerned, you aren't my brother. Not anymore. Not after what you did. You're dead to me."

Stunned into silence. That phrase was wildly overused. People threw it around, taking the words at their face value. They didn't comprehend what it really meant or what it felt like. No, it was not being able to speak. That was where the misconceptions started. It wasn't being able to acknowledge what you had just

71

witnessed, not being able to process thoughts on the matter. Your brain stopped functioning, refusing entry to the stimulus. It was ungodly. Like the feeling you get when you fake a smile, when you grin and bear it. You pretended to let it go, pushing it the recesses of your mind to where it would sit and eat away at your soul, and then—only then—you allowed yourself to speak, to change the subject all-together. That was what being stunned into silence really meant. And that was why I replied, "I'm almost on empty," and turned into the gas station.

The thirteen year old girl retreated back inside the armor of the seventeen year old version of herself. Her expression resumed its robotic apathy with a slight flush in her cheeks. I didn't know where to begin, much less what to say to her.

The heat from the concrete parking lot swept up into my face as the door opened, causing my eyes to burn and water. The hissing of the gas pump droned in the background as thoughts raced through my head. Sometimes, you forgot you weren't the center of the universe and everything ought to revolve around you. Sometimes, you don't realize that each and every one of your actions would bear a consequence. Sometimes, you were jarred into sudden realization of your own recognition.

The gas ran over by a penny—a damn penny! It stood alone, not even capable of two cents. It tarnished everything and epitomized imperfection. Blame the penny. Cast all your burdens upon it. Like it was the penny's fault that you did something wrong, that it was to blame for your mishap. One cent didn't matter. It was only *just* a penny.

The radio kept the disconcerting silence at bay both on the way to Anderson's Pharmacy and the grocery store. She wasn't feeling very talkative, and she answered my question about whether or not if she was going to come inside with head jerk. Based on her less than sunny disposition, leaving the keys in the ignition didn't feel like the smartest move. However, I did power down the windows for her convenience. I was just courteous like that.

I took a deep breath and prepared myself for the conditioned gust of air that would wash over me when the automatic doors glided to an open. The metallic rattling of buggy wheels over asphalt distracted me from crossing the barrier of the motion detector.

"There you are," said a voice that shouldn't be as familiar sounding as what it was. "You're running late today, Mr. T."

Ackerley pushed the buggy past, and the doors glided open. The anticipated gust of air washed over him, tousling his shaggy hair around his head. He turned and looked at me with the ever-present, goofy grin that promised all was right in the world. "Are you just going to stand there or are you coming inside?" he asked.

"Yeah," I muttered, crossing the threshold sans the usual gust of air I had become accustomed to. He offered the buggy to me with an overly dramatic gesture that was fitting of his personality. With head nod, I took the buggy from him and unfolded the shopping list as I steered toward the produce section.

Old Bitch No. 1 and her gang of clucking hens were nowhere in sight. I missed out on the weekly game of deception. Her questioning on whether or not I was Wilma's boy wouldn't happen. My artful skills of retributive deceit wouldn't be put to use. Not today.

The routine was caput, done, fineto. Even if things were to go back to the way they were next week, it wouldn't be the same. Not really. It was impossible for things to go back to the way they were once they had been altered, no matter if it be by fate or circumstance or sheer dumb luck. You couldn't stop the inevitability of life's upsets.

I glanced down at the list. There weren't any requests for meat. Not this week. I wouldn't get to mentally harass Lisa the Meat Specialist with an all-knowing smile when she asked if I wanted the usual.

I had no idea if the people I saw were usual people doing their usual routine of getting their usual groceries on a usual Thursday. They weren't *my* usuals. I wasn't one of them. The puddle of usual I had slipped in had dried up. The usual tree I had fallen out of was chopped down. The dogs were wearing flea collars, ridding themselves of the proverbial fleas of usualness. There wasn't anything usual about this day.

The out-of-body experience of being there but not really being there consumed me entirely. With a blink of an eye, the list was completely checked off and the buggy was full. I didn't know how I had come to be waiting in the cashier's line or how I even put the items on the conveyor belt. All I did was blink. That was it. Time changed, managing to speed up without my consent.

Beep. Beep. Beep.

"It sure has been a hot one," I found myself saying as though small talk was a normal occurrence for me. Like my system had glitched and discretion was tossed out the window right behind my weekly Thursday traditions.

Rhi smiled at me while she dragged items across the scanner, but it wasn't the usual saccharine one as before. It was a smile of an alliance, of camaraderie against the summer heat. She wasn't dropping irrelevant tidbits about herself. She had become completely relevant.

Right then and there everything changed. I crossed the borderline into the territory of friendship. I kissed anti-sociality goodbye. It was no longer small talk. It was a conversation.

"Let me guess," she said comically. "You aren't paying with cash, are you?"

"How'd you know?" I asked with a chuckle. I actually fucking chuckled. Who in their right mind chuckles? Only older men with chubby cheeks who have had too much to drink at dinner chuckled. What the hell was happening to me?

"Our reader is broken," she informed, holding her hand out. "I'll have to scan it for you."

Reluctantly, I handed the bankcard over. There would not be any espionage delusions of grandeur. There would not be a simple-minded thrill of simplicity. Nothing was the same. Everything was different.

As much as I wanted to hold on to the things I could count on, I knew it was time to let go. Here was how I saw it: you should hang onto the rope with a tight grip as long as possible, but when it was time to let go…you had to let go completely. You couldn't release one finger at a time in an attempt to make things last—that only caused you to slip and stumble. You couldn't let the gravity cause you to lose your grip. You had to be the one who decided to let go. It was the only way you'd land on your feet.

And so, I let go. Both hands opened up, and I let go. I wished Rhi a good day, and I obliged when Ackerley asked if I needed help with the groceries.

The buggy wheels rattling on the asphalt alerted Raleigh of our arrival. She'd had her feet sticking out the window, but she withdrew them. Looking straight through me, she focused on Ackerley. "Hey," she said with a coy half-smile.

"Hey, Raleigh," he said as I opened the trunk and started putting groceries in the back. "Are you enjoying your summer vacation so far?"

"I guess," she said, shrugging her shoulders. I guess her flirtation technique relied heavily on being somewhat off-putting and mysterious. "You?"

"I can't complain," he said with a laugh. He put the remainder of the groceries in the trunk and closed the door. "Nice seeing you, man," he said, turning to look at me.

"Yeah, you too," I said. Raleigh looked back and forth like she was trying to figure how we were friends.

"I apologize for him not offering you a tip," Raleigh cut in, turning all the attention her way.

"I'm sorry," I said, patting my pockets to pull my wallet out. "Let me see—"

"Don't bother," Raleigh said, holding out a couple of wadded up dollar bills.

Ackerley politely denied the offering, but Raleigh insisted he take it. She smiled a lovesick, preteen girl smile and dumped the wad of bills into his palm. Loose change fell from the confines of the dollars, bouncing onto the pavement.

"Don't worry about it," she told him as he bent down. "It's just a few pennies."

"Just because it's a penny doesn't mean that it's not worth anything," he said, standing upright. He smiled at the both of us as he pocketed the tip, and then he went back to work.

I am the catcher.

I was sleeping as the sun rose on the horizon. I was sleeping as the hands on the clock ticked. I was sleeping as the day crept overhead. I was sleeping as the sun set on the horizon. I was sleeping as nighttime fell with relief. I was sleeping as moonlight tiptoed in through the window. I was sleeping as my head rested against the pillow. I was sleeping as my eyes fluttered to a close. I was awake.

A sharp intake of breath zipped in-between clenched teeth.

I was falling. Forever falling. Forever waiting for the concrete of the sidewalk to scrape my knees. The world circled around me. Trees blurred into green as the horizon tilted. The sky, the houses, the church steeple. Everything spiraled out of control. Faster and faster.

Trees. Sky. Houses. Church. Trees. Sky. Houses. Church.

Treesskyhouseschurch.

Treesskyhouseschurch.

Treesskyhouseschurchtreesskyhouseschurch.

Faster and faster and faster they spun out of control. Momma, I promise I didn't run. I was a good boy like you told me to be. Treesskyhouseschurch. Daddy, I swear I was a good boy. I even minded my manners. Treesskyhouseschurch. I didn't do anything wrong. Please.

A melodic symphony struck up a complex score. Treesskyhouseschurch. The tune of my every afternoon. Treesskyhouseschurch. My heart pounded in my chest. Treesskyhouseschurch. It was too late. I was too late. The cartoon started without me.

Trees.

Sky.

Houses.

Church.

Eyes.

Hand.

Fear.

—

A sharp intake of breath zipped in-between clenched teeth. I awoke with a start of disorientation. Cold sweat clung to my forehead while sheets clung to my body. Sunlight had invaded the night, filtering in through the window and dancing across the floor.

It was one of those mornings where you shuffle from the bed and straight into the shower only to suddenly recall the fact that you lived in a house with five other people. The hot water had a lifespan of a minute, two minute tops, before it turned lukewarm. Then cold.

After what had to have been the shortest, quickest shower in history of all showers, I heard the hustling and bustling coming from downstairs. A multitude of many voices were speaking ill-fittingly garbled conversations. I feared that I knew who they all belonged to, but curiosity wasn't going to get my cat killed by walking into the middle of the battlefield of relatives. I knew better.

The only problem: sneaking out of the house completely unnoticed, which seemed highly unlikely. A quick scan of the upstairs hallway revealed Memphis sitting at the top of the stairs. Her brown hair was unruly. Like she had been running around playing before she had come to be sullenly perched on the step.

She was slumped over with elbows propped on her knees, her face squished by her hands. Her eyes cut over to me as I took a seat beside her. "What's going on down there?" I asked in a low voice, trying to keep quiet.

"People completely ruining my day. That's what's going on down there," she said with an exaggerated sigh. She was quite the precocious nine year old.

"I couldn't have said it better myself." I mimicked her and slumped forward, resting my elbows on my knees. "I wonder how long it'll take them to get everything together for Decoration."

"Lord only knows," she said, rolling her eyes. "All those old women down there were making such a fuss over me. I hate it. I was happy as can be running around and playing, but then I just had to come inside. Goodbye fun. I reckon that's just a part of life though."

"How do you figure?"

"Some days, life is fun and you get to play out in the sunshine. Other days, it's unfair and you have to come inside. I guess you just have to make due though. Ain't that a stinker?"

"Hmmm," I said, shaking my head and smiling. "Did anyone ever tell you that you don't look like a Memphis? I swear you remind me a character in a book I've read."

"Don't be silly," she said. "I most certainly look like a Memphis."

"What does a Memphis look like then?" I found her personality amusing and wanted to egg her on. She has grown and changed so much in the past years. She claimed she remembered the way it was before I went off to college, but I knew she had to be lying. She was only saying she did for my sake...so I would still feel like her big brother.

"You tell me," she said simply. "You're looking at one."

"Kid, you're a hoot."

"For your information, I am not a kid. I'm almost ten years old, thank you very much."

"My apologies, miss." I bowed my head.

The thought of staying in the house was all-together depressing, especially with the frenzy in the air. "What do you say to getting out of here and going to the park?"

"I say I'd rather enjoy that." She gave me one of those baboon grins and stood up. She went from being sullen to right as rain in no time. Kids—or young ladies as she preferred to be called—were capable of such feats. Those types of things diminished with age.

It was Memphis's idea to tell not our mother where we were going but our father instead. He was holed up in the garage with the other male relatives who were forced to tag along with their wives. They drank beer and shot the shit while the women busied themselves with making unbelievably gaudy flower arrangements. It was a quick and easy setup. A hush fell in their conversation (some things weren't meant to be heard by tiny ears) as she slipped inside and filled him on our agenda, and then we were ready to go.

The weather was perfect. A soft breeze swept across the park, keeping the heat from smothering us. We had the place to ourselves. Memphis wanted to swing, and so we swung. Then, she wanted to ride the merry-go-round, and so we merrily went around. From one piece of playground equipment to the next, we went. Just a big brother and a kid sister running around and playing games. Just two kindred spirits taking on the world together.

That little baboon was a handful, and keeping her pace was tiresome. Both of us collapsed into the grass with beads of sweat plastering our hair to our foreheads. With eyes closed, I tried to soak up everything around me, to keep it locked in my memory: the sound of our breathing, the smell of fresh cut grass, the wind whispering through the playground.

"What do you think they're doing back at home?" I asked, keeping my eyelids shut. I wanted to remember the sound of her voice, the sound of childhood.

"Best guess is that they are running about like chickens with their heads cut off," she stated, and then she let out a giggle. "I bet you anything that they are like, 'Oh boy, y'all. What do you think about this lovely arrangement of flowers? It's amazing how these don't look fake at all, don't ya think?'" She changed a tone to insinuate she was someone else. "Nah, I can't tell they aren't real at all. Now-now, they're pretty as picture!"

"Or maybe something like this," I said, and then I tried to mimic my grandmother. "Charlotte, we need to get the food together. Ya hear me? I'd just die…I would just *die* if anyone thought bad about me, I mean, our family. Let me just climb down from my horse and help you with that."

"Or…or…," she trailed, laughing her head off. "Hey, y'all. What can we think of to do for about five 'ours out in the graveyard? We'll torture them youngin's by makin' 'em sit there with nothing to do while we busy ourselves with talkin' about useless stuff." She changed her tone to sound something like our grandfather. "Lola, I think I might drive that there tiny car. It hasn't seen the light of day since our last parade. Shoot, I may even do a couple donuts just for kicks and giggles."

I snorted with laughter. That old Memphis was such a hoot. I didn't care that she was nine years old. She was one of the few people who didn't hold anything against me. She was pretty much the only friend I had.

The dry grass crunched underneath her weight as she sat up. Surely she wasn't ready to play some more, was she? I was still trying to catch my breath. "Look, it's Rhiannon," she said.

"Who?" I asked, sitting up and looking to where she was pointing.

"Our neighbor," she enunciated as though I was a bit on the slow side, and then she waved energetically.

Sure enough, Rhi was on the sidewalk at the park entrance. She snapped a picture, and then lowered the camera. There was no telling how long she had been standing there. I raised my hand in greeting, and she did the same. And with that, she continued on her way to wherever it was she was headed.

"She's nice," Memphis said.

"Yes," I agreed. "I think she is, too."

Memphis was wise beyond her years. Her view of the world was unique to say the least. She saw more than most people, and I most certainly trusted her judgment of character.

"Where were we?" she asked. "Ah, yes. We were discussing ice cream."

"We were, were we?"

"I do believe so." She nodded her head quickly, causing her hair to dance around her. "Now that I think about it, you even mentioned something about buying me some."

"You don't say?" I laughed out loud. "My memory fails me, but I trust yours. Come on, we'll go get some." I stood up, holding my hand out to her.

"I knew you'd see it my way," She said gleefully said as I pulled her up.

If only I were to be so lucky to see it her way.

Two ice cream cones later, we were back at the park. Memphis decided she wanted to see the ducks, and so we went to the pond. She chased the geese around and around, making funny noises. I said to her, I said,

"You're a riot," and she replied, "Just watch this." She sped off around the pond, flapping her arms and clucking as though she were part of the flock. The sugar rush was coursing through her system, and she was loving every minute of it.

Crossing down to the edge of the water, I could see the perfectly mirrored reflection of the sky. The world. Memphis flapped her arms over to me, sound effects and all. She stooped and picked up a few rocks. "Let's skip some," she said, holding her hand out for me to take one.

"Ladies first," I offered.

She pulled her arm back and flung the rock. It sailed through the air and bounced off the surface of the water, shattering the mirror reflection. It was just one of life's upsets. The rock skipped once, twice, three times as the ripples spread out.

It was my turn. I reared back and let the rock roll off the tips of my fingers. It skipped once before sinking like the stone that it was, but its ripples still distorted the picture. "Dadgum it," I said, editing my language for her sake.

"Ain't that a stinker?" she said, shaking her head.

Our ripples were overlapping, spreading out, and connecting. Everything was connected. The mirrored sky, the pond water, the film of pollen on the surface —

everything was part of something else. Like it all had a purpose and formed a bigger picture.

"That was fun while it lasted," she said, wiping her hands on her shorts. "Say, are we about done here?"

"I guess I am if you are."

My face was starting to tingle with a sunburn. Even though going back to the house meant having to put up with all the people, at least there would be air conditioning—what little my mom was willing to use. Plus, there was a lock on my bedroom door.

"Good, son. Good." She mimicked our aunt Derenda. "I gots to get back to the house. You know, it's almost time for my stories." She made a motion and slapped one hand into the palm of the other. "I can't be missing my stories. I *just* can't. I tell ya. I just can't."

I promised her we'd be back in time for her afternoon cartoons, not to fret. She walked with a hitch in her step, her strides quickening. I told her to slow down, that there wasn't a reason to rush.

"Now, I ain't got all day for you to lollygag around," she called over her shoulder, pausing at the entrance. I caught up to her, but she held her hand out to hush me before I could say anything. "Do you hear that?"

"Hear what?"

"Open your ears."

Straining to listen intently, I could make out a whimpering sound. It was faint and coming from somewhere nearby. We exchanged puzzled looks, and then glanced around the street.

"I think it's coming from there," she said, pointing at the trash can closest to us. Being every bit bigger than her britches, she strutted up to it and yanked the lid open. Just like that.

"Hold up," I managed to say. "There's no telling what it could be."

"I am *not* a child," she huffed.

Peering inside, all that could be seen was nothing but garbage. The whimpering came from somewhere near the bottom. I had a pretty good idea as to what it was, and I instantly regretted what I was going to have to do, what Memphis was going to make me do one way or another. With a breath held while I tried not to gag from the hot garbage heated by the summer's sun, I forced myself to stick a hand down into the disgust. Ugh. It smelled god-awful. It was all I could do not to hurl.

Fingers grazed a fast food bag, and the whimpering sounded again. Bingo. Gently lifting, I pulled it free. Whatever was inside was heavy and rolled around making more noises as I sat it on the ground. Suddenly, I thought of how stupid it was for me to have done so. There was no telling what was in that bag. "Stand back."

Did my kid sister listen? No. Her head was right above my shoulder as I opened the bag. She squealed a high-pitched squeal right into my ear. "It's a puppy!"

Someone had dumped off a puppy. Literally, they threw it away. Its eyes were barely opened, and its brown coat was coated with black grime. That didn't stop Memphis though. She held it close to her chest, cooing and trying to calm it down.

"What is this world coming to? I tell you…some people just make me sick," she spat out in a whisper. Like the puppy might understand what she was saying.

"I don't know." I shook my head. I really didn't know how someone could do such a heinous act to something so innocent. Like it was just another piece of garbage. How could someone look into its face like it didn't matter and throw it away? How could they throw it over into the trash can knowing that a slow, miserable death awaited it?

"I'm going to take you home and clean you up and you are going to have a family that loves you and I will be there for you and nothing will ever change that. I promise," Memphis said as she kissed the puppy's head. "Right, Phoenix? I can keep the puppy, right?"

Her eyes were full of such compassion that it made me want to cry. How could I say no? The puppy deserved the right to everything she'd promised. It didn't deserve to be cast aside. It deserved an all-encompassing love, and damn it…I was going to make sure it did.

"Absolutely," I said, my voice going rough. "You're exactly what that little feller needs."

I am nobody too.

Everybody thinks they are a handyman. Everybody claims to have the right tools in their belt. Everybody swears it can be fixed. Everybody promises it'll be like new. Nobody understands the meaning of the word "irreparable." Everybody thinks, and nobody considers.

It's not your fault for having delusions of grandeur. It's just how this world works. They say ignorance is bliss, but wise words don't change the fact that fighting a losing battle only results in heartache. Don't waste your time trying to restore a former glory. Accept that it simply can't be done. Take all those broken pieces and reassemble them into something new altogether. Learn how you can stop it from being broken again. That's all we can do. That's the only way to move forward.

Small steps are all it takes. Small step after small step after small step. It may not seem like much to the outside world, but it's the only way to make progress.

You have to get your footing before you can walk, and then walk before you can run.

The small steps aren't momentous occasions in the journey, no. They slip by without announcement and leave you feeling strong enough to face a new day. It could be the smile of a stranger or the way your head hits the pillow just right before you fall asleep or the joy of reading a book underneath a shade tree on a summer's day.

Under thus said tree, the air was cool and inviting. A soft breeze lightly picked up the corner of the book's page, letting it dance before falling back into line. Even though I had read the book countless times, it kept sucking me right back into the literary world within its binding as though I were a virgin unknown to its context.

The pages were worn underneath my fingertips as I flipped one after the other as the protagonist took his journey; it was all about the small steps. As with every good book, the ending came much too soon, and I read the final words on the last page. It was saddening to have to leave the world behind, but it wasn't goodbye forever. Just because the book ended didn't mean the story had to. That was one of the greatest things about books. Rereading kept the characters in your heart, where they continued to live and breathe as you made your way through life, as you grew-up. With them, you were never alone.

Excited yips of a puppy were carried by the wind, distracting me from the contemplative reverie. Memphis and Mr. Faustus, as she so aptly named him, were roaming around the backyard as they had previously done the past few days from sunup till sundown. She had her mind set on teaching him tricks.

"Listen here, son. I told you to sit and stay," her voice echoed around the side of the house. "Now, son. Now-now, how many times do I have to tell you?"

I couldn't help but to laugh at her stubbornness. She'd begged and pleaded until our parents said she could keep the puppy. Like there was any other doubt that they'd succumb to her cuteness.

She was saving up her allowance to buy Mr. Faustus a collar and one of those little pet beds so he could sleep in her room. I did have some money saved up, so why not help her out? After all, I swore to myself I would help. The entirety of my bank account was supposed to go toward moving out and starting my own life, but I highly doubted that would ever happen.

Picking myself up off the ground, I noted the pleasantness of the weather. It was nice for June, and walking to the pet store seemed as good a plan as any. After depositing my faithful companion onto the bookcase in my room, I started down the sidewalk leading into the main part of town.

I wasn't touring the neighborhood today, not again at least. It was peaceful to quietly observe en route to the pet store. Mrs. Thomas was tending to the flowerbeds along her front porch. She was an overly enthused gardener with more shrubbery than necessary.

As if some unknown force made her aware of my presence, she looked over her shoulder. She smiled and casually threw up a hand in a wave. The new dog nudged against the outstretched arm, wanting to play. She tossed the stick with a sigh. Like she hoped she could be left alone to garden in peace. The dog brought it back in no time flat, and the scenario repeated itself. It was a battle of determination.

Looking both ways before crossing the intersection of 3rd street and Dogwood Lane, I noticed that Lisa the Meat Specialist's car trunk was opened. A snicker escaped from my lips as I thought on the possible reasons why. My best guess? She was airing out her trunk to keep the dildos from melting into a big, mutated glob of penis. The thought alone was disturbing yet altogether hilarious. I just couldn't belie—

"What's so funny?"

My attention turned from Lisa's car. Rhi was crossing the street with the camera swinging from her neck. Like it was her accessory of choice.

"Um...." I debated on whether or not to tell her, and then I decided the junk in the trunk was something I didn't feel like sharing. It was just between Lisa and me. "Nothing really."

"Fine," she said, acting all defensive. "I didn't want to know, asshole." She held a hand over her eyes and shielded the sun. "What are you doing out here anyway? Stalking the neighbors?"

"Guilty."

"Your secret's safe with me."

"Good to know."

I took a step forward, and she took a step forward. That awkward laugh lurked onto the street corner with us. You know, the one that happens when you try to move around someone in your path only for them to do the exact same thing, making it impossible to pass. We were both headed the same way.

"Where are you going?" she asked as we ventured together.

"Thought I'd check out the pet store," I said with a shoulder shrug. "You?"

"I need more batteries." She brought her hand up to her chest and tapped the camera for emphasis. "I've been burning through them like nobody's business."

"For what?" I asked out of sheer curiosity. Normally, I steered clear of conversation that might involve getting to know someone. Once they told you their story, it was only customary to return the favor, and I wasn't one for customs.

"You might think I'm an overachiever...." She trailed off, looking down at the camera. "There's this photography scholarship with a deadline the beginning of August. I want to get a jumpstart on the future, so...I've been taking pictures for a portfolio, but it needs a theme."

"That doesn't make you an overachiever," I admitted, squinting my eyes against the sun as I looked into the distance. "You have to plan for the future."

"I suck at planning," she said indifferently. "I have all these pictures I need to go through, but I feel like I'm missing out on the opportunities if I'm analyzing all the candid events of the past few weeks."

"Sometimes, you have to follow through," I found myself saying in a half-hearted attempt at advice. "You might've missed something you overlooked when you saw it the first time."

"Uh...yeah," she said distractedly. "Right over there is where the most popular girl in school lives."

Following her line of sight, I looked across the street. The house had looked different the day I dropped Terri off. It'd been raining, and I didn't get a good view of it.

It wasn't the nicest on the block, but it wasn't the worst either. To say the least, it was nothing memorable—just average.

"Terri Lynn looks like a damn toad. She's only popular because she croaks the best when she's on her back." She overdramatically roared with laughter as she cracked herself up, making it embarrassing to be seen next to her. "You don't even know the best part! Her father is a pastor! You can't make that shit up!" She finally managed to contain herself, and lowered her voice. "I've taken a few candid photos of her. Maybe I can build a portfolio around her and call it 'Whore of a Holy Man.'"

"Now's your chance to get a few more," I pointed out as Terri emerged from the house wearing that too tiny bikini and carrying a towel.

"Damn it to hell," she said. "If I hadn't gotten carried away during Ack's birthday party and used all the juice in the only batteries I had left, I sooooo would."

It took a second, but I remembered his mentioning of a countdown to legality. "That's cool," I commented, wondering if he had some big blowout like most kids his age do.

Rhi carried on the conversation by herself as we continued past Terri's house and down the sidewalk. She was the type of person who didn't need the other to participate. A few head nods were all it took for her to keep right on talking. She mentioned how she surprised Ackerley with a cake and how they've always celebrated his birthday together with just the two of them.

"Why is that?" I asked. I wondered how long they'd been dating.

"Do you ever feel like you are on a different level than everyone else? That's Ack and me. We're so over all the fake-ass people around here pretending like they are a big somebody."

My only response was raised eyebrows as a go-to look of contemplation. Do you know the feeling you get when you instantly clicked with someone? It was like you had known them your whole life. It was hard to explain, but I could tell we were all on the same page. I didn't really know them, but I knew enough to know who they were. I knew that we were on the same side. We were all one in the same.

"You're different from everybody else," she continued as her flip-flops smacked her feet. "I've known it ever since that party."

I screwed my face up and looked over at her, silently asking what she meant. "You didn't jump at the opportunity to sell some exaggerated version of yourself," she explained. "Hell, you didn't care who we thought you were, much less what we thought about you." She shrugged her shoulders as a shy smile crept across her face. "That should count for something."

"Glad you don't think I'm an asshole, then," I said sarcastically. When in doubt, make a witty remark. That philosophy had gotten me through life so far. Why stop now?

She replied with an arched eyebrow as she said that the verdict was still out on that one. The slightest edge of flirtation was beginning to develop, which meant a change of subject was in order before it became uncomfortable. Wasn't she and this Ackerley kid dating? I rewound back a few minutes to something she'd mentioned, and said, "It was nice of you to surprise him."

"Well...." She bit her lip as she looked at the sidewalk like she was internally debating on something. "If I tell you something, you have to promise not to say anything."

It was a known fact that gossip led to drama, but that didn't stop me from promising not to breathe a word of it to anyone. Who would turn down undisclosed information?

"If I hadn't done it, he wouldn't have a birthday," she said. "Not a real one anyway."

"What do you mean?"

"Long story short is...." She took a deep breath like she was about to confess something she'd been holding inside of her. "His mother got pregnant at a really young age, and she raised him by herself. When Ack was nine, she started dating this guy. A year later they were married. His mother and stepfather started this new family, leaving him out of it like he didn't belong. Sure, they 'celebrate' his birthday, but that doesn't mean anything."

Her face was unreadable, but there was a gleam in her eye. It was hard to tell if she was heartbroken over the situation or if she was glad to be telling it to a third party—namely me. It just goes to show that first impressions weren't what they were always cracked up to be. People were more complex than they appeared, and I had misjudged Ackerley. That goofy grin of his wasn't a promise that all was right in the world. It was a wish that everything would be. I should've recognized it when I had first seen him. It was the same grin I'd used to bear it.

The flip-flopping was all that could be heard as we walked in silence. I didn't know what to say. How were you supposed to respond when someone dropped a bomb like that? The best I could do was to grimace and deliver a guttural sound that showed I understood exactly what she was saying.

I am poetically justified.

They say you should save your virginity for someone meaningful. They say you'll always remember your first time. They say it'll be magical. They say. They say. They say. Who the hell are "they?" Fuck them. They were always telling you how to live your life. They don't know anything.

No, I didn't save my virginity for someone meaningful. Why should I have? The way I'd seen it, I was a sexless non-virgin. I sure as hell wasn't pure, not after what happened. Why do you always have to remember your first time? I wished I could forget mine.

Being intimate with someone was too hard of a concept for me to imagine. I had to drown out my thoughts with alcohol before I could even think about actually doing it. I wanted to have sex. No, I wasn't desperate or hard up. I wanted to experiment. I wanted to see if I could do it—if I could go through with it.

I tried to get out of my own head, but I had kept asking myself where I was supposed to put what. Even with loosened inhibitions, some things couldn't disappear. I'd tried to be a different person. Like someone I'd seen in a movie. It wasn't me having sex — it was someone else. Everything was happening so fast, and I didn't have any control over it.

She'd kept making all these noises. It was completely distracting, and I couldn't concentrate. Then, she'd started rubbing her hands all over my body. That was when the flashbacks overcame me. I wasn't nineteen any more. I was a ten year old boy who didn't know what was happening. I didn't understand what has going on or who was touching me. I was scared beyond belief.

I'd started trembling and sweating profusely. My chest hurt, and my breathing grew short. Between the smothering breaths and the pounding heartbeats in my ears, I'd started to get sick. The room was spinning. My stomach hurt, making me dry heave. It felt like I was dying.

It was all I could do to keep myself from falling apart. I remembered locking myself in the bathroom, wrapping my arms around my knees, and rocking back and forth. It was there that I decided I wouldn't — couldn't — allow myself to fall victim to intimacy ever again. In hindsight, I had experienced a panic attack over the situation.

I wished I didn't remember it, but it was hard not to. Especially on rainy days when there wasn't anything better to do besides think. Being cooped up in the house for days on end was enough to drive anyone crazy. There were only so many times you could watch daytime television or search the online job boards. Hell, there wasn't even a place worth venturing out into the gloom to go. The curse of the monotony was full-blown. All I could do was think.

I was sprawled out on the floor with the side of my face scrunched up and resting on the hardcover of a book. I had attempted to start it, but it'd been half-assed. I couldn't pay attention. The same sentence was read over and over again without anything sinking in. I gave up and just lay there, becoming lost to thought.

At my junior class's pre-senior/beginning of summer party was where I had my first kiss. Seventeen was rather late for a teenage guy to have their first kiss, but I hadn't been like the other horny guys my age. My libido hadn't been skyrocketing out of the roof, and I hadn't cared about getting a piece of ass.

The kiss was with the cheerleader I had taken to prom. It was a quick peck on the front porch swing, not a heavy make out session. There were no fireworks or feelings down in my loins that made me want to jump her bones. It was merely two sets of lips mushed up against one another. Just clammy and altogether awkward as hell. That had been all I could focus on.

I thought that maybe it was one of those things you had to get used to, but I never did. Since my freshman year of college, I've not kissed or done anything sexual. There was no point in it, I swear. It was just one of the things I had come to accept. In part, I felt asexual. Like I wasn't attracted to anyone.

Playing self-psychologist all these years had seriously warped—the sudden sound of a door opening in an otherwise quiet upstairs broke the masochistic reverie. I was in a daze, blinking and trying to make sense of everything. From the spot on the floor, shadowed footsteps could be seen as they crossed in front of my room. Then, I could hear the shyness in Jackson's voice as it sounded down the hallway. "Raleigh?" he asked, softly knocking on the door.

"What do you want?" she hollered in a muffled voice.

"I was...I was just going to ask you if you could...if you would take me to town," Jackson said timidly. It was as though he already knew what she was going to say.

"What for?" Still, she could not be bothered to open the door.

"I, uh, there's this new video game...."

"You are such a geek!" She even went as far as to throw in a laugh to punctuate the exclamation. "You need to get a life. I've got better things to do."

"Oh, okay," he whispered and treaded lightly down the hallway back to his room.

I felt sorry for him. Honestly, I did. All he wanted was a video game. He shouldn't be ostracized for wanting the chance to escape life for a few hours at a time. There was nothing wrong with that. I knew exactly how he felt.

I peeled the side of my face off the book cover and sat up. He hadn't bothered to ask me, and I couldn't help but to wonder why. Suddenly, I had the urge to prove myself and find out his reasoning. I tracked his steps and knocked on his door.

"It's open," he called. "Come in."

"So, how's it going?" I asked stupidly, shutting the door to a close. I had never been into his room, and the situation felt oddly formal.

"Oh...." He looked at me for a few seconds like he was surprised to see me. "Nothing really."

I waited to see if he would ask me as he'd done Raleigh, but he turned away and stared fixedly out the window into the pouring rain. "I, uh, I couldn't help but overhear," I said, trying to be nonchalant. "Don't let what she said bother you. Don't listen to her." I started to move toward him but stopped myself. "That's the only way she knows how to hurt your feelings." My words felt all jumbled like I wasn't making sense. I was experiencing word vomit. "What I mean to say is — "

"That she's a bitch?" he asked with laugh.

"Yes, that was a bitchy thing for her to say," I agreed with a little laugh. The atmosphere was less tense with the lighthearted humor, so I decided to fish around. "What was it you wanted her to do?"

"There's this new video game I wanted to buy," he explained, turning to look at me. "I've been saying my allowance."

He went on to describe what it was about and how long he had been waiting for it. I was completely lost, but I nodded my head like I understood everything he was saying. It was plain to see how much he had his heart set on it. With our mother planning a reunion of hell at our grandmother's and Raleigh being, well, Raleigh, I was the only other option.

"I don't mind giving you a lift…all you have to do is ask," I pointed out.

"I figured you wouldn't want to."

"Grab some shoes and we'll go." I nodded my head at the door.

Needless to say, we were both soaked by the time we reached the car, but I didn't mind. It was welcomed if it meant getting out of the house to actually do something. I played nice and let Jackson listen to whatever radio station he wanted as we drove through the rain-washed streets. Seeing him bob his head as he sang along under his breath was quite the sight to see. Usually, he was reserved and silent. Like he was trying to make himself invisible.

There was this whole different side of him I had never seen before, not saying that I had been around to truly know. I think that by knowing that someone was there, someone who understood him was what made the difference. Maybe things would've been different for me if I had known the same.

The store in town was one of many in a chain across the South. The decorations were ostentatious, the paint job was over-the-top, and the choice of lighting would have been more suited for an amusement park. The whole building was visually nauseating to say the least. I couldn't fathom why I'd wanted to work there so badly during the summer before college.

The rain had slackened to a drizzle, and there wasn't any need to make a mad dash inside. It felt more civilized to casually waltz up to the glass door and open it rather than jerk it off its hinges in an attempt to take cover. Jackson took off in a quest for the videogame while I drifted aimlessly down the aisles.

The store was unexpectedly crowded. The consistency of the dreary weather was enough to make anyone want to change it up and seek a cure-all for cabin fever. With so many people, you'd think there would be a buzz of mindless chatter; however, it was strangely quiet. Every single person was walking around, intently focusing their eyes from shelf to shelf. The atmosphere was akin to a church or a museum, and it was highly uncomfortable for the most part.

Ever had that feeling that something was about to happen because it was too quiet? That was why my eyes were wide open as I drifted through the aisles. Apparently, there was such a thing as being too alert. Paranoia kept you looking over your shoulder. It made you forget to look where you were going, thus making you run smack dab into something you didn't see.

"Oh, sorry," I said, staggering to keep my footing. "I didn't see you...."

My words stopped short. When you bumped into a cardboard cutout and apologized for doing so, a feeling of complete stupidity mixed with humiliation washed over you as you realized (A) it was only cardboard and (B) you just caused a scene.

"That has got to be one of the funniest things I've seen all day," said a voice off to the side as I tried to upright the superhero game promo. "But I have been standing around in a dead grocery store. So, I guess that doesn't really count for much."

A hole to crawl into and die would have been most appreciated. I hated—no, I loathed bringing attention to myself. My cheeks flushed as I slowly turned around. Ackerley was on the next aisle over, and he was watching me with that ever-present grin of his.

"So, uh, yeah. You've been at work? That's cool," I said conversationally.

"Nice attempt at changing the subject," he said, shaking his head from side to side. Like a parent did when their child did the darnedest thing. "Yeah, I had the morning shift today."

"At least you got out of the house." I nodded my head and glanced around the store, trying to shake all feelings of embarrassment. "This rain sucks." Really? Had I really just made small talk about the weather? Ugh.

"I hope it's going to be pretty tomorrow like they say it is," he said with a sigh. He looked over at me, and I could see a bulb flicker with light above his head as his smile widen with an idea. "You want to go geocaching?"

"Geo-what-ing?"

"Geocaching," he corrected, getting excited. "It's like a scavenger hunt. You use a GPS and find stuff people have hidden. Rhi and I are going tomorrow. You should totally come with us even though you're a muggle."

"That sounds, uh, fun." Not to mention kind of weird. Trekking around in the heat and looking for whatever it was you had to find didn't sound very appealing. And why did he call me a muggle? "I'll think about it."

A crestfallen expression formed on his face by my less than enthused response, which made me feel bad for raining on his parade (no pun intended). Who knew what I would feel like tomorrow? I didn't know why, but I gave him my number and told him to let me know. Might as well write "social nicety" on my forehead.

Ackerley's gaze focused behind me, and then he made a parting gesture before disappearing into the next aisle.

"I'm ready to go," Jackson said, his voice materializing from out of nowhere.

"Did they have the game you wanted?"

"Yes," he said angrily. "But the lady at the counter won't let me buy it. She said I'm not old enough."

After quickly weighing the options as to whether or not it would be responsible of me to get it for him, I decided it could not be any more damaging than what was already accessible on the internet. I'm surprised he didn't ask me to do it already. "Go get the game. I'll buy it for you."

He didn't need to be told twice. Turning on a dime, he made a beeline to the right section. It was just a video game, but that didn't make it any less important. We all had our little vices for handling the pressures of real life.

"Phoenix Harper?" the lady at the counter said with a shrill voice. "Is that you?"

"Uh...." I grasped for words. Her face looked familiar, but I couldn't place her.

"It's me!" she exclaimed, patting her chest with her hand. "Caroline."

My, my...how far the mighty had fallen. No wonder I hadn't recognize her right off the bat. She used to claim her golden locks were natural, but a good three inches of black roots were showing. Her face was certainly plumper, and by that I mean she had either gained a hell of a lot of weight or was with child. Her hands were adorned with fake nails, and there was a ring on her finger.

"How have you been darlin'? I haven't seen you since you moved off to college." Her tone was so bright and cheery as though we were still the best of friends.

"I just graduated," I said tepidly. I was in no mood for catching up with a backstabber.

"I graduated about a year ago myself," she said, smacking a piece of gum. "Finally got my associate degree, and I've been promoted to manager." She said it with more pride than necessary. Like it was of the highest honor to be made a manager of this chain store and have a two-year degree in the time span of four years. "You got a rewards card?"

A worst case scenario played in my head and I shook it side to side. What if I had gotten the job that summer? What if I had attended the local community college? I would've ended up just like her.

Suddenly, I didn't care that she went around my back and swiped the job right out from under me all those years ago. The bitch had practically done me a favor. It didn't mend the broken bridge, and it sure as hell didn't make up for what she'd done.

"Do you remember Beau Austin?" she asked, sliding a form across the counter.

She was bound and determined to strike a conversation. Without looking up as I wrote down my basic information, I gave a grunt to show that I did. How could I forget Beau Fucking Austin? He had been the head honcho, all-star quarterback. He'd been the one who humiliated me at the graduation party that summer. God, I hoped he'd gotten fat and started balding.

"I'm Mrs. Caroline Anderson-Austin now!" she declared, waving her fingers on her left hand to showcase the ring. "We have a baby on the way!"

She got knocked up by the ex-high school hero. I bet he was working for his father in their family logging business. That figured. It was just one of many key factors in dealing with small town life. Some people stuck around. Some people tried to relive their glory days. Some people settled.

"Well, congratulations," I said with fake sincerity. "I hope you get everything you deserve, Caroline."

"I appreciate that," she said, laying a hand on my arm. "I really do."

"Here." I stood upright, pulling away from her touch and handing over the paper.

She took the form and leaned in, lowering her voice. "There's no, ya know…hard feelings, right?"

"Whatever do you mean?" I smiled big and acted as though I didn't know what she was talking about. Bitch. Of course, there were hard feelings. In fact, the hard feelings were harder than hard. Like concrete. Why would there not be? I trusted her to keep a secret—my secret. What had she done? She blabbed it to Beau Fucking Austin at that party.

Jackson stepped up beside me and laid Mutated-Space-Ninja-Zombies on the counter. "Caroline, could you ring this up to me? We're in a hurry. Thanks." With a satisfied grin, I slid the video game across to her so she could do her job. Putting her into her place was poetic justice at its finest, and it deserved to be commemorated accordingly.

Friendship's Obituary:

All those adventures with all the laughs,
Memories of old flood my mind.
During a brief period of time,
All was right while everything was fine.
Friendship is a tie that binds
With its illusive ropes of eternal life.
It's saddening to have lost touch.
My eyes itch to well up.
Yet, I will not allow those tears to ever be cried.
There is a reason why I cut all of those ties.
Of a death most foul, friendship dies.

I am the road less traveled.

I awoke with a start, gasping for breath. A book fell beside the lounge chair with a thud. The ceiling fan slid in and out of focus as it spun haphazardly in the breeze. The air was suffocating, and a trickle of sweat ran down the side of my face.

Waking up from an ordinary nap always had a sense of stupefaction, but waking up from a nap to the heavily intoxicating aroma of the neighbor's daylilies and the sweltering heat of late afternoon was even more so. After days on end of dreary weather, the sun was trying its damnedest to send the temperature through the roof. I cleared my throat and tried to swallow, but my tongue stuck to the dry palate.

Sitting up with a wince, my skin peeled from the plastic of the lounge chair with a sticky rip. Leaves on the trees danced in the stifled breeze, and a drone of bees bumbled along the rafters of the rooftop. Ever watched one those movies where someone woke up to find the world had ended without warning, leaving that person as the only being left alive? That was what it felt like sitting there on the back porch. Like I had slipped through the cracks of the world's untimely demise.

A feeling of grief still resided in my soul. The dream was fresh in memory, and I couldn't shake it. They had grown more prominent as the summer dragged on and intensified with the heat. I needed to clear my head, to just stop thinking altogether. Running wasn't the smartest idea due to the current condition of it being hotter than hell outside, but the chance to drown out thoughts with a speeding heartbeat and overexerted lungs was far too enticing to care about what was and wasn't a good idea.

A gurgle of a boiling pot echoed off the tiled floor as the backdoor swung shut. The smell of a roast being cooked wafted through the kitchen as my mom busied herself at the island with a knife and cutting board. With a shoulder pinning the cordless phone to her ear, she was gossiping away while she sliced and diced one carrot after another.

"Can you believe what she wore to service on Sunday? The nerve of that woman!" she whispered in a gasp. Whoever was on the line clucked on while my mom pursed her lips and mmhmm'd.

Holier-than-thou Southern Baptists were the worst. They would smile at your face but stab you in the back the instant you turned around. Despite their friendly promises, that was the only way they "had your back." Anybody and everybody was fair game, and they'd throw you under the bus for their own selfish betterment. If you wanted to survive dealings with those self-righteous hypocrites, you had to follow three key rules: **(1)** Always keep a watchful eye over your shoulder. **(2)** Keep your friends close and your enemies closer. **(3)** Never trust a word they say.

"Momma said that she actually volunteered to help with the church picnic! Do you believe it?" she sputtered, and more clucking noises ensued. "I know it, honey! She's about as crazy as ol' Derenda if she thinks she can fit into our fellowship!"

There she was running her mouth to God only knows who. Ten bucks said it was Nadine, my uncle Royce's wife. What happened to that judge not lest ye be judged stuff they were always cramming down everyone's throats? It truly was hard to have faith in people when they didn't practice what they preached.

I grabbed my running shoes and disappeared out the front door unnoticed. It went without saying that it was hot enough to fry an egg on the sidewalk. I had a strong feeling I'd regret what I was about to do five minutes down the road, but I was too damn stubborn to change my mind.

Ever had that feeling where someone was watching you? It felt as though needles were prickling the back of your neck. Like an uncanny sixth sense of sorts. A nonchalant scan about the street located the source of the pinpricks. Eye contact was made. Son of a bitch.

Mrs. Thomas from next door expectantly met my gaze. What was I supposed to do? A head nod and a smile of acknowledgement weren't going to be my ticket out of this one, not this time. I didn't know what she wanted, but it had to be something. Her eyes said so.

"G'd evening, young Mr. Harper," she called.

Slowly, I forced my legs to walk up the pathway leading to the front porch. The flowerbeds she'd been working on were finished. Big, bright blooms were a vast and crowded sea of color. The strongly fragrant daylilies hung heavy, tickling my nose.

"How are you on this fine day?" she asked with a tender smile.

I didn't know why, but I knew she really wanted to know how I was. The way she stared so intently as she waited on my response was as surreal as surreal could get.

"I'm good," I answered, and then I hastily dusted off my manners. "Thank you for asking, ma'am. How are you?"

"I can't complain." She shrugged her shoulders and gave an airy laugh. "I could, but focusing on life's negativities would ruin the beautiful day I've had."

Beautiful day? That wasn't the adjective of choice I would use. Muggy, humid, or even the stankness of the devil's armpit would better suffice for an accurate description.

"I...uh...your flowers are nice," I murmured, nodding toward the beds along her front porch for emphasis.

"Not of my doing," she said simply. "I merely planted them. They took it upon themselves to be, as you say, nice."

My lips rolled inward as I widened my eyes. No clue as to what to say.

"You look like you could use a nice, cold glass of sweet tea." She reached over to the pitcher sitting on the table by her rocker. Before I could object, she had already poured a glass. "Please, have a seat and make yourself at home."

She rocked back and forth, gently singing under her breath while I sipped the sweet tea. Usually, I had a knack of overriding all sympathetic tendencies, but Mrs. Thomas was sincere. I figured it wouldn't hurt to entertain her for a few minutes by accepting her invitation. There was some shred of humanity left within me (sarcastic laugh inserted here).

"Congratulations on graduating college," she said encouragingly. "That's quite an honor, young man."

"Thank you, ma'am." I didn't know how she even knew about it. It wasn't like my parents were bragging or anything.

"That little sister of yours informed me." She cut her eyes in my direction as if she'd read my mind.

"Memphis?"

"That'd be the one. She stopped by here just the other day with that puppy of hers. Wanted to schedule a play date with my Jasper." She laughed, shaking her head. "Said her big brother, the college graduate, rescued him. Oh, she just went on and on about how much she wanted to be just like you when she grew up."

I slowly nodded my head, unsure of what else to say. Why would Memphis want to be like me? Hell, I didn't even want to be like me.

"I was just like her at that age, you know? Spunky and full of spirit. I used to run around with the neighbor boy, TC. We would spend each hour of the day to its fullest. One time...."

cue flashback music

121

Mrs. Thomas:TC and I were playing down at my father's old barn. TC claimed he was a real cowboy and that girls couldn't be cowboys. "Who'd be the ones needin' the rescuin'?" he reasoned. Well, that just burnt my biscuits. I told him that real cowboys could jump onto a running horse. "That's easy," he said to me. I knew TC was a big ol' baby and wouldn't try it, but he was bound and determined to prove he could. TC was the stubbornest boy I had ever met. I didn't think he would go through with it, but he did. He had me bring one of my father's old mares through the barn, and he climbed up to the hayloft. He jumped alright, but he tried to chicken out at the last minute and missed the horse completely. Oh buddy, that ol' TC landed in a great big pile of horse manure. The look on his face...I cried from laughing so hard. I knew TC wasn't a real cowboy....

fade back to present day

It sure did sound like something Memphis would do, and I couldn't help but to join in on her laughter. Old Mrs. Thomas was a hoot just like my kid sister.

Sitting on the porch and listening to her reminiscence was actually enjoyable. As long as I was willing to listen, she was happy as can be. Like all she needed was someone who cared enough to pay attention.

The rocker I was sitting in probably belonged to her husband. Maybe she just needed to hear it creaking back and forth on the porch beside hers so she wouldn't feel as lonely. Life could bless us tremendously, but it could also take away whenever it felt like doing so. What did children used to call it on the playground? Being an "Indian giver" or something like that? While the term was politically incorrect, there was no better way to describe it.

She fell silent as her rocker creaked back and forth. Jasper was sprawled out beside the chair, and he twitched his hind leg with a grunt. The breeze danced with the chimes, and their steps clattered as they twirled. The ice in my empty glass chinked, melting in the heat of the evening.

"Thank you for the tea, Mrs. Thomas, but I really should get going if I want to get a run in before it gets dark." I sat the glass on the table and stood. "I really enjoyed hearing your story."

"I enjoyed sharing it with you," she said with a smile on that weathered face of hers. "You are welcomed anytime."

"Have a good evening," I said, turning to the steps.

"On your way out, could you do me a favor?"

I knew there had to be something that she wanted; however, I didn't mind doing her a favor, not anymore. "Yes ma'am."

"If you would, could you drag the bags of potting soil at the side of the house to the backyard for me? I would do it myself, but it'd take me forever."

"Sure thing," I told her. "I don't mind."

She thanked me again, and then she disappeared inside with the empty glasses. There were just two bags of potting soil that needed moving. No big deal. I grabbed both bags and hoisted them over my shoulders. They were heavier than they looked, but I managed. The closer I got to the backyard the heavier they seemed to grow.

As soon as I got around the side of the house, I dumped one bag onto the ground and then the other. After days of rain, the bags had managed to absorb water. The absorbed water turned the potting soil into a muddy mess. This muddy mess now caked the front of my shirt.

I eased it off over my head and tossed into the garbage can at the curb. It wasn't worth cleaning; some stains were permanent. Shoes gritted against the sidewalk as I turned to head the direction leading away from town, away from the time-capsule of a past.

The slanted rays of sunlight cast shadows of relief from the heat. A hint of twilight's approaching coolness doused the atmosphere as my feet pounded toward the outer limits of the subdivision. There wasn't much to see as far as the postcard certifications went. The sidewalk disappeared right where big plans for expansion had fizzled out, leaving barren lots of land with overturned trees. It was impossible to make out the contractor's original intentions for the property. The undergrowth grew wild, mixing with the redness of the clay dirt and engulfing the fallen trees. Mother Nature was reclaiming her brethren.

Most residents (i.e. my mother and my grandmother) called the back of our "lovely, highly esteemed" neighborhood an eyesore, but I liked the rawness of the countryside. It was untainted by the wear of assimilated perfection. If you listened closely, you could hear the wind rustle through the trees and the babbling of a creek as it fed into the river running along the side of town.

The road cut its way through the terrain, winding around an unkempt pond and up to a cul-de-sac on a hill. It was a nice, little spot with great views. My calves were burning by the time I reached the top. The circle of pavement was usually void of life, but someone was sitting with their back turned my way and looking at the river. I'd recognize that mess of blonde-brown hair from anywhere.

"Jesus!" Ackerley gawped as he turned around. "What the hell are you doing? Streaking? Put some more clothes on. God."

"I assumed I wouldn't see anyone." I locked both hands together and rested them on my head. So far, I've been accused of stalking and streaking. What was next?

"Y-y-yeah, uh, well, uh...," he trailed off, looking away and clearing his throat. "Uh, you know what they say about assuming."

"Ha." I gave a short laugh at his fluent sarcasm as I took a seat on the ground close to him. He shifted uncomfortably like I smelled bad. Maybe he was agitated by my presence. I knew how bothersome it could be when someone disrupted your solitary confinement. "If I'm interrupting something, I can leave you alone."

"I don't mind," he said, plucking a blade of grass and rolling into a ball between his thumb and forefinger.

We sat in silence, taking in the view. It was the perfect place to sit and think—to just be. The river flowed under the bridge and out into the horizon. Its surface reflected the oranges and pinks as the sun slowly set behind the mountain range. A boat was making its way upstream, its engine whining against

126

the current. A light breeze crept by, bringing relief from the humidity.

"My dad has always wanted a boat, but my mom is dead set against it," I offered in a notion of small talk as I watched the rippling water in the powerboat's wake.

"Why?"

"Your guess is as good as mine."

He shrugged his shoulders and nodded his head in thought. Silence resumed taking the lead in the conversation, but then Ackerley got a word in edgewise.

"So...," he said, expelling air from his lungs. "I guess you didn't want to go today."

"What?"

"Geo-cach-ing." He stretched the syllables to make it sound like three words as if I were a halfwit. "I left you a voicemail this morning."

"Oh, yeah," I said, suddenly recalling his invitation. I shrugged my shoulders. "I forget I have a phone sometimes. Sorry."

"You're weird."

"Thanks."

"Seriously, how do you forget something like that?"

"I never use it."

"Don't you have any friends from college?"

"Not really." I copied him and plucked a blade of grass. "While I've been put out to pasture in this godforsaken town, they are too busy living their lives to be bothered with keeping in touch."

"Did you ever think that maybe you are the one who's not keeping in touch?"

As much as I hated to admit it, he was kind of right. The truth was I hadn't made any of those lifelong friends you heard people rave about when reminiscing on their college years. To be honest, all I had to show for that span of four years were acquaintances who I couldn't care less about.

"This hell hole isn't so bad when you have others who feel your pain," he added, flicking the balled up blade of grass at me. "We should hang out or something."

"And do what exactly?" I asked, arching an eyebrow with skepticism. Why on earth would I want to hang out with an immature teenager?

"I don't know…." He cocked his head and smiled. "Rhi's parents are going out of town tomorrow night, meaning she's going to have the place to herself. Come over and hang out with us."

"Maybe—"

"Don't be such a fucking stick in the mud."

"You have such a way with words."

"I know, right?" He let out a boastful laugh. "Say you'll come over."

Maybe it was the extended exile paralleling Napoleon's Elba. Maybe it was the fact he'd made a valid point. Maybe the road of solitude was getting long and weary. Either way, something caused me to make plans to hang out the following night.

The last rays of sunlight were fighting to stay in the sky as twilight set in. An edge of coolness tickled my body, reminding me of just how undressed I was. It'd be smart to get a move on and head back, but a part of me was curious as to why he was there. I lost the battle of tact. "May I ask you a question?"

"I don't know. Can you?"

"That's not the way the grammar joke goes."

"Details, details," he said, waving has hand.

"Why are you up here?"

He pointed below to a car approaching the bridge. "Just…just watch," he added, his voice growing somber.

The headlights shined on the beams of the bridge. Each one was briefly highlighted as the car crossed, and then it returned to its darkened state as the next one was bathed in light. Like one door closing led to another door opening. It wasn't anything spectacular, but it was captivating to say the least.

"For the headlights?"

"Yes…and no. It's really just a part of it," he admitted. "I, uh….I come here when I just need a break from life." He bashfully turned away like he was self-conscious about dropping the suave, mastered pretenses and just being himself.

"What do you mean?"

"It's hard to explain." He went silent as he watched the fleeting headlights. "It's like...it's like when you fall in love with a song, you know? At first, you love it so much that you play it over and over again, but then the radio starts playing it repetitively. The song is everywhere, breathing down your neck. You begin to hate it and go out of your way to avoid it until eventually its memories have faded...." He trailed off as another car crossed the bridge. Doors closed. Doors opened.

"Then, there comes that day...that day you hear the song after all the bad memories are gone. It's then...it's right then and there when you realize why you fell in love with it to start with."

His voice dropped down to a whisper as he looked out into the settling darkness. "Yeah...life's like that."

I am a cat in the dark.

It's funny how when you actually had to put thought into clothing that you immediately decided you didn't have a thing to wear. Any other day, you could just throw open your closet doors, grab the first thing you laid your eyes on, and be good to go. See what thinking gets you? Sometimes, you had to tell yourself to get a grip and throw something on so you wouldn't be running late.

And so, I was on Rhi's front porch in jeans and a t-shirt with my hand poised to ring the bell. Quick as lightning in a summer storm, the door opened and I was jerked inside. The sudden transition into low lighting was blinding. All I heard was a quick "Did anyone see you?" as the door thudded to a close.

"Why does it matter?" I replied, blinking away the darkness. Rhi didn't answer the question. Instead, she stretched on her tiptoes and looked out the window. "Hello? What's going on?"

"Checking to see if Martha Gibson saw you," she explained, turning away from the window. "She has nothing better to do than spy on everyone. She takes it upon herself to inform my parents about everything I do."

"I know exactly who you're taking about." Old Bitch No. 1 was a pain in everybody's ass.

"Come on," she instructed, motioning for me to follow.

From the looks of it, Rhi's house wasn't expertly decorated by an interior designer or modeled after the latest trend as my mother preferred. The furniture was un-cohesive odds and ends. There wasn't a place for everything, and everything wasn't in its place. It wasn't fabricated into looking like a model home ready for potential buyers to traipse through, no. Rhi's house looked like someone actually lived there.

She led the way through the kitchen, out the sliding glass doors, and into the backyard. The view from my bedroom window didn't do it justice. White lights were strung up around the yard. With dusk settling in, they shined and shimmered off the surface of the swimming pool.

"You actually showed up," Ackerley declared from the poolside. He was dangling his feet in the water and sipping from a beer bottle. "Shocker."

Rhi plopped down onto the concrete patio and dipped her legs into the water, leaving me standing there. Talk about awkward. I didn't know whether to follow her example or sit on one of the lounge chairs. Making decisions on the spur of the moment wasn't me. I had to at least think before I acted. Making matters even more so awkward, I stepped toward the lounge chair but stopped myself with an obscure body jerk. I was officially out of my element.

"Are you just going to stand there or are you going to sit down?" Rhi asked with a girlish giggle, patting the concrete in an invitation. Her personality had done a complete turnaround. Since when was she all prissy?

"Yeah. Okay." My words stumbled out. Shoes were slipped off, and jeans were rolled up. Taking a seat between the two of them, I dipped my feet into the water. It had been heated from the day's sun and felt like a warm bath.

"You want one?" Ackerley asked, directing the attention back his way as he tilted the bottle toward me.

An eyebrow arched with skepticism as I eyed the bottle in his hand. "Illegal drinking? Nice."

"You're not going to tell...are you, Mr. Harper?" He laughed and tilted his head back, finishing off the beer.

"Here," he said, grabbing a bottle at his side and holding it out to me in an offer.

Remind me why I was here again? They were each tolerable when they weren't with the other, but together they fed off each other's energy. Beggars couldn't be choosers though. The way things were headed, a migraine wouldn't be out of the realm of possibilities. Why the hell not? A cold beer was exactly what I needed if I was going to have to put up with their immaturity. I took it from him and twisted the cap off, sucking the foam.

Rhi flipped her hair over her shoulder and gave me a funny look. "Soooo, I heard you like to show off your hot bod," she said flirtatiously, causing Ackerley to cough and spew beer from his mouth.

"Excuse me?" I asked with a sarcastic laugh, cutting eyes toward him. His cheeks were flushed, and he was giving Rhi a loathsome look that not only screamed for her to go straight to hell.

"I did *not* say you were showing off your 'hot bod,'" Ackerley sputtered, unable to meet my gaze. "I just said you were practically fucking naked like you owned the damn place or something. Jesus."

"Right," Rhi said, rolling her eyes. "Whatever."

The tension between the two of them was thick. Obvious, too. Something was clearly gnawing at their emotions. It was shaping up to look like a long night.

Maybe I should orchestrate a reason to go home, but that would entail me *actually* having to go home. If I had to choose between playing referee for these two or sitting in my room alone, there was no competition. I finished the beer without a second thought.

"So...have you looked through any pictures yet?" I asked, trying to clear the air.

"Actually, I have," she said, shooting Ackerley a mischievous smile. "Which reminds me, I need you to sign something saying you give me your consent."

"My consent for what exactly?" I gave a timid laugh as some sort of apology for being confused. It was one of those character flaws some people had. The need to apologize for something they couldn't control was illogical. Did its irrationality stop it from happening automatically, if not involuntarily? No. Did it stop people from expecting to hear that you were sorry for something you couldn't help? No.

"In case I use a picture of you, duh."

"Consider yourself lucky," Ackerley interjected obvious sardonicism, taking another long swig from the bottle. "She tricked everybody else by agreeing to take pictures at the church picnic and having everyone sign a consent form."

"Uh...excuse you," she scoffed. "I'm a very resourceful woman."

I nodded my head in agreement and finished off the beer. The slightest buzz could be felt, gurgling deep inside with an edge of relaxation and laughter. God, I hadn't drunk alcohol in forever. During the last year of college, I took it upon myself to be mature and responsible. So, I gave up drinking and smoking in order to prepare for the future—a future that was clearly never going to happen. Fuck it. Dire consequences weren't possible, so why not have another one?

Silence exuded from the poolside. Have you ever been in a situation and not known what to say? It was too silent and uncomfortable. You got lost in your head, deeply thinking while the weight of the silence bears down on your shoulders. The fact that I was actually sitting with two high school kids and drinking beer made me laugh. No, it wasn't one of those sarcastic har-de-har-hars. It started out as a breathy snort that quickened. Then, the chuckles grew more prominent. Gut-wrenching laughter ensued, intensifying the awkwardness. The dumbfounded expression on both of their faces caused me to shake with a silent wheeze. I couldn't help it.

"What the hell is your problem?" Ackerley spat. Like the concept of him being a potential cause to my "problem" was both vile and bitter.

Maybe it was the alcohol talking or maybe it was the weirdness of the whole night, but either way I felt high for the first time in a long time. "It's just that here I am with you two," I said after I'd collected myself.

"Why do you say that?" he asked defensively.

"Yeah, what's the deal, asshole? Huh?" Rhi playfully kicked water in my direction, reverting back to her teasing nature.

"No, it's not that," I said, holding up my hands to pacify them. "I just feel so much older and shit."

"Jesus, man. You aren't that much older," he pointed out with annoyance.

"I can see where you are coming from, though," she empathized surprisingly, causing Ackerley to roll his eyes at her attempt to showcase a serious demeanor. "I bet it's like that phrase 'been there and done that.' You've experienced college and all that. I guess we seem pretty juvenile in comparison...."

"I wouldn't say either of you are juvenile," I said, bending the truth. Their antics and overt personalities were all a front they used; however, I saw right through it. Like I said, I paid attention to detail. "How can I say this? Um...I guess it's just that we don't have the same experiences, not that it makes a difference because I don't think it should. You see, who a person is relies on the lessons derived from the, for lack of a better word, stuff they've had to go through. There isn't a requirement exactly on what experiences a person should have in order to be considered an equal. Some have experiences that others do not, and some have experiences that will forever change them. Some experiences are unfair. Some leave their mark."

A mouthful had been said, so I stopped talking. Silence followed the wake of the rambled speech. Climbing down off my soap box, I mumbled, "I get carried away sometimes. That probably doesn't even make sense. I guess I talked myself into a hole."

"No," Ackerley said as he met my gaze. "I couldn't agree more with what you just said."

"Care to share what you've learned, wise ass?" she asked with a mocking smile as she leaned back onto her elbows, completely disregarding what Ackerley had just said.

Phoenix's Guide to Life:
Tips, lessons, and advice from personal experience.

- Who you are in high school does NOT matter in the real world
- You will change more times than imaginable
- Your priorities will never be the same
- Never drink more than you know you can handle

- Do NOT expect someone to take care of you when you're shitfaced
- Life is nothing like the movies
- Nothing is perfect
- You will be let down
- Where you come from does NOT affect where you're going
- First impressions never matter

Please note that the aforementioned material is entirely subjective. These are advisory opinions derived from one Mr. Phoenix Harper's experiences. Following through with these tips does not guarantee a happier and/or better life.

"That's just about all I can think of right now."

I finished off the second beer with a gulp as they each nodded their head, appraising the tidbit of advice I offered from twenty-two years of existence. I wanted to tell them that because you had a college degree didn't mean you'd get a job. Just look at me. I couldn't even get a job at a fucking department store.

"No offense, but way to make the conversation get too serious," Rhi said, puffing her cheeks and expelling air with a sigh. "Let's inject a little life into this snooze fest with some music." She hopped up from the poolside and made her way toward the sliding glass doors.

As she disappeared inside the house, Ackerley leaned in and whispered, "Don't pay any attention to her. She doesn't do serious." His tone took on the sense of pretension as if she were incompetent.

"What's her problem?"

He leaned closer, his eyes never straying from mine. "Don't worry about her," he said, dropping the petulant behavior now that Rhi had left. "She's just being a bitch." He pulled the side of his mouth up into a smirk. I could smell the fermented beer on his breath as he continued, "Au contraire, mon frère...me and you though? We're on the same level."

What little alcohol there was had made everything intense. His brow arched with intensity. His eyes glowered with intensity. His crooked grin smiled with intensity.

"No offense, but your breath reeks," I said, unable to filter my thoughts.

"Yours ain't so great either."

With a lighthearted laugh, he broke the intimidating connection and looked down. He kicked his leg out and splashed water. Almost as though it was an involuntary response, I mimicked him and splashed water back. Bad idea.

Next thing I knew, we were tumbling through the air and into the pool. The world turned upside-down as water rushed over me. Arms and legs tangled together as we wrestled and dunked one another under in childish playfulness derived from alcohol.

"Ehem!" Rhi overdramatically cleared her throat. "If you two are done dicking around...."

I snapped my head around to look at her as she plugged an MP3 player into portable speakers. The dulcet tone of Rhi's namesake was carried by the summer breeze, giving the words wings so they could take to the sky. It was obvious she chose that specific song to make herself the center of attention. She smiled seductively and grasped the edge of her shirt. In a flash (no pun intended), she was standing there in her bra. Color me a million different shades of embarrassed. I averted my gaze as she dropped her shorts and looked over at Ackerley. He rolled his eyes and turned his back toward her, mumbling incoherently under his breath.

A dainty, little splash rang out in the night, and then water lapped the sides. I didn't know what Rhi thought she was doing, but she swam up behind me and jumped onto my back. "Guess who?" she whispered into my ear with a breathy voice. Like I didn't already know. Her...well, her breasts were pushed up against my back. Logically, there was only one guess as to who it could possibly be. What was the point of her asking such an inane question?

She laughed one of those girly giggles that seemed to echo into the night, and then she pushed away, making sure her body rubbed up against mine as slowly as possible. The sudden whoosh of cascading water drew my attention toward the other end of the pool. Ackerley had climbed out and was walking across the yard without looking over his shoulder. Rhi grunted with an annoyed sigh and followed after him. Like he was a child who needed consoling.

Between the beers, the warmth of the water, and the coolness of the night air, I didn't care what was going on. Contentment was found simply by floating on my back and looking up into the night sky—just being.

The lightning bugs were out, flashing across the sky without haste or urgency or desire to be somewhere else. The neon spark of yellow was stunning in front of the night's canopy of darkness. I was reminded of childhood and roaming all over the yard trying to catch them. Oh, how I wished that they didn't have to flash. I wanted them to shine that breathtaking glow forever. What you wanted from life didn't matter though. It was unfair like that. If I've learned anything, it was that nothing in life was meant to last.

I am the ant.

A sharp intake of breath zipped in-between clenched teeth. Rough concrete of the sidewalk scraped into my knees. The world was lopsided, tilting above me. The hand. The hand jerked me down. The hand—the hand tightened its grip. The eyes. The eyes told me everything was fine. The eyes—the eyes were lying.

Fear.

Hand.

Eyes.

Church.

Houses.

Sky.

Trees.

A melodic symphony's complex score reversed. My heart pounded frightened beats. The hand released its pressure. My knees buckled, meeting the concrete.

143

Blood lessened and lessened as the pain ricocheted into nothingness.

Churchhousesskytreeschurchhousesskytrees.

Please. Wrong anything do didn't I. Boy good a was I swear I, Daddy. Manners my minded even I.

Churchhousesskytrees.

Be to me told you like boy good a was I. Run didn't I promise I, Momma.

Church.

Houses.

Sky.

Trees.

Slower and slower. Everything spiraled into control: the church steeple, the houses, the sky. The blur slowed into focus. Trees. Such pretty trees with such pretty green leaves. I was falling up, up, up. My head was spinning, spinning, spinning.

Both feet wobbled. The hand released my arm. Balance was caught. I was upright. The world. The world stopped turning. The world stopped spinning. The world stopped.

The hand. The hand jerked my arm. The hand pulled me down. I was falling. Forever falling. Forever replaying as the world circled around me. Trees. Sky. Houses. Church.

The words. The words rang out. The words were deafening. The words took my breath. The words choked me. The words hurt me. The words sliced through me. The words.

"I bet you like cartoons, don't you? C'mon on inside…it's okay. I promise."

=

A gasp rattled through the darkened room as I bucked against the mattress with an arched back. Ghost pains shot through me, throbbing with memories. The sheets were tangled and clinging with nightmare sweat. Blood slushed against veins with frenzied heartbeats, drowning out the silence. Breaths were short-lived gasps, rattling through lungs. Like a dog panting for relief. Inhale. Exhale. Inhale. Exhale. Inhale. There would never be any relief.

The heat of the summer, the heat of small town life, the heat of remembrance—the heat was getting to me. Dreams were growing unbearable. Memories were slipping through the cracks, weakening the levies. The art of repression was drying up as life grew increasingly magnified.

Burning. I was trapped inside the house where no one called home, burning from the heat. How much longer could I last? Flames danced around me. My eyes filled with their light. My body scorched from their heat. The magnification—the magnification was burning me.

I am the tortoise.

Associative memory (ə'sōsē͟ātiv 'mem(ə)rē): *noun.* Remembering a previously experienced event, item, day, etc. by thinking of another, thus linking the two together.

In laymen's terms, it meant one thing made you think of another thing and so on and so forth. I had an associative memory by nature. Examples: **(1)** Every time I got ready for bed, I thought of a cartoon I'd watched when I was a kid because one of the characters joked about combing his hair for all the girls he was going to meet in his dreams. **(2)** Whenever I saw, smelled, or thought about seafood, I thought about my grandfather. **(3)** The scent of used books always reminded me of the library at the elementary school I'd gone to.

According to the definition of associative memory, the reason why my eye twitched when my mother said my name in a sugary-sweet tone was because I associated it to the act of someone buttering you up for a favor. Like I was a damn dinner roll.

"Phoenix," she cooed, leaning against my bedroom door. "When was the last time you got out of the house? Hun, I bet you are about to go plum crazy being cooped up in here."

That right there, my friends, was the hook, and the bait was my bereavement. It was the prelude to the favor. First, she had to entice me to get me on her side.

"You know, if you want to get out and get yourself a little fresh air," she began, waving her arms toward the window for emphasis, "then I'll give you some money to do so, darlin'."

And now, we waited. The fishing lure dangled in front of me as I weighed the options. Do I snag it knowing what will happen, or do I stretch it out for as long as possible while her patience wears thin?

"The girls are coming over here soon," she added, tugging on the fishing line and causing the lure to dance. "We're planning for the big Fourth of July cookout. If you wanted to help with that, then you are surely welcomed."

In other words, most of the women on the block were coming over to gossip and cluck. With my dad working his last day before the holiday vacation, it would be her last day of freedom before she would have to cater to his needs 24/7. It wasn't that she only wanted me out of the house, per se. She wanted my brother and sisters out of the house, too. What better way to do so than trick me into believing I needed some fresh air and have my siblings tag along?

And so, I weighed the options and decided taking my brother and sisters to the movie theater would cause less bereavement than being in a house full of dangerous levels of estrogen. Why a movie? Because for about two hours we wouldn't all have to try to "get along" with one another (i.e. factoring in Raleigh and the eclectic accessory of teenage bitchiness, which was ever-most-prominent in her day to day wardrobe).

The movie theater in town was located at the town's small shopping center, which everybody and their brother referred to as the "mall." It was a five cinema multiplex that stuck out like a sore thumb. With its vibrant paint job and futuristic décor, it was the only extravagant building in the plaza. Due to it being summertime in conjunction to the temperature reaching a degree more reasonable for the pits of Hades, the place was crawling with teenagers milling around in their vain attempt at socialization. Everybody had the same idea. Great. Just fucking great.

No sooner than when we piled out of my SUV, the over-countrified twang echoed through the parking lot. Terri the Variant was all gussied up for the evening with **(A)** her bleached hair in big, hairspray-plastered curls,

(B) jean shorts that looked more like underwear and a cleavage baring shirt that left nothing to the imagination, and **(C)** enough makeup to make a clown cringe. Now, that was what you called classy right there.

"Raaaaaliegh!" she drawled, placing her hand on chest in an "I do declare" gesture like she was some Southern belle. Please. The only type of belle she was got rang every hour on the hour, if you caught my drift. "What are the odds of seeing you here?!"

"Seeing as she was texting you while we were on our way here, the odds are pretty good," Jackson muttered under his breath.

"Hello there, Phoenix," Terri said, battling her heavily mascaraed eyelashes. It looked as if she had road tire lining her eyes.

A tight-lipped smile and a head nod was the best I could do by way of greeting. I couldn't stand that girl. Sometimes, you got this feeling right when you met someone and immediately didn't like them. Contrary to popular belief, I seldom instantly disliked a person. Though, I was frequently unfriendly, but that was a-whole-nother topic altogether.

"What movie are we going to see?" Memphis asked, tugging on my arm.

"I want to see the space movie," Jackson said, reading the show times.

"There's that new romantic comedy we should all see!" Terri exclaimed, literally bouncing in her heels.

"Uh...." Memphis put her hand on her cocked hip. "Listen, I don't know who you think are you, but no. I am not about to watch that mushy gushy crap."

"Excuse me, small fry? What did...," Terri trailed off, forgetting all about her comeback as something caught her eye. "Sweet Jesus, it's that weirdo in our class."

Of course, we all turned around to look like the nosey people that we were. My definition of weirdo ranged along the lines of being dressed in all black or something of the like. I scanned the parking lot. There weren't any ensembles of darkness. All I saw were normal-looking people blending into the crowd.

Raleigh smiled and ran her fingers through her hair, primping herself up. She raised her hand in a little wave at whoever it was, and then Terri cocked her head around so fast it could've given her whiplash. Still, I didn't know what was going on. Talk about being completely out of the loop.

"Oh my God," Terri said, looking at Raleigh with wild eyes. "Are you shittin' me? How many times are you going to talk about this? He's probably dating that other freak he hangs out with, if *that*'s even what he's into. You are so much better than him. He works at a fuckin' grocery store for God's sake."

Raleigh's smile faltered. Who made Terri the queen bee calling all the shots? Why in the hell did high school kids think they had the right to exert a sense of authority over others? If only they knew. I had a pretty good idea who they were talking about. Normally, I minded my own business, but she really pissed me off for some reason.

"Terri, I thought your father was a preacher. Does he know you not only dress like a prostitute but also cuss like a sailor? Show a little respect and watch what you say," I said slowly and evenly, nodding my head toward Memphis. My kid sister didn't need to extend her already large vocabulary.

Raleigh and Terri both eyed me strangely. Like I was an inanimate object that had suddenly decided to speak. "Uh," Terri said acidly. "Come on, Ral. Let's go see *Cloud Nine and Rising.*" She shot me a death glare and tugged on Raleigh's arm. I heard her say something along the lines of me being a douchebag as they walked away. Lovely.

I turned around to see Ackerley walking up to us. Nothing about him said "freak," not even in the slightest trace. He was a nice-looking guy with symmetrical features. Sure, he might've been a loner, but that was because he didn't force himself to fit in. Teenagers were cruel—that was all there was to it. He was a decent guy, and he didn't let the fact he had a bad home life burden him down. The way he kept his head held high made all the difference. That was the only thing which really mattered.

"I'm going to watch that space movie," Jackson called over his shoulder, starting toward the theater.

The need to shout for him to be careful or to wait in the lobby after the movie ended skipped through my head, but I figured it was implied. He was at that age where he knew what he was doing. Besides, the thought of playing the older brother still felt new to me.

"We seriously need to stop running into each other like this," Ackerley said jokingly, clapping me on the back. Yeah, the friendly salutations were also new to me, too.

"Hi!" Memphis said before I could form words in my mouth. She tilted her head up to look at him. "Who are you?"

"Hello, little lady," he said with a grin and squatted down to eye level. "My name is Ackerley."

"It's nice to meet you," she said, holding out her hand. "The name's Memphis. I'm almost ten years old."

"Boy howdy, you're practically already grown up! I'm certainly honored to make your acquaintance, ma'am." He took her hand and shook it. "May I ask what you and your brother are up to?"

"I'm hoping he will take me to see that there newfangled animated movie. Maybe you could come and watch it with us? " She cut her eyes up to me, her face reading a question mark.

"Sure," I said, smiling. She could carry on a conversation with a brick wall. "You're welcomed to join in on the fun if you want."

"If you're sure your big brother doesn't mind, I would be most honored." He smiled up at me and winked. It was clear that he was falling under that crazed baboon's spell. He never even stood a chance.

"Of course not," she said, flicking her wrist in a pish-posh gesture. "My brother is the best big brother in the world. Have I ever told you about the time he saved Mr. Faustus?" She grabbed Ackerley's arm and led him toward the theater, going into the story of how Mr. Faustus had come to be a part of the family.

I followed behind them, shaking my head. Memphis was going to talk his ears off before it was all over with and done. Ackerley didn't seem to mind though. He played right along with her and reacted dramatically with facial expressions to everything she said. He wasn't a freak at all. You could tell a lot about a person by how far they were willing to go out of their way for the sake of someone else. In this case, he was willing to entertain my kid sister when he didn't even have to be doing so. That said a lot.

When we got to the ticket window, I paid for his ticket and told him it was my treat, not to worry about it. It was the least I could do. I had a feeling something was off about him being alone in the first place. Why wasn't he with Rhi?

Neither Jackson nor Raleigh were anywhere in sight as we walked to the designated screening room. Memphis had Ackerley by the hand, pulling him behind her as she led the way up the stairs. It took her a good while to decide on where to sit. She had to have the perfect seat in the perfect row in the perfect section. Finally deciding on the ideal seating arrangement, she plopped down into one of the cushioned chairs and pulled Ackerley down onto the neighboring seat.

"May I ask you something?" I whispered overtop Memphis's head.

"Shoot."

"I couldn't help but notice you weren't with your partner in crime."

He closed his eyes and took a deep breath like he was stressed and needed to calm down. "We just...I, uh...we've been spending too much time together," he explained. "It's to the point where we are both getting on each other's nerves."

"I understand."

"Usually, we hang out the night before the Fourth and celebrate, but we kind of got into it the other day. She left early with her parents to go see some family...so I thought I would catch a movie by myself."

154

"I'm sorry that you two are fighting." I really was sorry, too. It was hard to imagine the inseparable twosome being separated.

"Don't worry about it," he said with his usual grin. "This is fun, and I'm enjoying myself. Thanks for the concern, man."

"No prob—"

"Shh!" Memphis cut me off as the hum of the projector filled the air. "The previews are my favorite part."

Lights dimmed as the projector rolled the film. The screen blared to life with a green hue, announcing that the following preview had been approved for all audiences. The movie hadn't even started yet, but the previews were building up to something good. They created a buzz of excitement in the darkened theater as all eyes were glued to the screen in anticipation, eagerly waiting for what was yet to come.

And so, we all three sat there for one hour and forty-five minutes while an animated rabbit tried his best to outwit his friend but fell victim to hubris. The cartoon was chock-full with witty phrases and retorts, giving it an effect of trying too hard. There were even double entendres and references aimed at an older age demographic that could be misconstrued to mean something, for lack of a better work, dirty. Was it something new? No. Just go back and watch the cartoons of your youth and you'll notice references and sexual euphemisms that you didn't notice way back when. It was amazing how those little altercations of perception could distort the overall image in your memory. Sometimes, you just had to let yourself be open to the possibility of it all to see the bigger picture, to see something from a different perspective in order to pick up on the smaller details.

"Are you coming to the neighborhood cookout?" Memphis asked Ackerley as we exited the screening room. She had made us sit there while the credits rolled because she wanted her money's worth. It was one of those times where it was easier to just go along rather than argue.

"My family is…." He trailed off, and then he looked down at her with a smile. "If you promise to save me seat, I promise to be there."

"Pinky promise," she demanded, holding up her hand and outstretching her little finger. "And no backsies."

"I promise," he said, locking fingers. "I never back out on pinky promises."

"We shall see if you are true to your word, mister."

She grinned a grin that stretched from ear to ear, and then she darted off toward Jackson and Raleigh in the theater's lobby. Thankfully, Terri the Variant was nowhere in sight. I guessed she left Raleigh high and dry as soon as their movie was over. Just went to show you what kind of friend she was.

"Thanks for, ya know," Ackerley said, shrugging his shoulders.

"Don't mention it."

"I guess I should be getting back home. You will be there tomorrow, right?"

"Yeah, there isn't anything else to do."

"Cool," he said, stepping to the side door. "I'll see you then."

Before I could shout a parting phrase, the door was swinging shut and he was gone. Memphis shouted for me to hurry up, that she had to get home and check on Mr. Faustus. I loved her to death, but she could drive a person crazy if she unleashed all her cute, quirky personality traits at once. I supposed that was the reason why some things were just fine in moderation.

On the way home, I noticed the same old sign standing right before the bridge, warning truck drivers about their clearance. It was one of those things that had become part of the background as the years had stretched on, and I hadn't really paid attention to it. It was there, but it wasn't present—if that made any sense at all.

The paint on the sign was battered and weathered. It had giant lettering that read **WARNING: TRUCKS THAT HIT THIS WILL HIT BRIDGE**. These little, I didn't know what the correct term was but I referred to them as metal dangly things, hung from it.

Just seeing it called forth a memory from my youth: I didn't know why, but every time I would pass underneath those metal dangly things I would say to myself, "That's a mouthful of words. You'd think that they could have shortened it or something." Still, time had lapsed and the sign stood there with its mouthful of words, cautioning big rig drivers.

Wouldn't life be so much easier if it came with warning signs? If only there were big signs with a mouthful of words and metal dangly things so that we could check to see if any danger lay ahead. If only.

I am standing outside the gates of Hell.

Deep in the heart of Dixie where junebugs arrived a
month behind, the Fourth was being celebrated to its
finest. Sulfur Springs Park was packed with Sulfur
Springs' residents. Sunshine beat down upon sweaty
brows with slanted rays as a bluegrass band plucked
strings on a makeshift stage.

The swing set's chains groaned and creaked as legs
pumped faster and faster. Airy laughter of children
fluttered with reverberating sweeps. Like birds
stretching their wings and taking flight. Little tufts of
dust rose as they chased after one another, frolicking
through the playground with glee and delight.

Camping chairs were sprawled out in the shade of
canopies. Red and white checkered tablecloths swayed
in the virtually nonexistent breeze. There was food, and
there was plenty of it. Gas grills sizzled in the
background as animated chatter rose and fell in the tide

of conversation, drowning out the slightest traces of silence.

How the residents of our neighborhood could manage to carry on a dialogue when they barely spoke to one another during the remaining 364 days (365 if you took leap year into consideration) was astounding. For one day during the summer, differences were pushed aside as folks were united in camaraderie by their love for "America the Great." Blah, blah, blah. It was all for show. It was as fake as fake could get. People only grew overtly patriotic for one day during the year—just like when they became "holier than thou" when Sunday rolled around and the church doors were opened.

Irony. It was ironic that America's independence was being celebrated when the very foundation for which it was built upon was being torn down by one-minded simpletons. Sure, people were smiling and being polite to each other's faces, but as soon as they turned their backs...you know. The unification of so many hypocrites carrying on in their hypocritical ways and preaching their hypocritical morals was bound to bust Hell wide open. Those religious zealots could go there for all I cared. They would be right at home in the fiery pits of which they feared. Yeah...irony at its best.

I know what you're thinking. You're thinking that I'm some diehard atheist or that I hate America or that I bear the mark of the beast. No. You're wrong. Get a grip for cryin' out loud. Take the time to kindly remove your head from out of your own ass and see the bigger the picture. I just wanted to know one thing: **where is the love?**

The phrase "looking for love in all the wrong places" came to mind as Memphis and I wandered in search of her newly declared boyfriend. She told anyone willing to listen about how gorgeous he was. We weaved and bobbed through the sea of rednecks sprawled out on blankets and enjoying the somewhat cooling relief of evening as they listened to the bluegrass band. She had Mr. Faustus on a leash, and there was a festive bandana tied around his collar. He was none too pleased and refused to cooperate with her. She kept having to stop and say, "C'mon now, son." The whole stop-and-go ordeal allowed my ears to fall privy to the conspiratorial conversations racing about the picnic blankets.

From the journal of **AGENT FAWKES**
THE GATES OF HELL: *documented observations*

Mr. and Mrs. Anderson are lounging in collegiate, crimson chairs. Their expectant daughter and son-in-law are propped up on a picnic blanket of orange and blue.
<insert conversation script>

Beau Austin: *Hey babe, who's that guy? He looks familiar, dun't he?*

Caroline Anderson-Austin: *'Member Phoenix Harper?*

Beau Austin: *Ain't he that guy you told me about at that party —*

Caroline Anderson-Austin: *No! No, you don't know what you're talking about.*

Beau Austin: *Naw, I'm purty sure he is.*

Caroline Anderson-Austin: *You were drunk as a skunk that night.*

Beau Austin: *So what?*

Caroline Anderson-Austin: *You don't know your ass from a hole in the ground.*

<end of script>

Lisa Jacobs has on big, bulky sunglasses. She is sitting alongside three middle-aged women. They all four suspiciously glance up and then resume looking at the booklet shared between them.

<insert conversation script>

Middle-aged Woman #1: *So how real does this one feel?*

Lisa the Meat Specialist: *Oh honey, honey, honey. It's lifelike!*

Middle-aged Woman #2: *And you say it vibrates?*

Lisa the Meat Specialist: *Your G-spot won't know what hit it!*

Middle-aged Woman #3: *Ohhhhh! I'm excited just thinking about it.*

Lisa the Meat Specialist: *Trust me, ladies. The. Best. O. You'll. Ever. Have.*

Middle-aged Woman #2: *How much?*

Lisa the Meat Specialist: *You really can't put a price on heaven, can you?*

Middle-aged Woman#3: *You do have a point....*

Lisa the Meat Specialist: *But if you could, it'd be only $59.95. Plus tax.*

<end of script>

Sasha Travis has her blonde hair pulled back into a slicked down ponytail. Her eyebrows are furrowed and arched. She is sitting alongside her mother, who is fanning herself with a paper plate.

<insert conversation script>

Mother Travis: *Look at them Andersons being all uppity-uppity.*

Sasha Travis: *Caroline messed around and got herself knocked up.*

Mother Travis: *They ate supper before they said Grace. What'd you expect?*

Sasha Travis: *He only married her after he found out she missed her period.*

Mother Travis: *She's nothing more than plain ol' white trash. That's what she is.*

Sasha Travis: *She should've had the decency to have it taken care of like me.*

Mother Travis: *That prude Bethany Anderson is too uptight for that.*

Sasha Travis: *Thank the good Lord I have a mother like you.*

<end of script>

Martha Gibson is perched upon a chair with an attached umbrella shading her sagging face. Her eyes are darting back and forth between members of the crowd as she carries on a conversation with an elderly woman.

<insert conversation script>

Old Bitch No. 1: *She had the nerve to volunteer for Wednesday night service.*

Church Hen: *Cluck?*

Old Bitch No. 1: *Yeh-huh. We ain't needin' no help from bastard bearing sluts.*

Church Hen: *Clucky.*

Old Bitch No. 1: *She made her bed, and now she's got to lay in all that filth.*

Church Hen: *Cluck.*

Old Bitch No. 1: *Lola's amazed that woman don't bust in-ter flames during service.*

Church Hen: *Cluckity-cluck-cluck!*

\<end of script\>

John Hughes is wearing his fez hat and sitting with his arms folded across his chest. He is not paying attention to the conversation between his wife Lola and an unknown, middle-aged man.

\<insert conversation script\>

    High Horse Lola: *There he is.*

    Unknown Man: *Let's take care of this right now.*

    High Horse Lola: *Phoenix Harper, we need to have a word with you.*

Cover has been exposed.

Mission has been compromised.

END OF JOURNAL ENTRY

After dismounting her horse, my grandmother motioned with a quick, "come hither" gesture. There was a pinched up expression on her face. Like she had sucked on a lemon or bitten into a piece of meat that still had bones in it. The unknown, middle-aged man smiled a fake-ass smile—the kind where all his teeth were showing and his lips were all thin and all you could see was his gums. With a mouth like that, "Gummy" would be the appropriate alias for him.

"Young man," my grandmother started, "what do you have to say for yourself?"

"How about you tell me what's going on first?" I retorted. "That'd help for starters."

"Do you have any idea who this is?" she asked, jerking her head toward Gummy.

"Nope."

"This here is Brother Lynn, Terri's father." She cocked her head with snootiness.

"Okay."

"Son," Brother Lynn/Terri's father/Pastor Gummy addressed me. "Now, Terri told me what you said to her. Now-now, I'm sure it's all a big misunderstanding, but I wanted to hear what you had to say for yourself before we decided on what to do." He placed a firm hand onto my shoulder, gripping tightly as he smiled a crazed smile. Gums galore.

I cut my eyes to his hand. He was squeezing for emphasis. Like he was showing me who held the power. "Do not touch me," I said maliciously, knocking his hand aside and taking a step to the side. "What do you mean by what I have to say for myself?"

Pastor Gummy looked as though he had been smacked. I didn't give a damn who the hell he was or if he ought to be respected simply because he stood in front of a bunch of uncomfortable pews and made longwinded speeches about eternal damnation to a deaf, dumb, and blind congregation.

"You watch your mouth!" my grandmother spat. Like she had any right whatsoever to scold me. That old bitch could kiss my ass. Fuck her and the damn horse she rode in on.

"What do you want?" I asked, looking to make sure Memphis hadn't wandered out of sight.

"Son, Terri told me you were rude to her last night. Said you insulted her greatly. Said you hurt her feelings."

"Well?" High Horse Lola huffed.

"I was merely stating the facts." I shrugged my shoulders with indifference.

"So you don't deny it?" She jabbed a finger in my face, and I swatted her hand away. I was trying to keep my cool, but she was making it fairly impossible to do so. Like the length of my temper's fuse was dwindling the longer I looked at her sourpussed face. I wanted to hit her. John just sat there in silence without a care in the world as he always did.

"We both decided you will apologize to her," Gums decreed.

Seriously? Did he really think I would apologize? Yeah, right...and pigs were about to sprout wings and take to the sky any minute now. "That will not be happening," I said, turning away.

"I'm sorry?" Gummy Gums reached out and grabbed my arm to stop me from leaving. "Maybe I didn't hear you correctly, son."

"Maybe *you* didn't hear *me* correctly. I said don't touch me." I jerked my arm away from his grasp. "I will not apologize simply because I am not sorry. Not the least little bit. Your daughter does have a filthy mouth, and she was using foul language in front of my little sister. Maybe you should take into consideration your own family before you nose around in other people's business."

A few steps were taken, and then I turned around. "And by the way, neither one of you have the right to tell me what to do. No one tells me what to do." Maybe I have control issues. So, what?

"Don't you walk away from me!" High Horse Lola hissed in a whisper. Like she was trying to keep her voice down in order to keep anyone from overhearing. She would have a heart attack and fall right off her horse if she was the hot topic of gossip.

I hope people did overhear simply because she deserved it. I had never listened to a word she'd said a day before in my life. So, why start now? I kept walking, closing the distance between Memphis and myself. Mr. Faustus was still stopping-and-going, and she was trying to be a stern parent.

"How many times am I going to have to tell you? I am going to need you to stop lollygagging around," she said, waving her index finger in scolding manner. She looked up as I stepped beside her. "Where have you been? I can't do a gosh-darned thing with this child! I give up." She untied the bandana in defeat and handed it to me with a sigh of exasperation. I couldn't help but to smile as I pocketed it for safekeeping.

Soft hoots of laughter came from behind us. A woman, probably in her mid-thirties by the looks of it, was stretching out a blanket in the grass. I wasn't quite sure who she was though. Her blonde hair was pulled up into a bun, and there was a strand of pearls around her neck. Talk about fancy, especially for a picnic in Redneckville, USA. She gazed up, her soft blue eyes catching the light and twinkling.

"I couldn't help but overhear," she explained with a smile. It was bright and luminous and beautiful. "I take it that she's your little sister."

"Yes ma'am," I answered courteously. See, I was a gentleman when it mattered. Don't go thinking I was a rude prick.

"She's darling."

"Thank ya, ma'am," Memphis said, standing tall. "This here is my brother Phoenix, and this is Mr. Faustus." She held her hand out to the woman. "And, I'm Memphis."

"It's certainly nice to make your acquaintance, Memphis." She shook her outstretched hand. "I'm Emma. Emma Arnold."

"Here, Mom," said a strained male voice who I assumed to be her son. He stooped and dropped an armload of camping chairs. "Eric's got the kids," he added, standing upright. "Phoenix?"

"Ackerley!" Memphis exclaimed with relief. "We've been looking everywhere for you."

"Hey, uh...." He was at a loss for words as he glanced between his mother and us.

"We're late because of me," Mrs. Arnold said apologetically. "It took me just about forever to get the brownies perfect." She held up a festive dessert dish covered with plastic wrap.

"I'll take those over to the food table," Ackerley said, taking the dish from her hand.

He left us standing there as he headed off without so much as another word, and Memphis trailed after him with Mr. Faustus at her heels. Mrs. Arnold smiled up at me with an "okay we're done here" smile. I nodded a departure and followed after them.

Memphis was relentless in her inane ability to talk the ears off anyone. She was talking ninety miles-per-hour about her upcoming birthday, how pretty his mother was, how many siblings he had, and why he called his father by his first name. Talk about giving someone the third degree. Memphis was far too innocent to fully understand the shortcomings of the topics she was pestering him with. She had no idea what it meant to be tactful.

Ackerley was being polite about the whole ordeal. I mean, he could tell her to shut up or mind her business, but he didn't. He smiled and carried on the conversation, trying to change the topic without her realizing it. It was plain to see how uncomfortable he was over the fact we had met his mother. Like his home life and social life were two separate entities that were insoluble and unable to mix. Just talking about his family seemed to cause his shoulders to tense up as though the weight of the world were upon him.

"Memphis," I said, cutting her off from shooting another personal question at him. "Do you want a brownie?"

"Does a bear do his business in the woods?"

Ackerley had peeled back the plastic wrap on the dish and handed her a brownie when her name was yelled out of the blue. Our mom was waving her hand, motioning for Memphis to come over to their canopy. She sighed and tugged on Mr. Faustus's leash, crossing the sea of picnic blankets.

Once she was out of earshot, Ackerley let out a deep breath. "With her being your sister and all, you wouldn't think she'd be such a talker."

"I see where you're going with this," I began as we walked up to the food table, "and you aren't the least bit funny."

"Don't deny my wit!" He laughed and bumped my arm with his elbow. "It was hilarious, and you know it."

"Says you."

I waited for him to comeback with some smartass remark as per his usual, but he didn't. His cheeks went flush, the redness stretching up to his ears. What was going on? My mouth opened to ask what had upset him, but then I overheard the conversation we had unknowingly barged in on.

Martha Gibson and her compatriot were at the end of the food table. They were standing in a stance that gave way to the fact they were none too happy. Their arms were folded over their chest, and their eyes were shooting daggers into the crowd.

"Look at her all dressed up," Old Bitch No. 1 said snidely.

"Ain't no amount of fancy clothes can hide the truth from the good Lord," Church Hen said with disdain. "I hope and pray to God she didn't bring refreshments."

"I wouldn't eat anything that woman made." Old Bitch No. 1 made a clucking sound of disappointment. "That Emma Arnold is whore and a half. That bastard son of hers must be here somewhere."

Ackerley's face was blazing. His grip tightened on the dessert dish with shaking hands. He chunked the whole thing in the garbage, and then he stormed off, brushing past the two gossiping hens.

"Excuse you!" Old Bitch No. 1 shouted. "This generation ought to learn a little respect."

If it would've been me, I would've ripped them both a new one. There would've been no way I could've just bitten my tongue and walked away. Hell far [fire]. After witnessing what just happened, my own fuse sparked. Temper couldn't be contained.

"Hey!" I called out, strutting up to them. "A hypocrite like you is the *last* person that should be talking about respect."

"How dare you—"

"Do you even know who that was?" I asked. "Your head is so far up your ass that I bet you don't. How's this for enlightenment? That was Emma Arnold's son. He isn't a bastard, and you would know that if you weren't both pathetic imbeciles."

"I ought to—"

"Save it for someone who actually gives a damn."

Just looking at the two of those holier-than-thou bitches made me sick. There was more I wanted to say. Oh, there was foul language and insults just itching to be thrown, but I refrained from doing so. I directed a death glare to both of them and silently wished them to the fiery pits of hell where they deserved to suffer.

Turning away, I set out to find Ackerley. There was no telling what thoughts were racing through his head. I had this overwhelming desire to find him, to make sure he was okay. I had to find him. I just had to.

I am a house of cards.

"How'd you know where to find me?"

Sitting in the grass beside the circle of pavement, Ackerley had his back turned on the river's bridge. His sights were set on town, on the park, on what he had ran away from. The algae-edged pond was lit up with the oranges and pinks of a slowly setting sun. A much needed breeze tousled the mess of blonde-brown atop his head. Like a father mussing his son's hair and telling him everything would be okay.

"A break from life," I whispered, my words growing soft. My eyes were trained on the tip of my shoes and the bit of gravel alongside the pavement. Emotions were foreign to me. My sleeves were never stained with the redness of truth and honesty. Squinting against the sun's slanted rays, I looked up. "Are...are you okay?"

Nothing. No answer. Instead, he drew his knees closer and wrapped his arms around them. Seconds that seemed like eternity had passed before he cleared his throat. "Did you know there's a car in the pond down there?" he asked. He cocked his head to look up but didn't meet my eyes.

He didn't want to talk about it, and I could understand why. So, I followed his lead. "I had no idea," I said, taking a seat in the grass beside him. "What's the story?"

"Hell if I know." He shrugged his shoulders and let go of his knees. "I used to make up these stories about it as a kid. It'd be cool if it there was some high-speed car chase and the bad guys plunged into the pond, or maybe these two people were in love and had to fake their death and run away because they couldn't be together." He plucked a blade of grass and rolled it between his thumb and index finger.

"I couldn't take the suspense anymore, so I asked my teacher about it one day," he continued. "She told me it was just an old junker that someone dumped off. There went my wild and crazy dreams."

"Teachers don't know everything," I offered. "Hell, my fourth grade teacher told me scientists experimented with a noiseless lawnmower and discovered that grass cried before being chopped down by the blades."

"I guess you're right....Who did she think she was by telling me that and crushing my imagination? I'd still like to think that it was just somebody who needed to get away or something."

His words lingered, weighing in the twilight. The last rays of sunlight fought to stay in the sky, reflecting off the pond below. The back end of the car was barely visible with tail lights and a rusted bumper jutting out of the water.

"What was it you said?" I had spoken the words attentively, cutting my eyes to the side. "There comes a day when all the bad memories are gone, and there isn't anything to ruin the moment for you, right? Well...some days are bearable. Some days aren't. That's life though...just a bunch of some days."

He contemplatively tilted his head to the side, taking me in. A smile sprouted upon his face, its petals unfolding and reaching up to his eyes. It wasn't the goofy grin he used to bear the weight of the world, no. It was a real smile. It was a smile of understanding, of realizing we were both coming from the same place.

"I, uh, I'm sorry that you had to hear...you know." His smile faltered, losing its wattage as he looked back into the horizon.

Down at the park, the bluegrass band's plucked strings could be heard with faintness, mixing with the wind and the sounds of nature. Flashes of light danced about while children played with sparklers as they grew impatient for nightfall to set in. Just like they'd always done in years past.

"Why are you apologizing?" I was dumbfounded — completely dumbfounded as to why he would be apologizing to me.

"Because." His cheeks tinged red, flushing up to ears again. He pursed his lips together tightly and stared straight ahead. The muscles in his jaws clenched. His Adam's apple bobbed as he gulped, swallowing his pride. "Because it's embarrassing."

It was easy to see that he was in a vulnerable position and it was hard for him. His eyes were glassy. Like he was trying not to cry. I might've been lacking well-quipped skills of the empathetic nature, but I could tell he was trying to get a handle on it.

"You know, this one time when I was little," I started, blurting the first thing that came to mind, "my whole family went to the beach. It felt like it took us forever to get there or maybe it was just the anticipation. I had never been to the beach before. I was so excited that I couldn't contain myself. We were staying in a condo, and there was balcony overlooking the water. I can still remember when they opened the door and I stepped inside. Bright light filled the room, and I could see the ocean water from out the sliding glass doors."

I paused for a second, making sure he was still together. He no longer looked to be on the verge of tears, but his face was unreadable. I took a breath and continued. "So, I took off running to get to the balcony. All I wanted was to see the beach, you know? Those maids sure did know how to clean windows. Low and behold, the sliding glass doors were closed. I plowed right into the glass with this echoing thud, and it knocked me flat on my ass. I wanted to cry from the embarrassment. My cousins ragged me about that for years."

He flicked the balled up blade of grass at me. "You kinda suck at this whole making a person feel better thing." His words said one thing, but the amused expression on his face said another. "I, uh, what they said wasn't anything I hadn't already heard anyway," he admitted.

Seriously? I didn't see how Christians could call themselves a Christian if they were doing everything that was completely non-Christian. Everything was circumstantial and ought not to be looked at one-sidedly. So, what if his mother had him out of wedlock? Big deal. This wasn't the 17th century. No one wore red-lettered badges for the world to see.

"It's all my fault." He rubbed his hands on the leg of his shorts. "If it weren't for me…if I had never been born, maybe she wouldn't have a name tarnished by an illegitimate bastard." He said the words with a stoic

179

expression, which didn't falter as he continued. "Sometimes, I think that's what she wishes."

What were you supposed to say when someone dropped a bomb like that? Did you offer your condolences for their loss of all meaning of life? Did you tell them to hang in there, to keep their chin up? What did you do if words were unable to express exactly how you felt? Were you even supposed to say anything at all?

I reached out hesitantly, unsure on whether or not I ought to offer some sort of sympathetic gesture. My hand danced above his shoulder, and then I gave him an awkward pat on the back. "It's not your fault," I muttered. "Don't ever think that."

His head swiveled around to look at me with eyes that had grown cold and detached. Like he was separating himself from the conversation. "I know that you know. Rhi so kindly informed me of what she said to you about my home life." The words bore no meaning. They were just words of defeat. They were a clipped statement delivered out of exasperation.

"I promise I didn't tell anyone," I said, letting my arm drop.

"You asked why we got into a fight. Well, that's why. She said that you knew how much of a screw-up I was. Said that you were only being nice because you felt sorry for me, that it was the only reason that…that I thought things were—"

"I'm going to stop you right there," I cut him off. "That is the biggest load of bullshit I have ever heard. I don't think you're a screw-up. Why would she say that? That isn't even remotely true."

"It isn't?"

"I'm not fake like most of the people in this town. I wouldn't pretend to be nice to you. Ackerley, I know where you're coming from. I can relate. In case you couldn't tell, I'm not the friendliest person in the world. If I didn't like you, I can guaran-damn-tee you that you'd know it."

He scrutinized me, his face softening around the edges. Like he had been wearing a poker face. Telling him that I could relate had been a slip of the lip. Now that I knew his story, it would only be appropriate to share mine. Only problem was…I wasn't ready. I wasn't sure if I would ever be ready.

A screech echoed into the night, and we both looked toward the park. The first firework had been ignited. It raced up, up, up into the darkened sky, arching in a curve and crackling. A color explosion owned the night as vibrant gold light burst forth in every direction. A million tiny, falling stars floated down to earth, leaving sparkling dust in their wake.

We both sat in silence as the first round of fireworks was shot. The sky was alive with dancing lights of blues and greens and reds. The air was laced with their smoke, bringing back the thrill of childhood memories from Fourth of Julys past. I closed my eyes and focused on the way the grass felt beneath me, the way the acidic smoke stifled my nose, the way the night air was cool but not too cool, the way my heart beat with excitement as the screeches rang out in the night.

It was spectacular moments that kept you alive— moments such as these that you could think back on and instantly recall every little detail. Those types of moments burned brightly. Those moments were fireworks in an otherwise darkened memory. Those moments were worth everything. They made all the difference.

The fireworks display came to a halt as the second round was set up, but the echoes remained; they did not go gentle into that good night. My eyelids flickered open to see Ackerley staring at me with the oddest expression on his face.

"Most people usually keep their eyes open so they can, you know, watch the show," he said, arching an eyebrow.

"I'm not most people."

"I've figured as much."

And, the smartass remarks were back. Everything seemed to be normal—about as normal as things could get, I supposed. His face lit up with an "oh, by the way" expression. Like he suddenly remembered something.

"The strangest thing happened to me earlier," he said, turning to face me. "I ran into Terri right after I got to the park. I swear to God she came up to me and was flirting. She said we needed to 'hang out.'" He had used air quotes as he talked. It was obvious what she meant by it.

Now, I wasn't a psychologist, but teenage girls were all pretty much one and the same. Just like 99.99999% of the human population, they tended to want what another had. Case in point: While Raleigh has expressed blatant interest in Ackerley, Terri was the kind of girl who only wanted something so someone else couldn't get it (you know exactly the kind of girl I was talking about—she was probably the homecoming queen or a head cheerleader or the most *popular* girl in school).

"If I never see her again, it'd be too soon," he added.

"Speaking of Terri," I recalled, slightly turning his way. "I saw Gum—I mean, her father today. He wanted to speak to me about what I said to Terri last night at the movies."

"What do you mean?"

"Right before you walked up, she was running her trap. I told her she needed to watch her language in front of my little sister…and I might've mentioned that she dressed like a whore, too."

"HA!" He laughed out loud and hard. "I bet her father was ticked. Knowing her, she probably twisted your words around and made it sound like you were a real jerk."

"His head was so far up his own ass. He wanted me to apologize. Like that's going to happen. Please. He had started to piss me off, so I started to walk away. Then, he grabbed my arm and shit."

"Grabbed your arm?"

"Like this," I said, reaching out to demonstrate how Gummy Gums invaded my personal space. I could still feel his grip, but I tried not to think about it. I placed my right hand on the upper part of his left arm and squeezed.

"T-t-that's, uh," he stuttered and then went silent.

He glanced down at his arm, and I let go. Maybe the grasp was too tight or something. Maybe I had invaded his personal space. I was completely and utterly awkward in most social situations. Definitely. With the moon being the only light source, it was hard to read his face.

A loud screech rang into the night, signaling that the second round had started. The moonlight caught his face as he turned his head up. Eye contact was made. A split-second glimpse toward the sky as it lit up with color was all it took for everything to change.

Lips. His lips tentatively pressed up against mine with shyness, taking me by surprise. They weren't cold or clammy; they were warm and trembling. The scruff on his upper lip tickled, but I couldn't laugh. I couldn't move. I couldn't stop him. I couldn't do anything. He exhaled a heated breath against my mouth, and then he pulled away.

Too much was going on. Fireworks were screaming to the top of their lungs. Acidic smoke was choking me. The cool grass was all I could focus on. It was the only thing that made sense. It was holding me into place, keeping me from drifting away.

Even though I was staring right at him, I couldn't see anything. Blind. Frozen. Paralyzed. Unable to process thoughts. Blink...all I could do was blink.

His lips met mine again with aggressiveness. Everything went dark. What happened to the moon? Did I close my eyes? Heartbeats drowned out the fireworks, screaming louder and louder as they overworked the veins. The coolness of the grass was ever most present. Its coolness was seeping through my skin.

His hand moved to my thigh. His hand. The hand. The hand was on my leg. The blackness blazed with life as each heartbeat thudded against my chest.

Trees. Thump. Sky. Thump. Houses. Thump. Church.

"Please, mister," I pleaded, pulling away.

I bet you like cartoons, don't you?

"I'm not supposed to talk to strangers."

C'mon on inside...it's okay.

"What did you say?" Ackerley's voice pulled me into the present.

My surroundings swam in and out of focus. I couldn't make sense of anything. Pain darted behind my eyes. I opened my mouth to speak, but I couldn't form words. I needed to get away—I had to get away.

"Phoenix," he called out as wobbly footsteps carried me to the pavement. "Wait." His voice drew near. "I-I-I'm sorry. I thought that...." He caught up with me. "Don't tell anybody. I'm sorry. I'm stupid. Please. Please, don't tell."

My feet were weighed down as though I were wading through mud. Each step was shaky. I stumbled. A hand grabbed my arm. The hand. The hand was pulling me. Down I went.

Trees. Sky. Houses. Church.

I won't hurt you. I promise.

Pain ricocheted through my body, racing alongside the speeding heartbeat. My knees cracked against the concrete. It hurt. It really hurt. I wanted my momma. I wanted her to make everything better.

Red—warm, wet, sticky red. Blood trickled down my legs. It was on my hands. It was everywhere. "Make it stop. Make the bleeding stop."

"Phoenix, you're not bleeding."

C'mon, son. Come inside. I'll get you a bandage for that booboo.

Sunshine was so bright, but then it was gone. It was dark. My eyes were blinded. I couldn't see. The church. The inside of the church was so dark. "Where are you taking me?"

Shhh. Now, we've got to be quiet.

"Phoenix, can you hear me?"

The room was stuffy. It was hot. I couldn't breathe. I didn't understand. It was dark. There were shadows. I was afraid of the shadows. "Please, mister."

That's it. Here, let me just take these off so I can see your booboo.

"Snap out of it!"

I promise I'm not going to hurt you.

"Dude, you're scaring me."

See, this doesn't hurt, doesn't it?

I didn't know what was going on. My knees hurt. I wanted my Daddy. I wanted him to make it all better. I wanted to go home. I had waited all day to go home. All I wanted was to watch my cartoon. "What are you doing to me?"

I said be quiet!

"Damn it, Phoenix. This isn't funny!"

The hand. The hand pressed against my mouth. The hand wouldn't let me talk. The hand made it hard to breathe. The hand silenced me.

Don't be afraid.

"Answer me! Say something! Anything!"

That feels good, doesn't it?

Breaths grew more rapid. Inhale. Exhale. Inhale. Exhale. Inhaleexhaleinhaleexhale. The moon swam into focus. Fingers clawed against the pavement. It was real. Everything was real. He was real. The shadow loomed over me. "Please. Not again. Don't hurt me again." I struck out, digging fingers into his shirt.

"Phoenix," the shadow said. "It's me. Are you okay?"

Ackerley was kneeled beside me. The gravitational pull of his voice thrust me into the present. He was blurry. No, I was crying. Tears were waterfalls. Fingers were clenching his shirt. I pulled him closer to see, to make sure. It was okay. He was Ackerley.

"I...." My voice croaked in a hoarse whisper, scratching the night. "I was a good boy."

I am the grass.

Aftermath has two definitions:

(1) Consequences and/or period of time after a disastrous event.

What does that first definition mean though? Let's break the word down. "After" means following or later in time. "Math" deals with lots of numbers, complex rules, and headaches (which you ask yourself whether or not if it will be of any use in the real world).

Logically speaking, "aftermath" means that it follows the math, right? You spend your time with addition and subtraction, multiplication and division, excusing your dear Aunt Sally, and learning the legend of Sohcahtoa. What then comes after all the hard work and determination? Is the whole greater than or less than the sum?

Maybe things don't add up or make sense. Maybe the end doesn't justify the means. Maybe you didn't get the answer you were looking for. When that happens, you're supposed to check the math. They always tell us to check our work. That's the aftermath. You take the time to see how you ended up getting what you got, why you arrived at that point, what factors played a key role.

Mathematics was my worst subject in school. I never listened to the teachers' instructions to check my work. Instead, the first answer I got was the answer I accepted. When my work was done, it was done. There wasn't any double-checking or making sure I did everything correctly, no. My damnedest was tried in order to avoid all the work that came after the math. Hell, I would end up so far out of my way just to avoid it. Distractions were so much more entertaining.

Once the calculations were done, going back was no longer an option. You cannot give back everything you've heard. You cannot erase what you've seen. You cannot take back the words you've spoken. You can't undo what has been done. All you could do was deal with the consequences.

I had to keep myself distracted from the aftermath. It had been days since fireworks owned the sky as the kiss took me by surprise. It had been days since the asphalt dug into my back as the world came crashing down through the gates of repression. It had been days since I desperately clung onto Ackerley and cried until tears ran dry.

Questions weren't badgered. There was no demand to know what was going on. Silence had exuded him as I slumped with his arms bracing me. He offered a shoulder to cry on, and that was more than enough. It was all I needed as the truth seeped through the cracks in the armor I had worn for years on top of years.

The math problem had been set up. Inside the parenthesis of a warped life, a little boy taught himself how to grow old. Collegiate freedom's exponent of four years made that little boy into a man. Memories were multiplied by harsh realities when he became the prodigal son. Who he had made himself into was stripped away by small town division. Summer's heat only furthered the confusion with the addition of a chance friendship. The loss of his sense of self was sealed with a kiss. Where did that leave the little boy?

My calculations did not provide an answer. Factors weren't all accounted for. There was only one thing left to do: the aftermath. It was time to check my work, but I couldn't. Not yet. I had separated myself from what compelled the surrender of the truth. I knew it was only prolonging the inevitable, but it bought me a few days at least. I wasn't sure if I would ever be ready to face him.

What did he think? What would I say? What was I going to do? Sometimes, the answers only imposed more questions—questions that would evoke answers I wasn't ready to hear.

He was due an explanation, but avoidance was so much easier. I kept pushing it aside, kept ignoring it, kept it all from being spoken into existence. The thought of formally sitting down in a formal setting with formal conversation as I formally bared my soul nauseated me. The whole damn thing was sickening and caused my stomach to turn. Like that feeling you get when you thought you we're going to vomit but couldn't. The only remedy was to not think at all, and the best way to do that was to keep myself occupied.

Distractions came in many forms. I could go running, but I would indubitably cross paths with him as I had countless times before. I could read a book, but forcing myself to concentrate on tiny, printed words while everything was churning on the inside would surely cause an unnerving sense of motion sickness. I could have done a lot of things, but all I wanted was the chance to escape. I wanted to live vicariously....

"Now, where was I?" Mrs. Thomas asked as she set down the pitcher of sweet tea. She brought the glass up to her lips and drank heavily, finishing with an "ahhh." She had been reminiscing about the good ol' days. She'd just needed someone to talk to, and I was more than willing to listen.

"You were telling me about the time you went fishing," I replied with a gracious smile. I've learned quite a lot about Mrs. Thomas and TC, the neighbor boy. Like how they spent their days playing cowboys and riding horses and playing mean-spirited tricks on some boy named Jimmy.

"Ol' TC and I were always trying to one-up the other, but everything changed that day we went fishing. I can remember it like it was yesterday...."

cue flashback music

Mrs. Thomas: The river smelled strong in that dry heat of late August. I refused to bait my own hook. TC laughed and said worms didn't have any feelings, but I made him do it for me anyways. We must've been out there for a few 'ours at least. I don't who was more stubborn, the fish for not biting or us for not backing down. Time dragged by slower and slower until TC got all fed up and called it a day, but then I felt a nibble. Finally! I was so excited and jumping up and down, but that dadgum fish was stronger than I was. TC got jealous and said I had to reel it in myself.

Talk about being angrier than a hornet. I was 'bout ready to let go and say the heck with it, but then Jimmy happened across the bridge and swooped in to help me. Now, Jimmy was from the other side of town. His dad was a doctor, and they had money. He didn't associate with the likes of us. Up until that day, I had always thought him snotty. We were just kids then. Barely even teenagers. We all thought we were too big for our britches anyhow…

fade back to present day

She took a long swig from her glass, and it clinked as she sat it down on the table. Her face looked younger and a little less weathered. I swear, I could see that little girl somewhere in there, meaner than a snake and full of life as she'd embarked on adventures in rural Alabama.

"That was the day everything changed. If it wasn't for Jimmy, everything would've turned out differently…."

She fell silent, losing herself in the memory. Her words trailed off in the light breeze of the afternoon, dancing with the chimes; their steps clattered as they twirled. A good deal of time had passed before the rocking slowed to a stop, and needles started to prickle the back of my neck.

"You've got the look of a man who has the world weighing on his mind," she pointed out. The lighthearted tone of her voice dropped. Her eyes filled with concern—sincerity.

Was it that obvious? It didn't matter how hard I tried to separate myself because some things were inseparable. My mind couldn't process anything. I couldn't wrap my head around what had happened. Years of stunning myself into silence had dulled the pain. Years of ungodly feelings had built and built. Then, everything came flooding back. He brought everything back. I didn't know why. Hell, I wasn't sure if I wanted to know why. Then, there was that kiss. That mental leap was yet capable of being made.

"I wouldn't say it's the world," I said with a sigh, leaning back in the chair.

No, it wasn't the whole world. It was just me in my world, and I had yet to let anyone in.

"That doesn't make it any less important, does it?" Her eyes held a revered stare. She gazed with intent as if to say she respected me enough to listen, to care.

It was my turn to talk, and she was ready to listen; however, I couldn't flat out tell her something along the lines of the following:

So, the other night the weirdest thing happened! I think...I think I had, like, an out of body experience. My memory is all hazy and shi—err, I mean crap— but I swear I went back in time to when I was molested. Oh, I know what you're thinking. Don't worry. It was nothing really. My parents said so! But if it was nothing...why does it feel like something, ya know? It's confusing. That's it! I'm confused greatly, ma'am. On top of all that, my friend kissed me. He was a dude, by the way. A dude kissed me. Imagine that! The funny thing is...I don't care about that detail, not really. I know it should bother me, but it doesn't. It feels so insignificant in comparison. Like just two sets of lips pushed against one another.... What's the big deal about that?

There was no way I could talk openly and earnestly with her about the topic. Even though I knew what had to be said out loud, my brain wouldn't send the signals to my mouth for the words to form. It was like a secret agent from K.A.T. was ordered to grab ahold of my traitorous tongue and tie it up to prevent any word spillage. It was all for my own benefit though. The last thing I needed was to slip in a puddle of slick truth and bust my ass.

I wanted to say that I didn't know, and I really didn't know anything. At all. Maybe I was afraid to speak my thoughts into existence. Maybe I was afraid my words would go unheard. Maybe I was afraid I wasn't important enough for anyone to care. Maybe a change in subject would help.

"What did you mean?" I asked after a few moments of internal debate. "What would've turned out differently if it had not been for Jimmy?"

Mrs. Thomas nodded her head in understanding. There wasn't that certain air of expectancy meandering between the two of us. She didn't try to pry things out of you. For that, I was grateful.

"You see, TC didn't like the fact that Jimmy was helping," she began, settling back into the gently rocking rhythm of her chair. "He got so mad that he waltzed straight up to Jimmy and slugged him." She gave a soft hoot of laughter that was both bitter and sweet all at the same time.

"If it hadn't been for Jimmy, TC would have always seen me in the same light. He wouldn't have seen me as something more than that tomboy who lived next door. If Jimmy had not been the southern gentleman his mother had raised him to be, none of it would've happened."

She sighed, expelling her lungs as she aired out the memories of the past. "From that day forward, the relationship between us changed. TC changed. He transitioned from that heathen who had always been my partner in crime into the young man that I began to fall in love with."

Her voice sunk heavily with remorse, and her once-weightless words succumbed to the gravity. She took steady breathes as though she were collecting her thoughts. Then, she sighed once more and continued on to explain what had happened.

"Over the years that followed, we grew closer. I knew—I just knew he was the one for me. Then the war came. That…that was when everything changed. That was when TC broke my heart and enlisted."

Mrs. Thomas changed from the old, weathered woman sitting across from me. In her place, I could see that young girl who was madly in love at a time in life when nothing was certain. She didn't know that happiness was taken for granted, that it could be taken away without a moment's notice.

"I was furious at him for breaking my heart. He wanted me to wait for him, to be there for him when he returned. But, I knew he was good as dead. I just knew there was no hope for his survival, for…for our survival."

A solemn looked flickered across her face as she remembered the past. "I cried my heart out every single day leading up to the day he was shipped off to Vietnam," she added. "My mother tried to reason with me. She took me out into the backyard the day I saw him off. She said to me, she said, 'Amelia, if you ever find yourself lost and not knowing what to do, then just look down at the grass.'"

She timidly stretched out a gnarled finger, pointing to her lawn, and then she continued. "My mother went on to say that the grass teaches us an important lesson that we take for granted. Despite being mown, cut down to size, trampled across—despite all those odds, the grass still chooses to grow. It keeps growing. It never gives up hope."

A nostalgic fondness shimmered across her face. Like she could still picture that day, that day from her past where her heart was broken and shattered into pieces, that day that echoed her mother's words in her memory. "My mother told me to be the grass, to never give up when I get knocked down."

And so, Mrs. Amelia Thomas and I both lapsed into silence as we rocked gently on her front porch. We listened to the wind as it danced with the chimes. We drank from our glasses of sweet tea, dampening our palms with condensation. We watched the grass as it chose to grow despite the odds. We watched the grass keep hope alive.

Aftermath has two definitions:

(1) Consequences and/or period of time
after a disastrous event.

(2) The new grass which grows after
a mowing or harvest.

The question is...

Which one do you let define you?

Do you let the disastrous event loom over your head
day in and day out?

OR

Do you choose to be the grass, to move forward, to keep
growing, to never give up?

I am cleaning.

There are always two types of people in life. It's really rather simple. The entire population can be divided into two sides. Either you are <insert one side here> or you are <insert other side here>. For instance: either you are a dog person or you aren't, either you can drive a stick shift or you can't, either you know what you want or you don't.

Get it. Got it? Good.

Then again, everything isn't so cut and dry. Not everything is black and white. Shades of gray are pertinent. While there may be two sides, that doesn't mean you have to choose between them. Like those ambidextrous son-of-a-guns who are both left and right handed.

Everything makes sense, doesn't it? You know which side you are on or which two sides you are straddling. The world keeps spinning and the sun keeps shinning and <insert synonymous sappy bullshit here> all because you know your place in the world. Tell me what happens when you don't know which two sides are the ones for which you are to choose between. What happens when you don't know who you are or where you belong? What then?

I didn't know anything anymore. Like you have been juggling so many things for far too long and you couldn't remember that *one* thing you started out with, that *one* thing you was able to grasp onto with both hands. I couldn't even remember the me I used to be back before Life made me a star attraction in her three ring circus, juggling to keep everything up in the air. No one could truly live while running around like a fool and none the wiser. Sooner or later, everything would come crashing down. It was definite.

Pointless. Everything felt pointless. What remained of the moving boxes were scattered about my bedroom floor, and it seemed foolish all of a sudden. I couldn't remember why I had refused to finish unpacking everything in the first place. What exactly was the point I was trying to make by refusing to do so?

I had nothing to prove. It wasn't as though the life I had before I sat in that hard, metal chair that made my ass go numb would pick right up where it left off. Like it knew I was all packed up, ready, and waiting for it to whisk me away. Maybe it was time to make a move though—a move forward. Maybe belated spring cleaning would do some good. Okay, maybe I was only looking for yet another distraction from doing what ought to be done. Sue me.

I opened the windows and welcomed a virtually nonexistent breeze into the stuffiness of my room. The ceiling fan turned haphazardly overhead as I sized everything up. Leaning towers of cardboard occupied half of the floor. Shit far [fire].

Looking at the whole picture was daunting— unbelievably daunting. Trying not to think about what came next, I focused on unloading one box at a time. Small step after small step led away from the impossibility of it all.

You would think that I would've accumulated heaping amounts of, for lack of a better word, stuff in four years' time, but you'd be wrong. My belongings didn't amount to some whirlwind of existence, no. The majority of the packaged possessions was...wait for it...drum roll please...books. I had boxes and boxes of books, all of which I had read at least twice.

The real me could be found with my nose in a book, reading on into the early hours of the morning. Being fake was the easiest route on which to escape. Being *that* party guy was a façade. Like I had become a-whole-nother person. Following my family's example, I submerged myself in to the world of fake. I fake laughed at every stupid joke and faked friendships with people who I never considered anything more than acquaintances.

I had been a big, fucking phony! The worst part of it all? It was the best four years of my life. I was Morris — just Morris. I wasn't reminded every single day of what had happened. I didn't have to deal with the past. I wasn't Phoenix Morris Harper, not for the most part at least.

And so, I unloaded all the books and put them on the bookcase where they rightfully belonged. My half-assed attempt at packing cracked me up. The remaining boxes were each labeled with "crap" or "junk" or "who cares?" scribbled in black marker. I didn't know why I thought it was so funny, but I laughed out loud (LOL).

Inside a box labeled "crap," the charger for my cellphone was tangled up with the cords of an old stereo. Why had I never looked for it after the battery had died way back when? Maybe it was because I had refused to unpack everything, to be officially moved back home. Maybe I was just as stubborn as the day was long.

Why not? I plugged my phone up, and it powered on. I turned my attention back to my boxed-up past. There was no telling what lurked in the remaining box of "crap," just waiting to be discovered, remembered. Before I could take a few steps forward, chimes rang out from my once dead cellphone. Color me surprised or maybe a nice shade of flabbergasted. I honestly wasn't expecting any messages at all, especially not the animated notification of voicemail(s) flashing across the screen.

Message (1) from caller: UNKNOWN
Congratulations on the achievement of your college degree. Would you be interested in furthering your educa—
MESSAGE DELETED

Message (2) from caller: Ackerley Dean
Mr. T, it's the bag boy. Do you want to go geocaching today? Give me a call back.
NEXT MESSAGE

Message (3) from caller: Caroline Anderson
Phoenix, it's Caroline. I didn't know if you still had your same number or not. Some of the old gang is thinkin' of gettin' together. You should totally come. Give me a call back! My number is—
MESSAGE DELETED

Message (4) from caller: RESTRICED NUMBER
You're a fucking jerk.
MESSAGE DELETED

Message (5) from caller: Private Number
Mabel? Ya there? Pick up the phone.
NEXT MESSAGE

Message (6) from caller: Private Number
Mabel, it's Polly. Lord, I know ya there. Pick up the phone. Now, I know ya there Mabel! Fine, I'll just talk to ya at bingo tonight.
NEXT MESSAGE

Message (7) from caller: Ackerley Dean
Phoenix…I-I don't even know why I'm calling your phone. You said you never check it. That's still weird, by the way (forced laugh). *Can, uh…can we talk about what happened?*
END OF ALL NEW MESSAGES

Nausea. It felt like I was going to vomit but couldn't. My stomach dropped as my heart jumped into my throat. A roaring screech echoed in my ears as brakes were slammed down on the thoughts straining to run rampant through my mind.

The phone slipped from my grip, and it bounced across the floor. Acting impulsively, I made a beeline to the box of "crap." No faster than you could say "distraction," I had dragged the stereo out and plugged it into the wall. I didn't care what CD was still in the player just as long as I couldn't hear myself think. I pressed the play button with an agitated mash and turned the volume up.

Synthesized beats from the 80s blared into existence, drowning the screaming thoughts nagging at my conscience. I closed my eyes and took deep breaths, listening—really listening—to the song. Music had a funny way of taking your mood and turning it 180° no matter if you were happy or sad or anywhere in-between.

Despite what you may think, I wasn't some cold machine. I did let loose from time to time. Humming the tune turned into a halfway sing-along, and that turned into full-fledged belting. It was dorky as all get out, but I didn't give a rat's ass. Sometimes, a random, singing-your-heart-out, jumping-on-your-bed, spastic dance was all it took to give you that feeling deep in the pit of your stomach that made everything feel okay. For that moment in time, all you cared about was playing air guitar to the extreme and banging your head just right. Like nothing else mattered in the world while you lived in the song.

I tore it up, son. It was the best impromptu concert in the history of all imagined concerts. My knees dug into the mattress as the song's last notes lingered in my bedroom stadium. Between the heavy breaths, I could hear the applause of the pretend audience as they praised me for rocking each and every one of theirs faces off.

Wait...the applause was NOT imaginary. A throat was cleared with an "ehem," but I kept my eyes squeezed shut. Damn it to hell.

They always say you couldn't embarrass yourself if you didn't care what people were thinking. Whoever they were, they didn't know Jack Schitt because it was downright (humiliating × embarrassing)^2 when someone witnessed you making a complete and utter ass out of yourself. You couldn't help but to care what they must be thinking.

"I can honestly say that was the last thing I ever would've thought I'd see you doing."

Raleigh's voice met my ears with a barely detectable laugh in the heavy dose of sarcasm lacing her words with its razor sharpness. I huffed in a half-snicker/half-snort, climbing down from the bed.

"Yeah, well I'm full of surprises," I began, looking toward the door but stopping short.

"I don't doubt that one bit," Ackerley commented. He was standing beside Raleigh, leaning up against the doorframe. That same goofy grin was on his face, but he looked different somehow. The blonde-brown shaggy hair of his was cut shorter, and there was an unreadable expression in his eyes. Like he was so sure of himself yet unsure of himself all at the same time.

I waited for the dread.

I waited for it to sink like stone in the pit of my stomach. I waited for it to weigh me down. I waited for it to engulf me. I waited for it to consume me entirely.

However, it did not.

I had been waiting in vain, worrying in vain. Seeing him standing there lifted a weight off my chest. I had been suffocating and didn't know it. And his presence was resuscitating.

He was Ackerley. He was the guy who had a good heart even though life had done its best to see otherwise. A thread of similarity bound us together. I could feel it anchored in my chest, tautly stretching toward him. He had significance in my life. He mattered—to me, he mattered. I didn't know why or what any of it meant.

Realizing I had been standing there with my mouth agape, I asked, "What's up?" It was generic. It was stereotypical. Leave me alone. It was the best I could do.

"Ackerley just stopped by to return something you left behind at the grocery store," Raleigh said gushingly, and then she smiled at me as if to say how much she liked him. Things between us felt the way they used to be. A split second later, the feeling was gone. Her face shifted back into its usual hoity-toity self as she remembered who we had become. "Well, whatever. I'm going to go tanning with Terri."

She retreated down the hall, her footsteps echoing the foreboding realization that I was alone with him. It was time to formally sit down and have a formal conversation as I formally bared my soul. What would he think? What would I say? Was I ready to let someone in?

"Are you going to invite me inside?" he asked, breaking the silence. "Unless you want me to wait out here while you stare at me with this look of confusion, which isn't very flattering by the way." He was most definitely a smartass. That hadn't changed in the past few days.

"Yeah. Right. Come in." I motioned with my hand. "I left something at the grocery store? I haven't even been there in while." In fact, I had forfeited the weekly ritual. It was one distraction I could do without.

"I lied." He smiled deviously and wagged his eyebrows. "You didn't leave something *there*, but you did leave this," he began, pulling out of his pocket the festive bandana that Memphis had handed me to hold onto. "I couldn't very well explain where I found it."

"I had forgotten all about that," I said, stepping toward him. "Where exactly did you find it?"

"Up on the hill where we—"

I lurched forward and clamped a hand over his mouth. I glowered at him with a "What the hell?" expression. He couldn't come busting up in here advertising that night to just anyone, especially not my family. I reached out and shut the bedroom door so we wouldn't be overheard.

My hand dropped from his mouth as the door clicked shut. A smile broke out across his face, and he said, "I was just going to say where we were watching the fireworks."

His presence was nerve-racking. My hands were fidgeting, needing something to do. I turned away and did the only thing I knew to do: I resumed unpacking the box of crap. It kept my mind from making leaps and bounds ahead of the conversation.

"I talked to Rhi, by the way. I was going to tell you sooner, but it was like you fell off the face of the earth."

"You did?" I asked, ignoring the latter part of his comment.

"We made up. I knew we would. We're best friends. I didn't tell her anything though. It's none of her business...."

Both gratefulness and amazement washed over me. I was grateful he didn't tell, and I was amazed how they could let bygones be bygones so easily. Not knowing what to say, a head nod of acknowledgement felt most appropriate.

I could feel the floor shift beneath his weight as he moved. I could hear his light footsteps as he walked about my room. I could see him out of the corner of my eye as he took everything into consideration.

"Did you rob a library?" he asked mockingly, nodding his head toward the bookcase.

"I like to read." I kept my eyes trained in front of me.

His steps propelled him closer to my side of the room. I could sense his eyes on my back as I rummaged around in the box. "Did you just move in here?" he asked, suddenly in close proximity.

"I guess you could say that."

"I care."

"What?" I risked a glace over my shoulder. He pointed to the box labeled "who cares?" and smirked. "You're more than welcomed to help. I've been procrastinating all summer," I offered.

It was weird having him go through my stuff, but at least it would keep his mind occupied a little while longer while I tried to regroup as I tried to unpack. So far, I had discovered exactly what the box advised: useless crap that could be stored in the attic.

"Suffocating," Ackerley said, disrupting my thoughts.

I turned to ask what he meant but noticed he was reading from a notebook—the notebook I had kept by my bedside to write down thoughts and ideas. Paralysis struck me as I stood there, unable to stop him from reading my personal thoughts aloud:

I'm suffocating.

All this cleaning makes me anxious.

Dirt is everywhere,

filling the nooks and the cracks.

I can feel it watching me as I clean.

Scrub, scrub, scrub.

Is it clean?

I don't think so.

Can I make it cleaner?

I hope so.

I'm suffocating.

My hands move with rhythm

as the stereo blasts

mindless music.

I hate it.

I hate cleaning.

Scrub, scrub, scrub.

Is it clean?

Is it shiny?

Is it brand new?

I don't think so.

"You write poetry?" he asked, raising his eyes from the notebook to meet my stricken stance.

"Sort of," I mumbled, reaching to grab the notebook from him. "I didn't intend for anyone to see let alone read it."

"They're really good." He teasingly pulled the notebook out of my reach and smiled. "What? Can't I read some more?"

"I would prefer you didn't."

"And if I do?" He took a step back and held the notebook up tauntingly.

"Fine." I shrugged my shoulders, admitting defeat upfront and turning away to the task at hand. "If you want you to, then go ahead."

His eyebrows knitted together, and then a sigh escaped his lips. "You were supposed to chase after me and threaten to beat the hell out of me unless I didn't hand it over this instant."

"What would be the point in that?"

"You suck at flirting."

My eyes darted over to him. There he stood, looking out the window. A red tent of coyness flushed his cheeks. He said it. Light was shed upon the situation. Hindsight bitch slapped me in the face with a sweeping hand of "how could I have been so blind?" The fight he'd had with Rhi made sense. The whole charade of showing off was both their attempts at flirting. With me. Of all people. Me.

"Flirting?" I asked tentatively.

"I, uh, I like you." He briefly made eye contact and looked away. "In case it wasn't obvious by my kissing you."

He liked me? Why would he like me? Did...did I like him, too? I knew I liked Ackerley, but I didn't know if I liked him like that. "Like" is such a funny word after you've rolled it around in your mouth more than a dozen times. It started to feel weird, and it didn't make the least amount of sense just like everything that was happening. He didn't badger me with questions or demand to know if I felt the same, no. I could see it in his eyes. He both knew and understood the inner turmoil swirling inside me. I could relate to him. We understood one another.

What was the big deal? Yes, I had feelings for him, but what those feelings meant was hard to define. Were they rooted strictly in friendship or was there something more to it? I didn't know if I was heterosexual or if I was homosexual or if I straddled the fence. I wasn't attracted to either gender, at least I didn't think so. I was experiencing an emotional impasse—a stalemate of sexual proportions so to say.

The first (and last) time I had sexual relations was with a female. It had only taken a couple of minutes for me to undergo a severe panic attack that left me fearing for my life. No matter how much I tried to deny it, the first (and only) time I experienced a kiss that brought something more than the feeling of clammy lips pressed together was with him, and shortly thereafter....

"Don't leave me hanging. Say something." He gave a shaky laugh, breathing out a sigh. "Anything."

The silence that'd fallen between us was both awkward and tense. Sickness sloshed around my insides, and the stress-induced bile hit the back of my throat. Word vomit gushed forth. I always said too much when I needed to say nothing at all.

"Your lips were warm, but they were trembling. I assume you were nervous. Your facial hair tickled, and your breath reminded me of the heat of the day." The words were measured, precise, and matter-of-fact. I was clinical in my approach.

"That, uh, that was my first kiss," he offered timidly. "Did I...did I do it wrong or something?"

It was true we hadn't known each other long, but I knew him well enough to know it was unlike him to put himself in such a vulnerable position. People were always judging others by how strong they were, but there was lot to say about someone who was willing to go out on a limb and show their weaknesses. Right?

He shouldn't have wasted that proverbial first kiss on me. He deserved better. I hadn't stopped him when he kissed me, had I? In fact, I was certain that I had kissed him back, had I not? How else would he have been encouraged to make a move? It was all my fault that the chain of events unfolded like they had. What the hell was wrong with me?

"You didn't do anything wrong."

I smiled to show him I wasn't patronizing or being condescending. If there was anything I hated worse than patronizing behavior, it was being condescended to.

"Then what, uh, what happened that night?" he asked, his eyes silently searching mine. "If you don't want to talk about it, then I'll understand. But, I'm here to listen if you need someone to talk to. You can count on me. I promise."

And so, we had come full circle. The time had finally arrived. He had told me his story. He opened up. He let me in. Now, it was my turn to do the same. He didn't demand an explanation. He didn't demand that I divulge the reasons behind my actions. He cared, and that made all the difference.

"Here," I said, motioning for him to sit down right there in the middle of my bedroom floor. I took a seat beside him and stared fixedly at the opposite wall, anchoring myself into place before I swam the churning waters of the past. "I think it's time I told you a story."

Was I afraid? Not anymore. Numbness had wrapped its inkling tendrils around my soul and pulled, detaching my heart from the events of twelve years prior. It was time to explain. It was time to surrender the truth. It was time to let someone in. That fact alone should've scared me, but I was weak from all the years of internal warfare.

"It all started when I was ten years old...."

I am dissonant.

We all have major regrets in our past. You know, those opportunities missed and risks that should've been taken. Not all regrets are momentous though. Maybe you wished you would've worn a different outfit for a date or ordered a different entrée from the menu.

Regret comes in many forms, many shapes, and many sizes. It holds different meanings for many people. Some may fantasize about what could've been while others may wonder what couldn't have been.

Sometimes, we regret the fact that we regret; second-guessing only shakes the belief in our actions, decisions, and reasoning. Sometimes, we regret the fact that we don't regret at all; no heartfelt remorse over our actions, decisions, and reasoning weighs on our conscience. Sometimes, we do both; we're trapped in the trenches while our head wages war against our heart.

Regretfully, I regret.

I regret the rape of my childhood. I regret feeling like an orphan in my own family. I regret closing myself off. I regret not being normal. I regret missing out on the me I was supposed to be. I regret not being able to see myself. I regret telling my story.

Regretfully, I don't regret.

I don't regret my actions. I don't regret holding a grudge. I don't regret closing myself off. I don't regret washing my hands. I don't regret running away to college. I don't regret letting someone inside my world.

Ackerley hadn't reacted the way I had always thought someone would. Like my parents had. Instead, he had listened carefully as I told my story. Rather than interrupting as silence spanned in-between the stumbling of thoughts, he had reached out and grasped my hand as if to reassure me that I was strong enough. I had felt his unsaid words of encouragement. No, it wasn't a homoerotic embrace or some shit like that. It was a friend showing that he cared.

When I had finished, he tried to look me in the eyes as he spoke: "Phoenix, I-I don't know how to even begin to tell you how sorry I am that happened...t-there is nothing I can say that will make everything alright because...it will never be alright."

His eyes slowly shifted, focusing on the floor as he became lost in thought. "Sometimes, there will...there will never come a day when all the bad memories are gone," he mumbled more so to himself.

It wasn't what he said but rather what he *didn't* say. I read in-between the lines. The past was incapable of being changed. You shouldn't regret things you had no power over. Everything, whether good or bad, is and forever will be a part of who you are. You just have to accept it in order to change your future.

Sometimes, it was easy to lose sight of that fact. Sometimes, the past clouded your vision. Sometimes, you don't allow yourself to see the bigger picture.

It wasn't that I regretted telling him but the fact he knew my truth. The words couldn't be taken back—they could never be taken back. I had bought into delusions of letting someone in, and I was experiencing buyer's remorse.

It felt like I was up at bat in a dilapidated baseball game. It was the last inning, and the bases were loaded. The pressure was on to see if I would win or lose the game. **STRIKE ONE**: I had told my parents, but they didn't believe me. **STRIKE TWO:** I had told my best friend, and she stabbed me in the back.

It had all come down to telling Ackerley. There was the final wind up, and then the pitch. I closed my eyes and swung. My breath was held as I waited for either the wood of the bat to crack against ball or the umpire's call of bad news.

Was it strike three?
Did I lose the game?
Was I out?

I am my father's son.

Kids say the damnedest things. They each have their own unique perspective on the world. Especially precocious, birthday girls like my kid sister.

Today was the day Memphis Harper turned a year older. She had been looking forward to the day of her birth, even bragging about <u>NOT</u> being a little kid. However, the realization of actually being a year older unsettled her tremendously.

When asked how she felt about turning ten years old, Memphis blanched and said, "Don't remind me! You're only as old as you feel, and I just so happen to feel as young and spritely as an eight year old."

When asked what she wanted to do for her birthday, she replied, "I was thinking about having a little shindig at the house, but…Lord, I don't feel like cleaning, and the mere thought of narrowing down a guest list gives me a sick, throwing up headache. I think it'd just be a better idea to have a quiet, family dinner out some place nice, don't you?"

And so, on the most special day of the year, her birth, the royal highness dictated we were to feast at the family-friendly themed restaurant in town. The other five members of the Harper family and I were crowded around a rather small table in the heart of the tacky kingdom known as Rancho Grande. It was a peanut-shells-on-the-floor kind of place. The decorations were remnants of a great clash of culture: the Aztecs of Mexico vs. cowboys of the Old West vs. pseudo-antiquity of 1950s America. Like a history book had upchucked and spewed onto the walls. It might've been called "redneck chic," but I called it like I saw it—the visual equivalence of a migraine.

Everybody and their brother had the same idea we'd had. You couldn't risk looking up from your plate; otherwise, you'd have a 95% guarantee of making eye contact with someone you possibly knew. A sea of chatter ebbed and flowed around our island of a table. Its waves crashed onto the conversational beaches, racing over the sand to fill in the gaps of silence.

On the next table over, Lisa the Meat Specialist was all dolled up and perched on the edge of her chair. She was leaning forward and engrossed in conversation with her dinner companion. Her date looked familiar, but then again everyone looked familiar in Sulfur Springs.

Of all the things to worry about, I found myself worrying about the junk in Lisa's trunk. What would happen if she found someone? Would she still be adamant in peddling fake penises? Why did things have to change? I wished everything stayed the same. If things could just be frozen at a specific moment in time when they were at their highest peak, then we wouldn't have to worry about the downside of that great big hill we like to call "Life."

"Raleigh," my mom said, her words slicing through the tide. "I was talking to your grandmother earlier, and she said that Martha Gibson said that her friend said that her grandson was going to start tutoring this fall. You could use some help in science."

"Uh," Raleigh began with a skeptical expression, "I had an 'A' in Chemistry last year."

"No, you had an 'A' minus." My mom sat down her water glass onto the tabletop with a clink. "If you are going to be valedictorian of your graduating class, you need perfect grades."

"Who says I want to be?"

"Raleigh Lee Harper, think about your future. Your brother was valedictorian, and he received a full-ride scholarship to college." She cut her eyes to look at me, her studious son with the *perfect* grades. "This family strives to be the best it can be."

There were so many things wrong with what she'd just said. I didn't even know where to begin contradicting her, so I bit my tongue. Studious was not the correct adjective to describe my stint in secondary education, no. Lonely was more appropriate.

Shrill laughter rang out through the conversation. It seeped under my skin, crawling all over me. How could Lisa the Meat Specialist just sit there and bat her eyelashes while her future was in the balance? How could she not care that she was jeopardizing everything? She wasn't who I thought she was. She wasn't that conspiratorial woman who told society to shove it. Fuck her and her fake laugh and her dildos.

"Troy, don't you agree?" My mom turned toward my dad for support.

"Well—"

"See, your dad thinks so, too. It's settled," she cut him off. Her eyes slid over toward Jackson. "What are we going to do about you? You need to get out of that room of yours. Join a sport. Do something. It's never too early, and extracurricular activities are what *make* a college application. They certainly helped your brother out."

Equal parts sympathy and jealously washed over me. I was sympathetic that both their lives were being controlled. No matter how irrational it sounded, I was jealous of the attention they were receiving. It wasn't like I desperately wanted them to notice me, but a little acknowledgement back then would've been nice, you know? Maybe a "You did great, kiddo," or maybe a "Keep up the hard work!" Hell, or even maybe—just maybe—something along the lines of "We're proud of you, son." That's what I wished they would've said. Back then.

It wasn't like my parents were never there for me, because they were. They just weren't *there*. My mom was always too busy running around like a chicken with its head chopped off. I didn't know when she had taken up painting, but she'd been trying to paint the perfect family for as long as I could remember. On the other hand, my dad was always working. He was either working at his day job or working in his garage or working on the yard.

My mom kept nagging and nagging, and then she nagged some more. She must've loved the way her voice sounded because she just wouldn't shut up. It was beginning to sound like nails on a chalkboard, and it was slowly becoming unbearable.

I risked letting my eyes scan around the restaurant in search of a distraction, which was found immediately. The waitress with blonde curls piled into a bun on top her head was making like Moses and parting the sea of chatter as she led three guests to their table. The tanned skin, the dark brown hair that tinted red in the sunlight, the light freckles across her cheekbones— all of it was familiar.

Both of Rhi's parents had tanned skin with the same dark hair, but she resembled her mother the most. There was—without any doubt—a heavy accent of Mediterranean heritage in their bloodline. Rhi smiled slyly when she made eye contact. Like she mentally exclaimed, "There you are!"

"Dear Lord in Heaven," my mom whispered, averting her gaze. "It's those people that moved in behind us. It's been what? Going on two years? They don't even have the decency to socialize with the rest of the community."

"Oh," my dad said disdainfully. "Alex is a good guy."

"Well, that Sandra Moreno must think she's better than everybody because—Sandra! Alex! How nice to see y'all out and about!" My mom smiled one of the fakest smiles in the history of fake smiles.

"Charlotte," Rhi's mother said, nodding her head.

Now that they were up close, it was easier to see the distinguishable characteristics that set Rhi apart from her parents. While her eyes were bright and cheerful, both her parents' eyes were tired and sad.

While my dad exchanged comments with Rhi's father about their job at the power plant, Rhi held up her camera and snapped a candid photo, taking me by surprise. I'm sure I was sitting there with my mouth agape as though I were some redneck buffoon. At least the photo would be authentic seeing as the high-class dining establishment was the setting (please tell me you've picked up on my sarcasm by now).

The waitress cleared her throat to remind everyone she was, in fact, still there and waiting to seat the Moreno's. Goodbyes were said, whether they were forced (the mother's) or friendly (the father's). Rhi leaned down beside Memphis and asked, "Do you know what I think a young, beautiful birthday girl like yourself needs?"

"I don't know," Memphis said, smiling broadly at Rhi's use of adjectives. "What do I need?"

"I think a young woman as pretty as a model needs her very own photo shoot," Rhi explained with one of those smiles that suggested that it was the most brilliant idea ever. "How about tomorrow? It'll be my birthday present to you."

"Hmmm...you know what? I like the way you think, Rhiannon."

Rhi flashed Memphis a smile and wished for her to have a happy birthday, and then she slowly met my gaze. "I'll be seeing you, Mr. T," she said with mysteriousness. Her eyes narrowed omnisciently, and her brow arched like it was saying, "I know everything."

She trailed off after her parents, leaving an invisible fist clenching my stomach in her wake. Slowly, it released its hold as she disappeared out of sight. There was no way she knew. He promised he didn't say anything, and I trusted him—I wanted to trust him for all it was worth, but still…. I couldn't help but to think of him and what he was doing right at that very moment.

"I just don't know what their deal is," my mom bitched. "Don't even have the common courtesy to be good neighbors."

I went to roll my eyes, but my dad beat me to it. Maybe in a different time or a different place I would've laughed, but Rhi's departure had unsettled me. He shook his glass, letting the ice cubes chink together. Like he wished he was drinking something a little bit stronger. "Trust me, Dad. I know exactly how you feel," I wanted to say, to empathize.

After eight years of pent up frustration and a self-imposed exile of four, we'd each went our own way. All of us being gathered together felt odd, surreal even. If I didn't know any better, I could've sworn we were all more like roommates rather than a family. We each came and went as we pleased, only seeing each other briefly in passing.

If I had to choose one parent over the other, I'd most definitely choose my father. No, it wasn't because my mother got on my ever-loving nerves, but because he believed me. Well, he believed me at first anyway.

Now would be the time to cue those chimes and flashback to what had happened that day. It was at a time right after our little family of three was brainwashed into going to the community church, right after my grandmother had sank her teeth into our business. My mother was the only one home when I had got there. Of course, she mothered me by hushing, shushing, and drying my tears.

Then, my dad arrived home. His tempered sparked after hearing the story I had to tell. He was angry—the angriest I had ever seen him. The look in his eyes swore to kill a man dead. I could still see his face in my memory.

Insert my bitch of a grandmother into the picture. All hail Lola Hughes, the greatest brainwasher this side of the Mason-Dixon Line. She convinced my mother I was making it all up, that Brother Covington was a well-respected pastor. She claimed we needed God in our lives.

In turn, my mother kept insisting it didn't happen until my dad began to doubt my claim. I think he wanted to believe her, to believe that something like that couldn't have happened to his son. Not no way. Not no how.

From that day forward, seeds of hate were sown. From that day forward, bitterness began to grow. However...from that day forward, my dad stopped going to church. Part of me wanted to believe it was his way of acknowledging the situation. Another part of me said, "Fuck both of them." The latter had won over my conscience.

"Can you believe the family reunion is in a few days?" My mother asked no one in particular. She was just talking to fill the silence. That was the kind of person she was. She just talked and talked and talked, unable to enjoy the silence. "It'll be here and gone before we know it."

"Thank God," my dad muttered under his breath and rolled his eyes, much to my surprise. Had he always been that way? I couldn't remember if—

A loud round of clapping echoed through the restaurant as a train of waiters and waitresses marched toward our table. A platter of ice cream and chocolate cake drizzled with chocolate syrup was placed onto the table in front of Memphis. Her eyes widened to the size of saucers, and drool dribbled out of her mouth as though she heard Pavlov ringing his bell.

"We have a very special birthday girl with us this evening!" one of the waiters bellowed while dropping a sombrero on top Memphis's head. "On the count of three, everybody join in for a good ol' Rancho Grande tradition!"

Tradition? There's a *tradition*? Are you shittin' me?

"One...two...three! YEE-HAW, Y'ALL!" a chorus of voices rang out simultaneously.

Stunned. I was sitting there in the hard, wooden chair, and I was stunned. They actually just yelled that out loud in the most exaggerated southern accent imaginable. Me = loss for words.

You know how in movies when something major was happening and everything was slowed down? While the picture crept by and a slow ballad of a song was played, the camera zoomed in on specific people for the sake of dramatic cinematography. That was what it felt like.

My eyelids blinked in-between subtle heart beats, taking in everything: Memphis's laughing face as she greedily looked at the cake, Raleigh and Jackson clapping along with fervent smiles, my mom being the doting mother that she was and pulling on my dad's arm for him to take a picture, my dad cutting his eyes down to her grasp with sheer repulsion flickering across his face.

There it was. There was the truth in the bigger picture. It could've slipped by without a moment's notice while you were none the wiser. There was one and one reason only as to why I picked up on my dad's look of repulsion. It was the look I gave the world.

Resentment transplanted itself onto my dad's face, its roots running deep. Surprisingly, I wasn't surprised. It was like when you cut yourself without fully realizing it. You could feel it stinging, and you knew something was wrong. However, you didn't pay attention to it, to what it meant. It was a dull, nagging sting that kept stinging until you looked down. There it was. There was the blood. Then, the pain came busting through the dull, nagging façade. It had been bleeding for a while. It had even started to dry and crust over. You washed it off only to reopen the wound, causing more blood to pour forth. Now, it was different. You knew you'd cut yourself. You knew you were bleeding. You knew where the pain was coming from.

I am the landslide.

The pen scraped across the notebook paper, cutting a line of darkest ink through the white blankness. A soft scratching sounded as the ball-point glided with the grace of a waltz, making cursive loops all about the college-ruled dance floor. On the count of three, box-steps were made.

Slow. Quick. Quick. 1-2-3. 1-2-3.

Breaths synced with the steps as the tempo quickened. Deeper lines of darkest ink cut across the vast white, scuffing the dance floor with their marks.

We all have fears.
Some may call them irrational.
Some may call them illogical.
Call them what you will,
but that doesn't make them any less or any more.
They are still there.

Like a stain that will not wash out.
They are still buried beneath the surface of your exterior.
Like a splinter embedded deep.
They are still sharp enough to pierce your confidence.
Like a thumbtack pinning grievances to your soul.

A soft breeze lightly picked up the corner of the notebook page. Lazily, it fell back into place as metallic clicks of a gate unlocking rattled into the atmosphere. The sun peeked out from behind a cloudy sky. Its rays were unable to cast down hellacious temperatures, but that didn't stop the fiery damnation that was Sulfur Springs.

Perched upon the topmost step of the back porch, I looked up from the notebook I kept by my bedside. Memphis was sprawled out on a lawn chair in the middle of the yard. A feathered boa was draped around her neck, and she twirled the end of it. Like she was fanning herself from the heat. Big, bug-eyed sunglasses belonging to our mother, who had paid an arm and a leg for them in order to fit in with the societal norms of her fellow hoity-toity Christian bitches, were artfully pushed up on the bridge of her nose with movie star elegance.

Rhi stepped around the side of the house with her camera bag in tow for the promised photo shoot. "Is that Memphis Harper the world-renowned model extraordinaire?" she asked, feigning star-struckness.

"I'm ready for my close-up, Misses Moreno!" Memphis exclaimed with a blasé tone, flipping her hair over her shoulder with flamboyance. "Make me young and eight again."

Have I ever said how much I wished I lived in my kid sister's world? Because I really did. Here she was without a care in the world as she enjoyed every moment of every day. Who wouldn't envy that? Not me, that's who.

"Honey, I'll make you look like you're still in diapers," Rhi said, sitting her bag on the steps beside me.

"Mah-vah-lous, dah-ling," Memphis sounded the syllables out with a fake accent.

Rhi laughed lightheartedly and tugged on the zipper, opening her bag and pulling the camera out. She flashed me a smile that said, "Your sister is absolutely adorable. You know that, right?" I nodded my head in agreement with her unspoken comment, returning her smile with ease.

That was what Memphis did. She made people smile with ease. She made me smile with ease. Just being near her made me feel human—normal. The corners of my mouth twitched. A faint pop of air sounded as my lips parted, paving the way for genuine sincerity. I could feel it. I could feel the actual smile in the depths of my soul as the smile I smiled reached my eyes.

I felt that sense of camaraderie with Rhi, and I wanted to ask her how Ackerley was but stopped myself. She would know that I wanted to know about him. My lips zipped before any words or thoughts of interest slipped out. Behind me, I could hear the pleading whine of a whimper. Mr. Faustus was standing on his hind legs and looking longingly through the screen door. I couldn't help but to feel sorry for him. His tail wagged into a blur when I reached to let him out. As fast as his four legs could carry him, he bolted down the steps, knocking over Rhi's bag in the process. She was too busy issuing exaggerated, clichéd modeling phrases as she snapped photo after photo to notice the mishap.

Contrary to both popular belief and my previous actions, manners were embedded in my DNA. I was, in fact, a southern gentleman through and through. Most of the time, I kept my manners to myself. Sometimes, I took them out for a test drive. Like now, for instance, as I bent down to retrieve the contents of Rhi's bag.

A photo album of Robin's egg blue laid splayed open and face down on the last step. The word "always" was written in a white, glossy calligraphy across the front cover. As if it were fragile, I eased it up off the step and flipped it over.

Staring up at me with eyes of familiarity was a little boy. Soft wisps of dark hair were captured in mid-step as they were dancing in an invisible gust of wind from the past. He smiled a toothless smile directly into the camera as he held up an outstretched hand, yearning for the person behind the lens.

Underneath the photograph of innocence was a caption with the same calligraphy as the cover. "Stephen" was written in elegant cursive, and it was dated roughly three years back. My eyes glided back up to the picture as his name reverberated in my head. His little, chubby cheeks said it all. I could see that spark of life. It was the same spark that emanated from Rhi like a blazing wildfire. There was a strong resemblance. Stephen had to be a relative or—

"Excuse you!" Rhi exclaimed, snatching the photo album from my hands. A million different expressions flitted across her face, ranging from anger to betrayal.

"S-sorry...the dog...steps...bag," I sputtered incoherently.

"I know you are just dying to see some of my work, but you're just going to have to wait like everybody else, buddy." She arched her eyebrow with obvious fake sarcasm like she was trying to cover her slip-up of emotions.

I had crossed a line, and she was doing her best to not let me know I'd done so. She hitched the bag over her shoulder and followed Memphis up the steps and into the house. I could faintly hear the over dramatic instructions to take some "artsy-fartsy" pictures on the staircase as the screen door slammed shut, cutting me off from the inside world.

What the hell had just happened? Why would she get so bent out of shape over something like that? I tapped my foot waiting for the voice inside my head to reply with some profound solution as to why Rhi went mental for a split-second, but I heard nothing. Nada. Zilch. Just white noise as the reception went out.

The best fix-it-yourself remedy I could come up with was a shoulder shrug. Sometimes, it was best to not put effort into a losing battle of problem solving. I slumped back down onto the steps and reached for the notebook. The pen started to dance as its ballpoint pressed against the college-ruled dance floor for an encore performance.

You may fear getting naked in front of someone.
You may fear being stripped of your clothing.
You may fear seeing the expression on the other's face.
You may fear letting yourself be scrutinized.
You may fear standing there in all your glory.
You may fear having no glory to bare.
You may fear hearing the thoughts they are thinking.
You may fear listening to the spoken truth.
You may fear showing the real you.

Footsteps thundered through the house, and then the screen door was almost torn off its hinges as a ball of fur and my kid sister shot forth into the backyard. Memphis must've tired of her Hollywood diva persona; she switched gears faster than you could blink. Now, she was back to her ten year old self—for the time being. If I've said it once, I've said it a thousand times: I wished I lived in her crazy, little world.

"That was fast," I commented with nonchalance as Rhi took a seat on the step. I wanted to test the waters to see whether it was safe or if my boat would capsize in her grudge-holding current.

"Your sister is something else alright," she commented as she eyed Memphis and Mr. Faustus playing some sort of made-up game of chase around the backyard.

"I couldn't have said it better myself." I laid the notebook down and cut my eyes toward her. "Thanks for doing this for her. I'm sure she'll be raving about how amazing the pictures are."

"No problem," she sighed, leaning forward and resting her elbows on her knees. "I love photographing the innocence of childhood."

Her words called forth the photograph of Stephen. I wanted to know who he was. I wanted to know why she was carrying around the album. I wanted to know why she regarded it such personal importance. I wanted to know everything, but I couldn't bring myself to ask.

"You know childhood is fleeting, don't you?" she asked. Talk about randomness. She was way off in left field or something.

"What do you mean?"

"Childhood dies...." She kept staring straight ahead, her eyes never leaving Memphis. "It just dies. You can never get it back. I wished someone would've told me that sooner or later innocence dies and everything you know can be taken away."

I found myself wanting again: wanting to tell her I wished the same thing, wanting to tell her I knew what she meant, wanting to tell her that innocence dies a death most foul. However, I refrained from doing so. She was obviously having a deep moment. Like she was the main star in a play and thinking aloud in a soliloquy.

"If you think back on a certain time in your life, you have all those memories that burn the brightest in your memory. You don't even have to think to recall the fact something happened or what took place. It just comes rushing forth, carrying every single detail—every insignificant, damned detail...."

Still, I didn't say a word. Rhi didn't look at me, not even with the slightest twitch sideways. She did glance down at her camera bag, and then she titled her head into the sky as though she were preaching to the clouds.

"I don't know why those memories hold so much importance, ya know? It's like there's some unknown matter of significance of that particular moment of that particular day. You can relive that moment over and over again, replaying it over and over in your head."

She shook her head slowly, solemnly. "That's why I take pictures. That's why I like to capture everything before it's too late, before everything dies. I just don't want to relive those moments that are stored away in my head. I want to relive every moment of every day as much as I can...because...because you never know what will happen, what moments will be taken away from you. I want to live in every single moment over and over again."

As her words echoed into the atmosphere and mixed with the soft hues of late afternoon, she heaved herself up from the steps and swung her bag over her shoulder. Memphis's excited squeals of laughter played in the background as a very somber Rhi turned her head toward my kid sister.

"She's special." Shielding her eyes from the sun, she looked back at me. "Please don't take her for granted...childhood doesn't last. She'll get older." Gravity pulled her eyes down toward the ground, and she muttered. "We all get older...."

I am falling down the rabbit-hole.

Charlotte Harper was in a snit so foul it made the worst of snits minuscule in comparison. She nagged about *this*, and then she nagged about *that*. She nagged about some things, and then she nagged about other things. Nag. Nag. Nag.

"Raleigh, I told you to watch your sister!" she griped when Raleigh plopped down on the couch and started flipping through the television channels. "Take her to the park or something. She's driving me ape-shit-crazy running up and down the stairs."

"Jesus Christ! Someone make that stupid dog to shut the hell up!" she snapped when Mr. Faustus whined for attention as she was getting food out of the oven.

"Jackson, put down that video game and go help your father out in the garage," she spat after the handheld game emitted a series of beeps. "Damn it! I can't even hear myself think!"

Ladies and gentleman, may I present to you...Mrs. Charlotte Harper!

Wife. Mother. Cook. Professed Christian. Taker of the Lord's name in vain.

Despite the obvious genetic traits, adoption was that universal solution to all my problems. I guaran-damn-teed you I was left on the doorstep of the nearest Catholic church swaddled in receiving blankets. Like I was Quasimodo and my birth parents knew I was bound to be a fuck up. Maybe they wanted me to have a better life than they could've provided. Maybe they'd had no idea I was going to be reared in the small town cesspool. Maybe my life would have been different if they had just kept me instead of throwing me away.

All of this *excitement* around the house was because of one thing and one thing only. Would you care to guess? I'll give you a hint: two words. First word sounded like "living." Second word sounded like "hell." Give up? FAMILY REUNION! But, it wasn't just a family reunion. It was THE family reunion. It was the fucking Hughes family reunion with my mom's side of the family. It was clones of two-faced, religious zealots molded after her mightiness, my grandmother. Not only would it be a living hell, it'd be like actually living in Hell...with a trailer pulled up in the expansive, fiery front lawn of Hitler's mansion of brimstone, which is located on Heinous Lane nestled in-between Stalin and a vacant lot reserved for one Mrs. Lola Hughes.

I could think of a million things I'd rather do instead of seeing my extended family. Root canals, elective brain surgery, having my right pinky finger snapped off with bolt cutters by the mafia, a prostate exam, plucking out each eyelash one by one with tweezers, tearing off each fingernail with a masochistically slow speed.... Need I continue or do you get the general idea?

Escape was the ideal verb of choice. My father escaped into the garage (he was probably drinking a beer and staring a hole into the wall). Both my sisters escaped out the front door (there was no telling what Memphis talked Raleigh into doing). My brother escaped out the backdoor (ten bucks said he was hiding from our mother's line of sight from out the kitchen window and playing the video game he was so keen on).

A wishful breath expelled itself, filling bubble dreams. I wished I could escape. I wished I could abdicate my bloodline. I wished I could run off and elope with the life I should be living. I wished I could figure out why I felt like a foreigner in a different land of emotions and feelings. I wished I could. I wished I might.

And so, it was me all my by lonesome against the nag-induced war. Raleigh left the volume on the television as loud as it could get, and the sound was mixing with nagging naggisms of my naggy-ass mother, Charlotte "The Nag" Harper. My eye tensed in preparation to twitch. My eardrums were 0.999 seconds way from imploding from the audial stress and putting me out of my misery. The war was still raging, and nag bombs were still dropping. I was ready to go AWOL.

So much was going on at once. If my life were a movie, it'd be a scene where high-pitched music would sound while the camera angle rotated out of control with tension building and building. I wanted to tell her to shut up, to shut her trap. It boiled and bubbled, surging through my veins. My skin crawled with the want, the desire to scream at her until no sound came out. I wanted to, but I did not. Losing control could not be afforded.

Instead, I took deep breaths and took pride in reflecting on the facts: the fact that I would be up and gone from the springs of sulfur, the fact that my life *would* get better, the fact that most church goers in this town would end up in the fiery pits of Hell with their own little house on Heinous Lane, the fact that it would devastate my mother if she knew how unhappy my father was, the fact that it would fracture her perfect family if I happened to up and announce that I was

247

sexually confused in more ways than one. Yes, I was reveling in the facts as I attempted to stare through the wall as though I was awaiting the power of x-ray vision to emerge.

A whimpered sounded as soft clicks were clicked on the hardwood floor of the hallway leading from the kitchen. As sad as it sounded, it was the most relieving sound I had heard all morning. It meant I wasn't alone. There was Mr. Faustus. He came tip-toeing around the corner as though he were walking on broken glass. His tail was tucked in-between his legs, and his puppy dog eyes looked as though they were watering up with the saddest puppy dog tears.

"Here, boy," I called, squatting down and patting my thigh. He regarded me with a scrutinizing stare through those puppy dog eyes of his. It wasn't like I was going to scold him for whining, for doing something he couldn't help. All he wanted was a little attention, a little acknowledgement even.

"Did your momma go off and leave you, huh?" Still, he was leery of my true intentions. His eyes grew wide and timid as he craned his neck, looking toward the kitchen. I had to extended my arm and stretch my hand out to scratch his head. That dog was skittish as all get out.

"Do you want to go outside?" Bingo was his name-o. I had said the magic word. His ears perked up at the mere mention of going outside. His tail untucked itself from in-between his legs and started wagging with excitement.

He excitedly padded after me as I crossed into the kitchen to get his collar and leash from the laundry room. Already learning how to survive the chaos that was the Harper family, Mr. Faustus turned his face away and gave my mom a cold shoulder as she angrily tackled tablecloths with an iron. I mean, why iron the tablecloths? I was quite sure that a get-together of hypocrites didn't call for starched creaseless-ness for which thus said hypocrites would devour their meal of one foot after the other.

Huffing and puffing as she sang a church hymn, my mom slammed the iron down against the ironing board in her vain attempt for perfect tablecloths. Would she ever learn? Some wrinkles couldn't be made smooth again. Some creases would forever remain creased.

"I once was lost," she crooned, "but now am found." The iron attacked the fabric with a hiss of steam as she haphazardly jerked it around. "Was blind, but now I se—GODDAMN IT!" she bellowed, dropping the iron as angry, red splotches erupted on her left hand. What did I tell you, ladies and gents? Hypocrisy at its finest, striking while the iron was hot. Pun fully intended.

If my life were a 30-minute comedic television show, the camera would close in on Mr. Faustus and me as we exchanged looks. Computer animation would arch his eyebrow to match mine as a silent, witty remark was exchanged between the two of us. A laugh track of an amused audience would play, and then that comically timed "wah-wah-wahhhh" would sound right before the show breaked for commercials.

After a word from our sponsors, we were back.

Mr. Faustus tore out the backdoor, pulling me with all his might in his haste to leave the house. If I didn't know any better, I'd say that dog thought lightning bolts were going to strike and he wanted to get as far down the sidewalk as possible before the well-deserved catastrophe occurred. Who'd blame him with all that blasphemous blasphemy at its finest? Not me, that's who.

The day was lovely outside from the bubble of family drama—no, make it a boil of foreshadowing yet to come. The sun was bright and twinkling with dancing rays of whitest light in a cloudless sky such a hue of blue it looked as though someone colored it in. Like someone grabbed a box of crayons and put sky blue to the test.

It was funny how life was shaded by colors, how everything was colored within the confining lines of who we were and who we were expected to be. Life was a box of crayons with twenty-four colors from which to pick and choose, but which crayon colored you? I'd be that crayon that was never broken, that was never used up. I'd want to be that whitest white. It was the only color that showed up on black paper. White was the only color that could cut a blinding light through the darkness.

If Mr. Faustus could read my thoughts with some canine sixth sense, he didn't acknowledge my sudden interest in the nature as if I were a pastoral poet with a knack for childhood arts and crafts. He tugged against the leash as if he were late for an appointment. Trying with all his might, he attempted to pull me along the block in the opposite route I had grown accustomed to.

I didn't care my routine had been offset by his change in direction. Besides, I was too engrossed in watching Mr. Faustus's spastic head bobs as his nose roamed all over the sidewalk to care about such trivial details as an alternative direction; there was more than one way to reach the same destination. He had practically glued his face to the sidewalk as he made that sniffing sound, taking in every smell he could suck in through his nostrils.

There wasn't a mailbox, fence post, bush, or random inanimate object left unturned by his olfactory sniffs of discovery by the time we had made turned the last corner of the block. Mr. Faustus was still going strong, yearning to be leash free to do as he pleased. He was still a puppy, but he had some strength. A few more

251

weeks or so, and Memphis wouldn't be able to control him.

The very rational thought conjured up a very irrational picture of a comically cartoon Memphis who was frustrated in her attempt to walk a comically cartoon Mr. Faustus. Little speech bubbles filled with "@$#%@!!" as swear words. Just thinking about my kid sister's probable use of profanity in a time of stress caused a great hearty chuckle of sincere amusement.

Laughter made even the tensest of times a little bit better, and the weight laden on your shoulders lessened. The monotonous wasn't so monstrous anymore. The hellish heat wasn't so hellacious anymore. Sulfur Springs wasn't so sulfurous anymore.

I sure did feel out of my element. Before I could stop myself, my hand returned the "index-finger wave" as a pickup truck drove past. An elderly couple was sitting side by side on the bench seat, and the man had his arm around the woman. It was a very sweet gesture of undying love. I was talking cheesy, tear-jerking, romance movie type of sweet. That was what everybody dreamed of, wasn't it? To be old and still in love as though it were still the first time? Why did I even care?

The sighting of the rare old-and-still-in-love-couple caused vicarious nostalgia for the past. Without a second thought or so much as hesitation, I turned down the walkway. Mr. Faustus raised his head into the air, and his nostrils flared from intoxicating scent of Mrs. Thomas's daylilies.

Before I could take the first step onto the porch to knock on the door, I heard her aged voice resounding from around the side of the house and the excited yips of her dog. "Jasper!" she hooted with that lighthearted, airy laughter. I could just see the way her face lit up when she smiled and the way her eyes shined with that smile as her laugh fluttered. I found myself longing for her sincerity.

With Mr. Faustus at my heels, I took the walkway around the side of the house as I had done previously when she asked me to carry the potting soil earlier in the summer. The air weighed heavily with the aromatic smells derived directly by her green thumb the closer I made it to the backyard. Stepping around the corner of the house was like stepping into a completely different world from before.

"Mrs. Thomas?" I asked, looking around in amazement. She had been busy putting that green thumb of hers to good use. Bright, bold flowers covered the earth in a blanket of blooms, and I was awed by the magical feel of her garden.

"Mr. Harper," she called from the middle of the yard from where she was sitting in one of two white Adirondack chairs underneath a rather large shade tree. She closed the magazine she was reading and laid it on the chair arm. "Well, what a lovely surprise to see you. Please, sit." She motioned to the other chair—the chair I assumed belonged to her dearly departed husband.

How could she just sit there and casually flip through a magazine without so much as a care in the world, especially sitting alone in a matching set. I wished I could be that type of person. I wanted to be able to sit back and not have a care in the world as I paid my full, undivided attention to each glossy page. But, I couldn't just sit there and flip from one page to the next with an actual interest in what page article "so-in-so" was on or what came next with a flip of the wrist. I just couldn't. Here lately, my interest was fleeting. I could only hurry through a magazine, a book. It was like I couldn't wait to get to the last page so I could shut it, be done with it, be finished. I couldn't enjoy the simple pleasure of the story within. What kind of person did that make me? What did that say about who I am?

"Thank you," I said, crossing the yard. Mr. Faustus wagged his tail excitedly as he took in Jasper lying on the ground next to her feet, but Jasper wasn't as intrigued. He just rolled onto his side and regarded us through upside-down eyes with the pure laziness of a feline.

"How are you doing this afternoon?" I asked, taking a seat.

"I'm sitting here and enjoying the day," she said, looking around the yard. "Life is good."

"It sure is, ma'am."

I wanted to agree with her, wanted to believe in what she believed. I followed her gaze around the yard. The back porch jogged a memory of an elderly lady ambling down those steps as a dog danced around her with a stick in its mouth. Cocking my head, I looked next door to the house I lived in, to the place I was supposed to call home.

There was the window. There was my bedroom window in a house I didn't feel at home in. There was my view of the world.

Funny thing was…from the outside it looked like an ordinary, simple window. How was anyone supposed to know there was someone lurking on the other side of the pane? How was anyone supposed to know there was someone painfully looking out from the pane? After all, it was just an ordinary, simple window on an ordinary, simple house on an ordinary, simple street in an ordinary, simple town. Nobody would be any the wiser less the window were opened so they could see inside.

Being in her backyard felt more personal than sitting on her front porch. Like we were old friends. She was the grandmother I wished I had. She was the nurturing woman I wished my mother was. Through her eyes, I mattered. Through her eyes, I was worthy of life. Through her eyes, I could see clearly.

"Mrs. Thomas, will you tell me a story?"

"I would love to, Phoenix," she replied, reaching across and patting me on the arm. "Where did we leave off?"

"Your mother had told you to be the grass…."

"You know, I still remember the very day she spoke those words to me. I can still smell the way her perfume mixed with the wind. I can still see her hair dancing in the breeze. I can still hear her voice…."

Her voice caught in her throat, and I thought she was going to cry. I was prepared for her to cry, but cry she did not. Her eyes glistened as though she was about to breakdown, but she didn't shed a tear.

"My mother was a beautiful woman inside and out. I still remember her as she was that day, not the way she was when…when the cancer took her from me. I still remember that moment because she told me to never give up. It was in that moment she changed my life."

My eyes closed. A projector played the scene on the back of my eyelids. I could see a very young Amelia Thomas on the cusp of life and her mother before cancer robbed her of the life she had. My heart panged with the happy moment of sad longing. My eyes itched in their desire to cry. I wanted to weep for both her loss and her gain of understanding. I wanted to weep for that great love of a mother I didn't have.

"I never gave up," she continued on. "TC had been gone a good while before the days became bearable once again. At first, he wrote me letters, but they soon became few and far between. I kept hope alive for as long as I could...."

She cleared her throat and breathed deeply. "It wasn't until a year had passed that my mother started getting sick. She told me to be strong, to never give up hope. My father and I watched the life slowly die in her eyes. I tried to be strong, but I didn't have it in me to keep hoping. When the doctor said she didn't have long, I couldn't take it. I ran. I ran out of the room and down the steps and out the door and right smack dab into my future."

Her little, airy laugh fluttered, catching me by surprise. I didn't quite follow how she found amusement in the memory. "There stood Jimmy outside on the porch, waiting on his father to get done doctoring. Tears blurred my eyes, and I collided with him. Jimmy caught me from falling. I wasn't strong enough to keep a brave face. I sunk into him and cried my eyes out over the loss of everything I had."

"Jimmy...." A bittersweet expression shaded her face, coloring inside the lines wore by the years she had lived. It was the look of happiness in the time where sadness was all she knew. "Jimmy was there for me as my mother lost her battle. Jimmy was there for me as my mother was laid to rest. Jimmy was there for me when I needed him the most. Jimmy Thomas was there for me…and that made all the difference."

Mrs. Amelia Thomas had found someone to spend her life with despite the adversity of her trials and tribulations. She remembered the past with a cherished perspective, not with one of bitter remorse. She did not let disaster loom over her head. She chose to move forward, to keep growing, to never give up. She chose to be the grass.

And for that, I wept.

I am waiting to exhale.

Woe was me. After all the pent up frustration and dread, the day of living hell had finally arrived with a whimper rather than with earth-shaking cataclysms to suggest it was doomsday as I had previously anticipated. The sun had risen like it did on all previous Saturdays, birds had tweeted their promising song of usual morning cheeriness, and the day had begun without any whims of foreboding. Everything had a strangely bright disposition, and I didn't much care for it. It was like in those horror movies where at the beginning everything was all perfect and shit. Fast forward to the end where everyone was brutally slaughtered by a bitter man in a cheap, plastic, Halloween mask.

I absolutely did not want to go, but I was in a catch-22. Either I could go and endure it or I could skip out on it and listen to my mother nag about it until the next one, which could be *years*. The former was the lesser of the two evils, so naturally that was the reason why I had come to be sitting alone at a picnic table underneath the farthest shade tree and watching the show unfold behind Sulfur Springs Community Center.

The tragedy that was the Hughes family was weaved together in a tangled web of comedic proportions. I mean, the Bard wished he could've dreamt this shit up. Albeit, he was probably rolling over in his grave with pure jealously.

There were throngs of cousins once, twice, three times removed as well as great aunts and uncles. In other words, the majority in attendance consisted of people I hadn't seen since I was a child and had no idea who they were much less care about them enough to make fake-ass small talk. I didn't know much about my family, and I fully intended on keeping it that way. I took great pride in the efforts I'd put forth all in the name of disassociation. I've had quite the successful streak in keeping it up. Why ruin it now?

Keep a low profile. Keep your head down. Keep from making eye contact.

I kept chanting the mantra to myself in hopes I would be left alone. I had no interest in "shootin' the shit" with the men. I had no interest in catching up with the cousins I grew up with. I had no interest in being a part of the family.

I needed a distraction. After closing my eyes and clearing my head from everything that was going on, there was one interest I had in mind. Deciding to do something that I rarely did, my cellphone was in hand and a text message was being constructed.

Hell. No clue on what to say. What was the text messaging etiquette? Why was I so behind on the times? Should I key in something like "Sorry, I've not been very loquacious here recently" or "I'm confused as what the implications of everything might mean" or...what?

After a few moments of internal debate, the most appropriate and logical conversation starter was the ever so simple "Hey." It was short and to the point. Done and done. As I closed the cellphone, eerie feelings of someone being in close proximity—those weird, tingly feelings that seemed to crawl all over your body—chilled me to the core. Son of a bitch. I had forgotten a vital key point: *Keep alert.*

"Well, look who we have here," said a voice I hadn't heard since God knows when.

Easing herself onto the bench beside me, Derenda Hughes expelled a sigh that smelled strangely of liquor. My aunt was a 40s something librarian who was talked about behind her back for being single so late in adulthood. She had a no nonsense appearance that suggested she didn't care what she looked like.

According to High Horse Lola, she was the black sheep of the family.

"You graduated, right? They didn't kick your ass out or anything, did they?" Derenda asked, taking me by surprise with frankness.

"I, uh…I graduated," I managed to answer.

"Good, son."

What the hell? Her behavior was off-putting. She wasn't the aunt I remembered. The Derenda I remembered was a really scatterbrained woman obsessed with soap operas that my mother had made the butt of almost every joke.

"Look at them," she said, nodding her head. "They're all mindless sheep."

Ok. Hold the phone. Had I just heard her correctly? She had obviously been drinking. Who the hell has an open bar at a reunion? I didn't know how to properly respond to her statement. I just nodded my head, arched my eyebrows, and clasped my lips together with an "mmhmm."

"I snuck a flask in here. Momma would shit a brick if she knew."

Okay, now *that* explained a lot. Why was she confiding in me? Maybe Derenda wasn't this crazy, old bat my mother had brainwashed me into believing. Maybe she was resentful of the family just as I was.

Maybe we had something in common. Maybe I wasn't completely alone.

"I can't stand these pathetic bastards," she said. She shook her head with obvious disgust, and looked around our kinfolk. Her eyes darted judgmentally, and then her lips parted with a subtle intake of breath.

Sulfur Springs Community Center proudly presents in association with Lucifer himself

"The *Fucking* Hughes Family Reunion!"

narrated by **Derenda Hughes**

DH: Oh, just look at Nadine *(my uncle Royce's wife)*. She just thinks she is so high and mighty because she's eating a salad. Look at that expression on her face. See it? Her upturned pug nose, those fat cheeks that make her eyes squint, her wobbly chins. She thinks she's better than anyone because she isn't eating a hamburger. Miss Thang is on a diet. Big fucking deal. Her lard ass has been on that damn diet since she married Royce, and she is still as big as the broad side of a barn.

DH: Lookie there. It's momma's baby *(my aunt Lucinda)*. Momma has always thought she was the perfect one, the most special one, the one with the brightest future all because she married a politician and moved to D.C. and had the perfect blessing of twins *(my younger cousins Kirby and Brodie)*. Blah, blah, blah. That's all bullshit. Little Miss Perfect is going through a divorce because she caught her husband dickin' around. I don't know who took it worse, momma or Lucinda.

DH: Why, I'll be damned. Mr. High and Mighty himself *(my uncle Royce)*. You be careful if he comes around because he'll want something. He's a user and doesn't think twice about it. He makes me sick. I can't even stand his ol' stupid ass always thinking he knows what's best. You know, he got into a fight with daddy awhile back over who gets what after they die. Mmhmm. He sure did. Right there at Thanksgiving. Now, that was what I call dinner and a show! I about choked to death from laughing so damn hard.

DH: Look who's coming this way, it's Lola Junior *(my mother)*. Now, I know Charlotte's your mother and all, but...damn that woman's a piece of work. Look at her prancing around all proud and shit that she single-handedly helped momma.

Let me tell you, son. I just don't know how your father puts up with her fucking bullshit. Hell, I don't know how any of you kids put up with it. I don't blame you one bit for going off to college instead of staying around here like Hunter *(my uncle Royce's son)*. Now, I want you to promise me that you'll be different. Do whatever you can to distance yourself from this fucked up family. Don't be like me. Don't keep waiting and waiting...*burp*...and waiting your whole goddamned life.

She had fallen silent as she watched my mother make her way over. I was slightly taken aback. Honestly, I was more than slightly taken aback. Part of me was saddened by her brutal honesty while another part felt relieved to not be alone in my state of mind. Either she was going through a midlife crisis or she was cracking under the pressure from years of pent up frustration. Like she was Mount Vesuvius and wanted to wreak havoc of our unsuspecting, Pompeian family.

Was she really that bitter and remorseful about the family, our family? It was as though I had been visited by The Ghost of Christmas Yet to Come. Was being a bitter, 40s something single what I had to look forward to? Will I be Derenda? Better yet, am I Derenda?

"Hun," my mom said in an overtly, sugary voice as her skeptical eyes roamed all over Derenda's appearance. The atmosphere between the two of them grew tense. "Your father needs to some help with moving the cooler from inside. Could you be a dear and go help him?"

Her mood swings were enough to give someone whiplash due to the neck-breaking ups and downs. I nodded my head and stood, wanting to be anywhere but caught in-between their death glares.

"Derenda," she said as I walked away. "Derenda, Derenda, Derenda...what *are* we going to do with you?"

"Charlotte, Charlotte, Charlotte...I'll tell you what you can do," Derenda said in a cool voice that suggested an edge of sarcastic demeanor. "You can shove your head up your own ass for all I...."

Her words were lost as footsteps carried me out of earshot. A smile flickered across my face in agreement and appreciation. Preach it, Derenda. Preach it.

An odd, out-of-place weight weighed heavily in my pocket, tapping against my thigh. I wasn't accustomed to carrying a cellphone on my person. Did I have a new message? My curiosity got the better of me, and I checked to see.

There were three new messages—all from him. The first one read, "Hi." The second read, "Would you want to go out Wednesday night?" The third was a clarification that read, "Not like a date or anything, but you know…just the two of us hanging out."

The funny thing was I could hear his voice in my head as I read the messages. I could hear his pretentious ramblings as he asked if I wanted to hang out. I could hear the vulnerability in his voice as he clarified what he supposedly meant to imply. I could hear my own voice of reason agreeing to Wednesday night. To just hang out. That was all. What was wrong with that?

A frustrated sigh caught my attention as I stepped onto the awning leading into the community center. Raleigh griped a bag of ice in each hand as she tried to open the door, but she was out of luck in her futile attempt to twist the handle. Those southern gentleman manners that were embedded in my DNA surfaced, and I reached out to help her. Without so much as a thank-you, she stepped inside. I followed suit.

No wonder the reunion was being held outside. The community center felt like stepping into an oven. The air inside was stank with staleness. There was no bittersweet smell of AC, but there was a bittersweet ghost of its existence. Sweat immediately beaded upon my brow as I followed Raleigh toward the kitchen.

I resumed looking at the text messages as the awkward silence screamed at the top of its lungs between us in the deserted hallway. I now knew why people constantly kept a tab on their cellphones in such situations. Everybody needed a crutch for support, right?

As if they had a mind of their own, my fingers keyed in a response to text #2's question. "Sure. What did you have in mind?" Done and done. Nothing cataclysmic happened because I agreed to hang out. *See,* I told myself as we drew near the kitchen. *Everything is going to be okay.*

I spoke too soon.

The naggy naggisms of my naggy grandmother echoed off the kitchen's tiled floor. How did that saying go? Like mother like daughter or something like that? Raleigh and I hesitated outside the door, peering around the corner. Our dad was bent over the cooler as he tried to situate canned cokes. Lola was circling over him like the vulture that she was. Her teased up hair was dripping with sweat and sticking to her forehead. The inside the building was hotter than it was outside, but she should've felt right at him with the hellacious temperature. Zing.

"Troy," she nagged, "I told you to bring the biggest cooler you had. Why did you bring this rinky-dink piece of junk? Hmm? Hmm? You never listen. That's just like a man!"

Why was my dad just letting her talk to him like that? If it were me, I'd bitchslap the smugness off her wrinkly, old face. My hand shook at just the mere thought of doing so.

"I swear," Lola continued. "You are pathetic. I don't see why Charlotte married you. You're a good for nothing, worthless, sorry—"

"Lola," my dad interrupted through gritted teeth. "I said this was the biggest cooler I had."

"*This is the biggest cooler I had*," she mimicked. "You lie like a dog."

All this argument over a damn cooler—a damn cooler! What was more childish or shallow about bickering over a measly, insignificant cooler? It was absurd, ludicrous even. I felt as if I were watching two people skate on thin ice, and the ice was starting to fracture with splits and cracks. Very unstable. Very unsafe. Very ominous creaking as the cracks cracked under stress.

"Lies! That just goes to show you what kind of role model you are for your kids," she spat, wiping the sweat from her face with the back of her hand as she tried to salvage her hairdo. "No wonder that boy of yours lied about Brother Covington molesting him."

An invisible fist clenched my stomach. My eyes focused in and out of tunnel vision. I could feel Raleigh looking at me. I could feel the pins and needles penetrating from her stare, but I couldn't move. Hearing it spoken out loud was paralyzing. Hearing his name spoken into existence in relation to what happened made me feel as though I were in a cartoon and someone dropped a piano on my head causing me to see little, bright, twinkling stars. That was my life—just one big joke of cartoon where just when I thought things were looking up someone took pleasure in cutting the rope that held the piano above my head as it gently swayed with looming devastation.

Was I imagining things? Did someone press the "pause" button? Nobody was moving. My dad was frozen with a can tightly gripped in his hand. All I could hear was my heartbeat pounding in my ears.

"Shut up," he seethed through clenched teeth.

"What did you say?" Lola asked with a crazed expression in her eyes.

"Shut. Up." His voice grew louder, and he slowly stood. Still, he gripped the can.

"W-w-why, I never—"

"Shut up," he cut off her flabbergasted sputtering. "I've had enough. You hear me? I'm sick of this family. I'm sick of you and John looming over my head. I'm sick of the way my son got treated all because of you and your warped sense of right and wrong. Most of all, I'm sick of the way I let you control me all because I knocked your daughter up all those years ago. But not anymore. You hear me, Lola? Not anymore."

I was a deer in headlights. I couldn't move. I could only watch the speeding car.

My dad didn't get all up in her face. He didn't scream at the top of his lungs. He didn't throw the canned coke as I thought he would. He spoke with a clear, level voice—the same voice he had spoken to my siblings and me with whenever we had gotten into trouble and were being scolded. He popped the tab on the can, and took a sip as if he weren't in the middle of confrontation before he continued his scolding lecture to a very deserving troublemaker.

"I'm done. I'm finished. No more. So what? I knocked your daughter up. So what? I married her and supported her with the job John got for me at the power company. I've spent the past twenty-two years paying y'all back, and I'm done. I've wasted my life. I've ruined the relationship I had with my son. For what? Tell me. For what, Lola? Nothing. I've never been so ashamed of myself in all my life."

After all those years of holding bated breath, I could finally exhale—I had been waiting to exhale all along.

Thinking fast, Raleigh acted as though we just happened around the corner of the kitchen when our dad walked out. She held up the ice bags and made a comment about it being so hot with an exaggerated expression on her face while expelling a gust of air, which would've been "acting normal" if it had been a normal gesture for her to be so chummy. I, on the other hand, couldn't keep the shock off of my face. One look at the both us told him that we had heard everything. He nodded his head with an indefinable expression and walked out of the community center with even, measured footsteps. The door opened and closed with such a gentle thud that unsuspecting onlookers would be none the wiser of what had just happened. It was a quiet exit, but it screamed louder than ever. It echoed with finality.

We found ourselves following his even, measured footsteps out the front door. "Where do you think he went?" Raleigh asked, squinting into the distance. Her tone had lost all pretenses of teenage bitchiness. I didn't answer right way as I followed her gaze—both of us searching for our father.

For a brief moment, we were children stricken with the unsettling fact that our parents weren't just a mother and a father. They were actual people with lives that hadn't always revolved around us. For a brief moment, we were united together by the sudden realization that we were siblings with parents who weren't as we had always made them out to be. For a brief moment, things were back to normal between us. And a brief moment was all it took to restore the air of comfortableness we once shared.

"I have no idea," I finally answered.

Raleigh looked down and lifted her arms in a questioning shrug. The bags of ice were leaking, drip-dropping between us. The ice sloshed together with its slowly melting slush as she let her arms fall back to her sides. She longingly gazed once more toward the direction our father had gone, and then she met my stare.

No emotional, sappy music played while we suddenly found ourselves reunited after years of being apart. No discussion was held pertaining to the implications of the past or the outcome of the future. No words were exchanged at all.

Even though she now knew I had been telling the truth all along, she may not have forgiven me for running away. I didn't know what thoughts she was thinking, but she looked at me the way she used to—the way she had before I snuffed out the candle of my existence in her life. In those muddy green eyes of hers, I could tell she knew I wasn't a liar, and that meant more to me than the acceptance of my apologies. I wasn't dead to her after all.

I am an expatriate.

Laughter fluttered on wings of innocence in through the window. Neighborhood children raced around the yard in a mad dash to hide before "it" counted to twenty Mississippi. Everyone loves the childhood game of hide-and-seek, do they not? When the seeker starts counting with eyes tightly closed, that's when the spirit of the game begins. You take off in your search for the perfect hiding spot as the numbers are counted with anticipated echoes, filling the air with exhilaration. What could be more fun than spending hours outside in the dusk and hiding with the thrill of getting caught?

There is something about both the game and the risk involved that lends a sense of unadulterated excitement: the way your heart goes pitter-patter with a sense of levity, the way your breathing catches as you wait to be found, the way your eyes dart around in suspicion.

"Ready or not, here I come!" rings out with a declaration of determination.

Now, it was time to lie in wait. Now, it was time to see if your hiding spot was as good of a choice as you believed it to be. Now, it was time to see who would be the last one to be found.

The game can last for hours—that's one of the drawbacks about the childhood pastime. As the minutes tick on by, the hider gets fed up with being on pins and needles while waiting to be discovered. It's all an internal battle. Does the hider give up knowing they are too hidden for their own good? Should they give it another five minutes in hopes the seeker stumbles across the hiding spot? Do they keep the hope alive that the seeker hasn't given up the search or, dare I say, forgotten about them?

That's life though. You find yourself sitting there with controlled breaths while you wait—just waiting to be discovered or forgotten or rejected or cherished or needed or wanted or loved. You are waiting for life to happen so you can start living. You're waiting for that godsend of "Olly, olly, oxen free!" so you can come out into the open while remaining safe.

Maybe you're waiting in vain. Maybe you aren't the person who should be hiding. Maybe, just maybe, you're the one who ought to be seeking.

It had been far too long since I had last played the game. Minutes had turned into hours, and hours into days; years had begun to pile up. I didn't even know if I was the hider who was too damn stubborn to give up my hiding place or if I was the seeker who was too damn stubborn to cry out "Olly, olly, oxen free" in defeat. What was I supposed—

"Earth to Phoenix!"

Ackerley was standing outside the car and leaning in through the window. He had insisted that he drive, and I felt extremely awkward about the whole ordeal. I was the type of person who drove. I was the driver, not the rider. Allowing someone take the wheel while I relaxed against the passenger seat felt foreign—completely and utterly foreign.

"Are you just going to sit there or are you going to get out of the car?" he asked with that goofy ass grin on his face, and with it brought memories of bittersweet AC mixing with the smell of produce as he bagged groceries.

"Is there a reason why you brought me out here?" I asked, getting out of the car and looking around the all too familiar cul-de-sac on top the hill.

With a shoulder shrug, he squinted as he took in the departing rays of the setting sun. "According to my heavily detailed research, movies strictly imply that the most pivotal scenes take place with awe-inspiring scenery while sitting on a car hood."

Surreal. That was exactly how it felt to be hanging out with him. No, I wasn't talking about the same use of "surreal" that celebrities claimed when describing their experience winning an award or working on the movie or what the hell ever. I was talking about the real meaning of the word. It felt bizarre because we both knew what happened last time we were at the cul-de-sac but didn't mention it. Like it happened to people we didn't know anymore—two complete strangers.

It would be completely cliché for us to sprawl out on top of his car hood. Just cue some clichéd music while two friends shared a clichéd conversation about what was in store for the rest of their clichéd lives. Was there such a thing as too many clichés in Hollywood? Either way, they were overrated, so I chose to stand.

"Too bad the snow cone place wasn't open," he mentioned, leaning up against his car.

"I don't really care much for them." That was me for you—completely nonchalant.

"Aw, why not?" he asked. "It's like you're holding a nice, little smile in a cup. A secret smile only for you and the summer to enjoy."

"You live in your own idealistic world, don't you?"

"Be jealous."

The conversation felt forced between the two of us. Who were we kidding? The both of us knew the things that weren't being said and were too afraid to mention their implications. He knew my story, and I knew his. Here we were both well-versed with one another and unsure of the best way to proceed.

"What are you thinking about?" he asked without looking sideways.

"What do you mean?" I swallowed hard. Did he already know what I was thinking and was only asking to bring it into the light? Was he acknowledging the elephant that had accompanied us for the evening, who was sitting in the backseat listening to our chalked up conversation with an ear pressed against the window like the nosy bastard that it was?

"You just look like you've got a lot on your mind. That's all."

So many thoughts were buzzing around inside my head that I couldn't even enjoy the picturesque river flowing under the bridge and out onto the horizon with its surface reflecting the oranges and pinks of the setting sun. There were thoughts about anything and everything: him, the present, my aunt Derenda, the future, my father, the past.

"It's nothing much," I lied. "You know...just stuff."

"Stuff sucks. I hate stuff. I wished stuff never would've been invited." He cocked his head and grinned that ever-present grin that promised everything would be okay. "Stuff needs to leave us the hell alone."

He caught me off guard, and I laughed because...well, because it was quite hilarious with the expression on his face and the way he said it. It was one of those "you just had to be there" moments. A previously unknown weight lessened in the pit of my stomach as he laughed right along with me.

Pushing off the car, he stood tall and moved his arms in a half-jerk as if he didn't know what to do with them. "Raleigh was telling me about your family reunion the other day when she came into the store for some ice." He settled on burying his hands in his pockets. "How'd it go?"

Now, why would Raleigh drive all the way across town to get ice from that specific store when there was a gas station right down the road from the community center? Hmm, I wondered (sarcasm in case you haven't picked up on my sense of humor by now). Too bad her love interest wasn't accepting what she offered (see previous parenthetical statement).

"Eh." I shrugged my shoulders with apathy. "It went."

"I know exactly what you mean."

That was another thing I liked about him. I didn't expect him to understand, but he did. He understood more things than I ever could've expected out of anyone. Maybe I hadn't missed the pitch in the dilapidated baseball game that was my life. Maybe he wasn't strike three. Maybe he was a real friend first and foremost.

Standing there started to feel awkward. Like we were both waiting for something—anything—to happen. We were dancing an intense tango around the word we both didn't want to recognize, the word we both feared, the word that leads to insurmountable confusion, the word pronounced as "ho-mo-sex-u-al-i-ty." So what would it mean if I was gay? Even though it would mean I was attracted to the same sex, at least I would be attracted to *someone*. I wouldn't be alone in this world.

I didn't want to contemplate that implication yet. I was happy enough to have found a friend that hadn't ran screaming for the hills after I divulged my biggest hang-up to date. At least Ackerley wanted to be my friend. At least he empathized with me. At least he cared, and that was a first.

"Why aren't you hanging out with Rhi tonight?" I asked in an attempt to soothe over the conversational discomfort. "Aren't you two each other's shadow or something?"

"Ha," he said half-heartedly, looking the other way. "She's dealing with a few things regarding her family."

"What do you mean?"

"It's not really my story to tell, but…." He unburied his hands and nervously fidgeted them as an expression crossed over his face, signaling his internal debate. "Well, it involves her little brother."

"Stephen." It wasn't a question. It was a memory surfacing, a memory of a little boy smiling with a toothless smile directly into the camera as he held up an outstretched hand.

"You know about her little brother's death?" His tone clearly indicated he was taken aback by my knowledge of such private information.

"Death?" The word murmured between my lips. "I, uh, I saw a photo of him. I didn't know he had passed away."

"Shit." He took a deep breath as though he were about to jump off the plank. "Stephen has been gone three years."

The date of the photo jumped in the front of my memory. It had to have been taken right before his death. I could still see it clearly. I could still see the soft wisps of dark hair caught in mid-step as they were dancing with an invisible gust of wind. I could still see that toothless smile and chubby, little cheeks. I could still see that spark of life…that spark of life which had an expiration date for shortly after the photograph had been taken by the person for whom Stephen was reaching an outstretched hand toward. The realization hit me in the stomach like a sack of bricks.

"What happened to him?" I found myself asking in a dry-mouthed whisper

"There was a car wreck...." His words were spoken with clinical intentions, but emotion seeped around their sterile edges and choked him as it permeated the stillness of the subject. "It wasn't raining or nighttime or anything like that. It was during the middle of a sunny day. Their mother was on her way to pick Rhi from her old school. A drunk driver ran a stop sign. He hit them in the passenger side, and the force pushed her into oncoming traffic or something."

On a normal day in a normal town, the least suspecting thing happened to Rhi's family that caused their life to be turned upside-down. No wonder Rhi was ornery about the photo album. That explained her morbid melancholia, her claim of childhood dying and everything being taken away. "That's why they moved, wasn't it?"

"Yeah." He shifted his weight onto his other leg, and leaned against the car. "Mrs. Moreno still blames herself for the accident and wishes it had been her in his place."

No wonder her mother wasn't social. She was busy entertaining her own demons. If the death of her son was her cross to bear, then Sandra Moreno was a good woman. I couldn't fathom the feeling of having someone that had been a part of me die...the death of the life you helped to create. I knew it was masochistic for Mrs. Moreno to beat herself up over something she couldn't control, but it was romantic in a way. At least she cared enough—loved her son enough—to want to switch places so he would've lived. That was what a mother's love should be, right? Wasn't a mother's love supposed to know no bounds?

Tears. I could feel traitorous tears of treachery welling up. God, why was I such a titty baby? What was with all the waterworks all of a sudden? I never showed emotion. Showing emotion wasn't something I did. I strived to be emotionless. My eyes widened as if to stop the slip-up of tears from leaking and splashing down my face. Inhale. Exhale. Inhale. Exhale.

During my mental episode where I had lost my ability to remain calm, cool, and collected, Ackerley moved closer without my knowing. My tears and emotions were almost bottled up when I felt the pinpricks of his closeness. "Uh, I got something in my eye. I think a bug flew in it or something," I blurted.

"Damn those bugs," he commented with a wispy laugh as he turned to face me. He knew that I knew that he knew I was on the verge of crying, but he played right along in my game of denial; my family didn't have game night, but they had taught me how to be a pro in *that* game. That alone made me more appreciative of him. I didn't do well with conveying my emotions in the vernacular of spoken word. That was how things were done in the United State of Me.

He leaned in, and a flashback sparked like a firework shooting across the sky. My breathing caught as I turned into a statue of stone. It was infuriating that I was so impassive and weak. Hell, I couldn't even stand up for myself and stop him if he planned to k-kiss me. It was even more infuriating that I didn't know if I wanted him to or not. Most of all, it was infuriating that I didn't know—just didn't know anything anymore.

Instead of doing as I had thought, he hugged me. It was a cross between that awkward man hug consisting of one arm and a full hugging embrace, which made it even more awkward. I wanted to laugh, not at him but at what we must look like. Here he was leaned over and showing some sort of affection, and I was rigid and erect (bad choice of words).

It wasn't a very long embrace like I'm sure would've been portrayed if it were a movie scene; however, it was long enough. I could feel his heart beating. Lub-dub, lub-dub, lub-dub. It was pulsing blood through his veins, delivering oxygen to his brain and keeping him alive. He was alive. He was real. He was using his heart.

A light breeze touched my cheek, weaving in-between us with rhythmic sways as he let go and ended the embrace. Our silence was mutually agreed upon as we both pointedly gazed into the distance. The sun had set, giving way to the dark. Star light was star bright, and I saw the first star of the night. However, it was not that twinkling, proverbial star I had always seen. Unfamiliar was what it looked like—different. It wasn't the same as I had always seen in my own little world. It was a new perspective. It was the first star in a night sky blanketing a foreign land.

What happened? Had I been deported from the United State of Me? Had I been booted onto some far-off, distant island? Better yet, had I packed my own bags and left for Elba on my own accord? I waited for that little voice in the back of my mind to answer, but it was my heart who replied: lub-dub, lub-dub, lub-dub.

Napoleonic Heart:

Nothing could have been changed,
But still I wished I would have been warned.
By the hand of naivety, innocence is brutally slayed.
I never imagined I would become this person.
Preparation was not taken for the knowledge I fell privy.
Promises were nothing but a traitorous tongue's cheap words.
Must you always push me to my utmost limits?
In-between all the hollow words we will never share,
Silence screams its loudest, most deafening.
You have become my greatest strength,
But also my greatest weakness—my greatest failure.

Freedom exuded me, but you spoke your part.
Since when were we on terms to speak?
Selective hearing no longer bodes well.
Over think, over analyze my actions—you make me.
If it were possible, my hate would consume you.
Why is your punishment of the cruelest kind?
Ignorance was thy bliss.
Why pry open thine eyes?
Ill-conceived thoughts brought upon an ill demise.
You are a fickle fiend—I swear it!
Banishment! Exile! Be gone!
Pack your bags, and do forget to write.
No, I did not mean that. Forgive me
Do not go. Please, do not ever go.
I could not live without you—I would not want to.
With only this pleading thought, from you I will then depart:
Promise me, my dearest Heart,
You will be stronger than strong;
You will be all I need to believe in.

I am saved.

"C'mon on inside…it's okay."

The hand. The hand jerked me down. The hand—the hand tightened its grip. The eyes. The eyes told me everything was fine. The eyes—the eyes were lying.

I was falling. Forever falling. Forever waiting for the concrete of the sidewalk to scrape my knees. The world circled around me. Trees blurred into green as the horizon tilted. The sky, the houses, the church steeple: everything spiraled out of control. Faster and faster.

Trees. Sky. Houses. Church. Trees. Sky. Houses. Church.

Treesskyhouseschurch.

Treesskyhouseschurch.

Treesskyhouseschurchtreesskyhouseschurch.

Faster and faster and faster they spun out of control. Momma, I promise I didn't run. I was a good boy like you told me to be. Treesskyhouseschurch. Daddy, I swear I was a good boy. I even minded my manners. Treesskyhouseschurch. I didn't do anything wrong. Please.

A melodic symphony struck up a complex score. Treesskyhouseschurch. The tune of my every afternoon. Treesskyhouseschurch. My heart pounded in my chest. Treesskyhouseschurch. It was too late. I was too late. The cartoon started without me.

Trees.

Sky.

Houses.

Church.

Eyes.

Hand.

Fear.

The world was lopsided, tilting above me. The words. The words rang out. The words were deafening. The words took my breath. The words choked me. The words hurt me. The words sliced through me. The words.

"I won't hurt you. I promise."

Pain ricocheted through my body, racing alongside the speeding heartbeat. My knees cracked against the concrete. It hurt. It really hurt. I wanted my momma. I wanted her to make everything better.

Red—warm, wet, sticky red. Blood trickled down my legs. It was on my hands. It was everywhere. Make it stop. Make the bleeding stop.

"Phoenix, it's okay. I'm here now."

The voice. The voice was new. The voice was familiar. The voice was male. The voice was coming from behind me. The voice came with hands. The voice's hands picked me up.

"I've got you. I promise you're going to be okay."

—

I awoke with a start, gasping for air in the darkened bedroom. My dream had changed, stopping before *it* could happen. Ghost feelings lingered where the hands had picked me up. Whose hands were they? Who else was there? The voice was already a faint memory, becoming lost to world of dreams and slumber. I knew that voice though—I was sure of it. Who...who saved me?

I am the family man.

"May I speak to Phoenix Harper?"

The clipped voice on the other end of the phone called forth a memory, and it clicked with the sharp clacks of high heels from the recesses of my mind. The act of trying too hard: short stature reconciled with pumps, a dress stretched tautly around the midsection, modern hair dyed an unnatural color. A point resounded: why try to be something you aren't when the whole world could tell who you were underneath the disguise?

"This is him."

"Ms. Wetherell here."

"Hello, ma'am. How are yo—"

"I've called in regard to the employment position," she cut me off, getting straight to the point. "Are you still interested?"

I had forgotten about the god-awful firing squad casting their formalities aside and embracing the triggers, firing rounds into my ego as it slid to the floor and bled out a puddle of esteem. It still pissed me off that Victims No. 2, 3, 4, and 5 had donned a bulletproof ego and orchestrated extravagant answers to the interview questions which had put mine to shame. That was such a notorious prank Monday had played.

What the hell? Why was I hesitating on answering her question? "Yes. Yes, I'm still interested in the position."

"I want you to come in for a second interview Friday morning at 10:00."

Friday? Hmm…what *was* I doing Friday? Oh, wait. I had no life. Of course my schedule was wide open. "I'll be there."

"Great. Friday it is."

The line clicked. She had hung up. At least it was on a *Friday* this time. Returning the phone to the living room, I couldn't help but to think that things were starting to look up. All hope for finding a job had been lost over the course of the summer. Okay, kiddos…what did you have when the demand for a product, let's say "optimism" for instance, greatly exceeded the supply of thus said product? A shortage. Right when I least suspected, I received some form of news. It wasn't necessarily good news, but it sure did have potential.

"Was that mom?" Raleigh asked from her spot on the couch. Her cellphone was glued to her hand as her fingers flew across the keypad.

"Nope," I answered, sitting down in the armchair.

Jackson was slurping down a bowl of cereal, and Memphis was sprawled out in the middle of the floor. Mr. Faustus was by her side while she stared at the television in a hypnotic daze as one of those morning cartoon shows for kids aired. The high-pitched voice of the main character plus the incessant cereal slurpage was enough to make my eye twitch. God, I hoped the show went off soon. Maybe I could trick her into changing the channel.

"I have better things to do than sit here and babysit all day," Raleigh complained, her fingers never skipping a beat in the rhythmic click-click-click of the text message.

"Like what? Shopping?" Jackson scoffed.

"It's none of your business, nerd." She gave him the evil eye, but I knew she wasn't serious (well...I think she wasn't anyway). Resuming her stare down with the cellphone screen, she asked, "When did mom say she'd be back?"

"She said a few hours," I lied. I couldn't help but to lie.

That usual routine of a sharp intake of break and waking up with a start was growing old, but none the less it was unfaltering and consistent. I had sought to lessen the disorientating fog by way of my usual method (a.k.a. going for a run), and that was when I heard the tail end of the argument from the staircase.

I'd heard the level sternness in my dad's voice, and it didn't allude to any confrontational tones. My mom's voice, however, was raised to the point I could make out a few distinct words in-between her naggy naggisms: Momma + said, reunion, your + fault, pathetic. There had been an audible huff, and then the back door had opened and slammed shut.

I had been sure that it was my dad that stormed out on his way to work, but he was sitting at the kitchen table when I walked around the corner. He knew I heard everything, and there was no use in trying to play it off. We had both known better. We had both nodded our heads in the guy code of mutual acknowledgement.

"She took her mother to a doctor's appointment," he'd explained without me having to ask. "I should really get going to work. I'm late as it is." He'd stood from the table rather stiffly as if the weight of the world was bearing down upon him. Like he was preparing to walk death row. "Remind Raleigh she agreed to babysit while she's gone."

After we'd said our goodbyes, I had drifted into the living room. The disorientating fog had been lifted by a harsh blow from reality, and I no longer found myself wanting to run. I just wanted to sit, and that was exactly what I'd done all morning with the exception of the phone call.

Even with Jackson eating cereal like a Neanderthal and Memphis singing along with the high-pitched cartoon character and the chimes of a new message arrival every minute, I didn't mind being with my siblings. It wasn't anything special or momentous or anything like that. We were just sitting around the house doing nothing, but we were doing nothing together like old times.

Five minutes into a third episode of the cartoon, which I had condemned to the fiery pits of Hell because the theme song went and got itself stuck in my head, Mr. Faustus's ears perked up as an engine sounded in the driveway. Mommy dearest was home. I stood and crossed to the window to see whether or not my bitch of a grandmother was with her. If so, I'd definitely be making one hell of a quick exit.

Correction: our mother wasn't home. Sitting in the driveway was my dad's truck, and behind it was a boat. At the risk of sounding like a broken record, it was surreal because…because it was so unexpected. Shouldn't he be at work? Seeing my dad with a sly yet genuine smile on his face and a hitch in his step as he bounded up onto the front porch was a sure sign of change, both in the now and yet to come.

"Guess who took the day off from work?" he called, opening up the front door.

I wanted to blurt "What's going on?" but stopped myself as I turned away from the window and looked over at him. I knew what was going on. I had known it the instant he had snapped at the family reunion.

He held up a key with an oval-shaped, foam keychain dangling from it. "I thought it'd be nice to have a boat," he said indifferently as if he just commented on the weather.

Of course, my siblings jumped up and put in their two-cents of excitement over the newest addition to our family's way of life, but I held back. I was awe-struck by my dad's actions. It was the first time I could remember that he'd done something he wanted to do, not what my mother insisted he do. My dad's actions spoke louder than words, and his newly acquired boat was equivalent to: **Fuck you!**

"I was thinking about taking it out for a little drive," he mentioned. His tone held no traces of excitement, and his poker face retained its cool. It was his eyes that gave away his exhilaration. They were lit up with that spark of life. He looked like a different man, a new man. The ties that bind had been laced and knotted, holding my dad hostage; however, they were wearing thin. He was growing restless under those restraints—the same restraints that bounded a little boy in a house where no one lived, where no one called home. If he could free himself, then maybe I could too.

"What do y'all say?" he asked, jingling the key with enticement.

And just like that, all of us were going boating, even Mr. Faustus due to Memphis's complaints that he was an important part of the family too. Did our dad mention anything about our mother? Nope. Did I feel the need to bring her into the conversation? Negative. Why ruin his fun with the thought of her?

Because of the arbitrary events of the day, I couldn't wrap my mind around what was going on. Everything was happening before I could process thoughts on the matter. It was as though we were in a movie and a key point in the plot of the storyline had taken place, and then the scenes unfolded at a fast pace to further the story along in a montage with riveting background music to strike a chord in the audience's heart. One minute we were standing in the living room, and the next we were piled up in his truck and on our way to the docks. Then, we were loading onto the boat before I knew it.

If I was remembering correctly, I had never been on a boat before in my life. Sudden unease washed over me as the water pitched back and forth. The only way I could describe the sensation would be to compare it to riding a Ferris wheel with the tilting and unsteadiness that nestles in the pit of your stomach from the fear of falling off. Um, yeah...I tightened the straps on my lifejacket, and then I double-checked Memphis's for good measure. You could never be too careful with that crazed baboon.

The engine started as I was checking her straps, and Mr. Faustus let out a fretful whine as he tried to climb into her arms. "I've got you," she cooed, holding him close and kissing him atop his head. "I promise you'll be okay."

I've got you. I promise you'll be okay.

The words swirled in my head and the wind slapped me in the face as we started off upstream, following the river out of town. Flashes of the dream clouded my vision in-between heartbeats. The voice. I knew that voice. Who was it? I couldn't think. The longer I thought about it, the less and less memorable the dream became. The voice was a fading echo in my memory.

With the mix of wind and motor droning in my ears, my mind was a blank slate. Like when you turned it to a television channel with no signal and the screen filled with black and white static while the speakers hissed. It was official. I actually liked boating. It allowed me to clear my head of all those pesky second thoughts derived from overthinking.

Upstream we went, bobbing along in wake of other boaters' waves. The scenery along the riverbank progressed from the overly fake postcard-picturesque to the unruliness that was nature at its finest. The landscape raced along beside the boat as the bridge leading out of town slowly came into view, growing larger and swimming into focus with each passing second.

It was funny no matter how many times you have seen something, all it took to change your perception was a new perspective. Everything you had always held to be true was warped and distorted as you filed new associations and memories and outlooks into that big filing cabinet in your mind. Seeing the bridge from below, I noticed the supports jutting into the water and the beams along the underside. I could see everything that was holding it up. There was always more to the picture than you thought. It was more than just a bridge leading out of town. It was so much more than something you had to cross over to get to the other side.

The first time I had my perspective altered, Ackerley had pointed out the headlights in the night as their light bathed the bridge. Like one door closing leading to another one opening. We had been on the hilltop cul-de-sac. I twisted in my seat to see if I could find his spot — the spot where he went, where we went. I couldn't see it from the river, but I knew it was still there. Out of sight didn't mean it was out of mind. No matter what people tell you, it never does.

It was on top that hill where my first real friend once told me that life was like a song you fell in love with. At first, you loved it so much that you played it over and over again, but then the radio started playing it repetitively. The song was everywhere, breathing down your neck. You began to hate it and even went out of your way to avoid it until eventually its memories have faded....

That same friend of mine went on to say there came a day when you heard that song after all the bad memories were gone. It was then. It was right then and there that you realized why you fell in love with it to start with.

Through deep thought's furrow-browed expression, I observed my family. There was Mr. Faustus, the one who was a "thrown away" puppy given a second chance. There was Memphis, the one who truly saw right through me and a hoot if I'd ever known one. There was Jackson, the one who used video games as a vice for taking off the pressures off adolescent life. There was Raleigh, the one who had been hurt the most by my reckless abandonment. Then, there was my father.

The revelation for why my dad had ignored my molestation still did not make it okay even though his hands were tied. I didn't know if I could ever forgive him, but a part of me wanted to. That should count for something, right? It was completely fucked up parenting, but…but it just wasn't my life that had been squashed and squandered away. The ties that bind had been laced and knotted, holding him hostage; however, they were wearing thin. If he could find the strength from within to free himself after all these years, then maybe I could too.

I am enlightened.

Today was Thursday, and my usual routine had been lacking. Over the course of the summer, I had shied away from the sheer simplicity of the simple-minded thrill. Raleigh had been more than eager to take over the reins so she could see her favorite bag boy. Little did she know that she was putting the cart before the horse on that one.

Due to Terri the Variant and her ways of variance, the reins had been handed back to me while Raleigh went to practice for cheerleading tryouts, which were scheduled for when Sulfur Springs High School opened its doors for the upcoming school year (seriously though…if you had to practice yelling and spelling out simple words, then whether or not you made the cheerleading squad wasn't your biggest concern). And so, I parked in my usual parking spot in front of the grocery store.

301

Miles dwindled into nothing more than mere footsteps as my feet followed the path across the asphalt. As always, hazy heat distorted the air with its vertigo-inducing wave. The store front looked as though it was melting, but there were no "if onlys" this time around.

Assured rather than timid footsteps led through the illusion and across the barrier of the motion detector. A cool, conditioned gust swept hair out of my face as the doors effortlessly glided open. I crossed over that threshold without hesitation despite the previously conceived notion that it was more terrifying than any circle of any Hell ever imagined.

I had arrived at my usual time. As I reached for a buggy, I noted the usual team of Rhi and Ackerley as they worked their usual shift of cashiering and bagging while the old church hens took their usual sweet time in the produce section. Some things hadn't changed despite my absence. Just because I didn't show up to play my part in the usual Thursday did not mean the usual ceased to exist.

Through the sea of clucking hens, I waded with a buggy and the more-so-wadded-than-folded shopping list. Like always, there stood Old Bitch No. 1 with her sagging jawline and beady, little eyes. "Aren't you Charlotte's boy?" she asked as I drew near.

The game of deception had restarted. Like we had both went back to the beginning. There was no passing GO or collecting $200—just starting over. Would it still be just as easy to deceive her as it had been when I first moved home? She pursed her mouth together while she looked me over from head to toe as she waited for my answer.

Martha Gibson was the retired principal of Sulfur Springs Elementary, and her actions were reason enough for the crude alias used in her reference. She was a hypocrite who practiced the opposite of what she preached, who itched to sink her dentures into the next big piece of juicy gossip. Maybe a little honesty would do the old broad some good. Maybe it was time to push pretenses aside. Maybe the joke had reached its end.

"I'm Troy's son," I answered as I pushed past her, carrying on about *my* business.

The shopping list was short and didn't request any produce; in fact, only a few things were listed. The thought of who had actually made the shopping list never really crossed my mind. I mean, of course I knew my mom made the list out, but I didn't realize it. It was as though she was ordering me with her precise, detail instructions written in hasty cursive. Like she was controlling my life from afar. I didn't need her stupid list to guide me step by fucking step, so I crammed it into my pocket and set off toward the meat section.

Lisa Jacobs was a butcher, and I often called her "Lisa the Meat Specialist." She sold sliced and diced prime cuts of beef, but it wasn't her only job. Lisa was a provocateur who had a fetish for dildos, which she kept a small inventory on hand in the trunk of her car. As far as I knew, she had flown under the radar of Sulfur Springs' moral police of church martyrs. Those who only knew of her side job were the ones in the market for a good, self-pleasuring time, and through word of mouth she got her business. While I wasn't a loyal customer of the junk in Lisa's trunk, I knew because I paid attention to the world around me. It was during first week that I had arrived home when I discovered Lisa's secret.

Because I had been away from home for the better part of four years, I had found it difficult to assimilate back into a life of living with my family. After dinner each night that week, I would drive around town listening to music and trying to forget which reality I actually lived in. There had always been this maroon car with the bumper sticker "BUTCHERS DO IT BETTER" parked in various spots around town where traffic wasn't so out of place. On the fourth night, I slowed as I drove past, and I witnessed the hurried exchange of cash and adult novelties out of an opened car trunk beneath the glow of a streetlight.

"The usual?" Lisa asked with that same smile of someone reveling in a double life as I slowed the buggy in reverie.

She remembered me. Why had I not seen it before? She had actually remembered my "usual" after all this time. She paid attention to the world around her. Here she was, a meat specialist of sorts, who was caught up in her double life, and yet she still remembered me. Was there more to Lisa Jacobs than just selling dildos and slicing up cuts of meat? Was she more than just a woman who worked a day job and spiced up her life with what I had assumed was a thrill from selling something as formidable as penis replicas?

Maybe she didn't need to work two jobs in order to survive. Maybe she was sick of her normal, day-to-day existence. Maybe she wanted an alternate life free from monotony. We were more alike than I thought. After all, she was a person too. Like me.

"No, thank-you," I declined with a smile, forgoing the all-knowing edge I had usually used. She had surprised me with her memory retention.

"Alrighty," she beamed as though she had no idea I had been judging her and using her business dealings for my own comedic relief. "Have you a good day."

"You, too."

My display of social niceties had opened the door to future socializing, but I was okay with it. Just because I thought I knew everything didn't mean that I did. Didn't Lisa just prove that? I didn't know. Working my way through the now mentally complied list, I wandered up and down the aisles.

There were the usual people doing their usual routine of getting their usual groceries. There was the woman with the big ass bun on her head meandering about in aisle two, but she was just a woman who happened to be Holiness. There was the bored stock boy shelving pinto beans on aisle four, but he was just a boy working his summer job. There was the indecisive old man analyzing several brands of laundry detergent in aisle nine, but he was just an elderly man who couldn't make up his mind. These people and I shared something. Not only was it my usual Thursday routine but also theirs.

So what if I had become one of them? So what if I had slipped in a puddle of the usual? So what if I had fallen out of the usual tree and hit every damn branch on the way down? So what if I had laid down with the dogs and caught those proverbial fleas of usualness? At least I wasn't alone in my usual. At least we were a part of something for a brief moment in time every Thursday.

I pushed the scarcely full buggy into the only cashier lane open. As usual, there was a good amount of people waiting in line. The minutes ticked by as I waited, but it was something I had come to accept. Sometimes, you had to accept the things you couldn't change, right? Wasn't that what being serene meant? Easier said than done...but wasn't serenity worth a shot?

The meticulous drone of the AC filling the air with a bittersweet odor of coolness played in the background as the beep, beep, beep rang out while Rhi dragged canned food across the scanner. Her brunette ponytail bounced animatedly as she nodded her head, and then she parted those overly glossed lips. "It sure has been a hot one," she said to the man in front of me.

What the hell? That was reserved for me. That was what she'd always said to me. That was our small talk that I didn't care about making.

"It's hotter than two mice humpin' in a wool sock," the man commented.

Rhi laughed a fluttering laugh, and then she dropped irrelevant tidbits about herself to keep the conversation going. How had I not noticed it before? Why had I not realized she carried on the same, scripted conversation with everyone that came through her line? How could I've thought that I was the only one she wanted to have small talk with? Her camaraderie against the summer heat had been imagined. The weekly occurrence I relied on to happen like clockwork was pretend—fake.

"Look who it is, Ack," Rhi said, dropping the saccharine pretense as I unload the few things onto the conveyor belt. "Mr. T strikes again."

"Hey," Ackerley said. Just an ever-so-simple "hey" as we made eye contact. He gave his goofy grin that promised all was right in the world when clearly nothing was right at all. That was just him though. He chose to smile despite life's adversities.

"Hey," I ever-so-simply replied.

"Guess what?" Rhi asked, dragging items across the scanner.

"What?"

"I'm finished with my photography portfolio for the scholarship application," she beamed, her ponytail bouncing with excitement.

"Well, congratulations. That's great." I guess she'd decided to follow through and go through all those pictures she had taken over the summer.

"It is," she began and then lowered her voice, "the shit. I'm evening making it into a slideshow. You better come watch it."

"Okay," I agreed. "What's it about?"

"All I'm gonna say is…you inspired the theme." She wagged her eyebrows in an attempt at mysteriousness. "You'll have to wait till tomorrow night to find out."

Beep. Beep. Beep. She scanned the groceries and slid them down to Ackerley to bag. No, they didn't pile up into a Himalayan mountain range awaiting his expertise. They were bagged into three bags and ready to go before Rhi could give me a total. He titled his head to the side with a playful smirk. Like he was saying, "See, I can do my job."

"It's $32.73," she declared. "Will this be cash or credit?"

Cash or credit? My fingers itched to pull out my wallet. The moment that had kept me coming back to the grocery story wavered in my memory: the reverberating click as the card was swiped, the screen blazing to life with reliable words, the secret code. Did I still want the simple-minded thrill? Did I still want to that brief instant feeling of being another person, of an alternate life washing over me?

"Will this be cash or credit," she repeated herself as though I hadn't heard her the first time.

Make a decision.

Make it.

Now.

"Cash," I answered.

Call me whatever you will because you won't blow my cover. There wasn't a covert affair. There wasn't a clandestine battle for superior intelligence. There wasn't an alternate life. I was just a normal guy buying groceries on a usual Thursday.

"Here you go," she said, handing me my change and the receipt.

I thanked her, and then we said our departing "see you laters." Ackerley hoisted up two of the three bags before I could say a word of opposition, but I hadn't been planning on opposing his help. I just grabbed the other bag and nodded my head for him to follow.

The whir of the gliding doors was the last thing I heard before the bubble of bittersweet AC burst. A rush of heat straight from the devil's armpit smacked me in the face. We crossed the threshold and stepped out into the humid, summer day. There was no need in looking back. I knew everything would still be there next week, but if it wasn't…it would be okay.

I am brutally jarred into sudden realization.

All appears to be right in the world when everything makes sense. The sun even shines brighter as it casts its light onto your life, reflecting a kaleidoscope of colors. But what happens when things don't make sense? How does the sunshine fare as it shines down on the new perspective that you did NOT ask for? What then?

It's like death. It's like missing a funeral. No one tells you that a turn for the worse had been taken. Hell, no one offers condolences—not one "I'm sorry" or even "my deepest sympathy." Nada. Nothing. Zilch. You are on your own to go at it alone as you stand in front of the grave with a sadden heart. Why had death swooped in on swift wings before life had the chance to live? Without your knowledge? Without your permission? No matter how big or how small or how significant, a loss is still a loss just the same. It's okay to grieve, to mourn, to weep. It's unsettling. You kneel before the

311

freshly buried earth and lay a flower the color of cheerful morbidity. No one told you. No one informed you. No one said you'd be too late for that last goodbye, to bid farewell to certainty—to everything you thought you knew.

This death, however, had been bittersweet. I had to say goodbye to all preconceived notions that I had not only once but also twice reconsidered since I had donned that mortarboard cap and choir singer robe. Just when I'd thought I figured the real world out, some unforeseen force twisted that kaleidoscope, changing the colors of my world...and it wasn't always bad. You just had to take it all in stride.

While Monday was the notorious prankster that it was, Friday was the week's saving grace. My job interview went surprisingly well. There weren't any bullet wounds. My ego had been spared. The idea of launching myself into the world had suddenly become very real—the possibility grew more probable. I wasn't saying it was going to work out, but at least it made me realize I still had a chance against the cold, cruel world. Goodbye feelings of hopeless inadequacy. Good riddance.

The ding, ding, ding of the open car door reverberated somberly in the midday heat. I picked myself up and put myself back together, stepping out of the car and dusting the metaphorical dirt off my knees.

It felt as if I had swallowed a brick, and it weighed heavily in the pit of my stomach. Was I regretful of my redeeming interview? No. The opportunity of change just had that effect on me.

The car door shut, silencing the incessant dings. An eerie feeling of something not being quite right settled over me. Something was out of place. Everything was too quiet. Like the world had come to an end in the amount of time it took me to unbuckle the seatbelt and get out of the vehicle, leaving me as the sole survivor of an untimely demise.

Of course my dad's truck was gone because he was at work. So was my mom's car. What else was missing?

Footsteps carried me around to the front yard. The windows were darkened in the house. Nobody was home. I didn't know where my siblings were, but I didn't want to go inside. I didn't want to be inside an empty house I had never called home with only my thoughts for company. Not today.

Talk about being deader than 4 o'clock. A lazy breeze gently blew, bringing with it soft chimes to disrupt the calm. That was when I felt it. Needles pinpricked the back of my neck in that uncanny sixth sense of sorts. My eyes nonchalantly darted next door, and there sat Mrs. Thomas on her porch like always.

I had some spare time before Rhi's slideshow presentation, so I thought I could use a little escape into the past. And so, I walked across the lawn—the grass.

As I drew near, I realized it wasn't the Mrs. Thomas that I knew. She wasn't wearing her usual gardening attire, no. She was dressed up a faded blue dress that looked like she had gotten it from a thrift store. On top her head she wore a small hat (pillbox I think they called them) of the same faded color. Was I dreaming? Did I die in a fiery car crash on my way home and didn't realize my soul was left to wander an earthly purgatory?

"You look nice today, young Mr. Harper," she called as I made my way up her walk. I had almost forgotten I was wearing khakis and a button-up shirt. I even had on those stretchy socks that were always cool to the touch when you put them on but hot and sticky when you took them off.

"Not nearly as nice as you do, Mrs. Thomas," I said with a polite smile as I stepped up onto her porch. Now that I was nearer, it was plain to see that she wasn't the usual Mrs. Thomas at all. She was wearing make-up, and I could see the young girl she was underneath the lines of life's years. On her lap lay a bouquet of the daylilies from her garden bound together with a white string.

"Oh! This old thing?" She laughed that same airy laugh of hers and soothed the fabric of her dress. "It's nothing really."

The heavily intoxicating aroma of the daylilies mixed with the breeze, and I could smell a faint trace of perfume. Mrs. Thomas was dressed up for something. Did she have a date? What was the reason for her sudden change in appearance?

"Please, have a seat," she said, motioning beside her. "I'm just waiting on my daughter to get here."

"I didn't know you had a daughter," I said as I eased down into the rocking chair.

"I don't suppose I ever got around to telling you about Kathleen, did I?" Her face broke into a smile of reminiscence. "She was such a blessing to me and Jimmy, but I'm getting way ahead of myself. Where did we leave off?"

"Jimmy had been there for you during your mother's...." I trailed off, unable to speak death into existence.

"Oh, yes," she said, rocking gently back and forth. "That's what made me see Jimmy in a new light. He wasn't that little boy from the other side of town. I didn't know what was going on between us. There was something about him that made me feel different." She laughed her same little flutter. "I guess you could say he made me feel complete, but I didn't realize it until much later. I still hadn't given up hope about TC, and my heart was torn."

"Did you ever hear from TC?"

"His letters had eventually stopped. Every single day I would wait for the mail, hoping I'd get a letter to prove me wrong. No letter ever came. First, my mother, and then TC. My father was lost in his own depression, and it would've been too much to bear if Jimmy hadn't been there. He was my friend through everything. The days passed by, and Jimmy was still there…he didn't go anywhere or leave me like everyone else."

She fell silent, closing her eyes as if she were trying to collect her thoughts. "A year had passed by before I realized Jimmy was the one for me. It had been at the Fourth of July picnic right here in town. He had asked me to go with him. Oh! I can still remember how nervous he was when he asked me." She shook her head with laughter. "You should've seen him. The way he fumbled his words. I couldn't help but to say yes."

In my mind, I could feel the lightheartedness the holiday brought about. I could see Amelia in a summery dress with Jimmy by her side. I could smell the summer encompassing them on their first date.

"One date led to another," she continued. "It took him a good couple of dates before he tried to kiss me. I was…well, I guess you could say that I was hesitant to let him. TC still panged my heart, but there was

Jimmy—the boy who had become my best friend, the boy who hadn't left me. I kissed him back, and it was unlike anything I had ever felt before. I can still feel that kiss till this very day."

She absentmindedly brought her hand up to her face, resting her fingertips on her cheek. "A year passed before we knew it. No one had heard from TC. It was like he had fallen off the face of the earth, and he was presumed to be dead. My heart ached with grief, not because I had lost my first love but because I lost my childhood friend. Jimmy was right there beside me though, and I couldn't help but to fall in love with him. The heart wants what that heart wants, so they say. There's no use in trying to change its mind."

The summer breeze danced with the wind chimes on the porch, bringing musical echoes into the otherwise nonexistent world. There wasn't a trace of life anywhere. No cars drove by. None of the neighbors were out in their yards. It was as though Mrs. Thomas and I were the only people left alive. The spoken words of memories had created a bubble around us, and it enveloped her in its nostalgia. Her eyes weren't focused on anything in particular. She was seeing into the past.

"Of all the things I can remember the most, it was the look in his eyes as he got down on one knee and proposed to me that summer. Me! Of all the people in the world, he chose me. I know daylilies aren't the most

317

romantic flower, but he had this big bouquet of them he had picked from his mother's garden and this little, velvet box." She looked down at her left hand with fondness. "It was this ring that was in that little box. Even after all these years, I still wear it. I can still see the look on Jimmy's face when I said yes. I can still see the wide-eyed smile of that man who loved me for everything that I was."

She breathed deeply, taking in the scent of the flowers on her lap. "We were married the following summer in his mother's garden when the daylilies were in bloom. Shortly thereafter, I became pregnant with our daughter, and Kathleen Lily Thomas was born the following spring. I was the happiest I had ever been in my life, but then…." She had trailed off, shaking her head in disbelief.

cue flashback music

Mrs. Thomas: Out of the blue, someone rang the doorbell one day. I opened the door to a ghost from the past. There stood TC. After all that time, he was alive. I didn't know what to think. All the air went right out of my lungs. There stood my childhood friend, my first love, but it wasn't the same TC. There was something gone from his eyes — war had killed something inside him. I was relieved that he was alive, but I was angry at him for everything he had put me through, for letting me think he'd died. He'd been out of touch for so long...he didn't know anything. He didn't know I had gotten married. He didn't know I'd had a baby. He didn't know I had kept on living life even after he had left. The look on his face when Jimmy came to my side with Kathleen....

fade back to present day

She twisted her wrist and looked down at her watch. "Kathleen should've been here by now. She knows how important today is. That girl takes right after her father."

"What is today?" I asked casually, feeling slightly intrusive.

"Today...." She smiled and looked over at me. "Today is my wedding anniversary. Every year I go and visit Jimmy's grave on this date."

"I'm sorry for your loss, Mrs. Thomas."

"It's perfectly okay, young Mr. Harper," she said, tilting her head to the side and smiling despite the talk of her husband's death. "A heart attack took Jimmy from me twenty-four long years ago. You know, he always promised he would never leave me, but he did.

And that's okay. I can still feel Jimmy's love in my heart, and I know he's waiting on me. That's what makes it easier. I just know he is waiting on me to come home, and home is wherever he is."

She smiled, but I wanted to cry. I wanted to cry for her loss. I wanted to cry for her strength at keeping hope alive. I wanted to cry tears of happiness because Mrs. Thomas made me finally realize there was such a thing as love in this world—the world I had thought I was completely alone in.

"Do I look okay?" she asked, patting her hair. "I want to look nice for Jimmy. This was always his favorite dress of mine."

"You look beautiful, Mrs. Thomas," I said with a hoarse whisper, trying to keep the waterworks in check. She was a beautiful person inside and out. I wished there were more people like her in this world, in this town, in my life.

"Thank you, dear." She squeezed my arm with compassion. "I always take these flowers with me. An anniversary without them just wouldn't feel right." She reached down and pulled out one lone daylily. An unreadable expression flickered across her face. "Nowadays, I take one for TC's grave, too."

TC's grave? She hadn't said anything about that. It was time for me to head on over to Rhi's, but my nostalgic curiosity got the better of me. "What happened to him?" I asked.

"Bless him," she said with sadness. "That war messed him up. He got so caught up in his own head and forgot about the life he had before he'd left. Something inside him had snapped, and he never was right again. I know he tried his best to act like it hadn't phased him when he came back, but I knew. I knew something had happened to that little boy I grew up with. The TC I knew was gone. He was no longer the neighbor boy. He was a man whose soul had been broken by war. He spent his later years devoting himself to God, but I guess he couldn't escape all of his demons. It happened a few years back. He never married, never had kids, never had a family. He was alone right up to the very end. He was alone with the thoughts of everything he'd done, and he ended up...I just don't understand why he thought he could find relief by taking a bullet to the head."

She twisted the daylily in her fingers as she stared down at it. "He wasn't right. War can do that to you," she explained, shaking her head with disdain. "I don't mourn the loss of the man he had become...I mourn the loss of the young man he was before the war stole him away from me. I mourn the loss of my childhood friend, Terrance Covington."

I am under the impression.

"Ladies and—err, I mean…gentleman and gentleman, are you ready?!"

Ackerley and I were seated in an ancient, oversized couch in Rhi's downstairs basement while she stood in front of us. A smile of anticipated triumph beamed across her face. She had spent all summer working on a photography scholarship before its August deadline and had decided to create a slideshow of the portfolio for our viewing pleasure.

"So, I had more than 500 pictures after all was said and done," she began, "and I had no idea what I could do with them or which ones I could use. Then, I remembered something Phoenix had said earlier this summer."

Huh? I had been listening to her, but the words weren't sinking in. They were going in through one ear and out the other. "Um," I said, trying to shake off the events of earlier. "I-I said something?"

"Remember the night when we were out by the pool?" she asked, to which Ackerley muttered something about more than he cared to.

"Yeah...yeah, sure," I said as I tried to call forth that night from my memory, but I couldn't think. There was a giant brick wall of an obstacle blocking all process of thought. Everything had stopped making sense.

"You said something that night, but I didn't think anything about it." She waved her hand as if she was trying to sweep aside the fact. "They were just four little words, but now I see their significance."

"What did I say?"

"Just watch."

With that being said, she turned out the lights and darkness fell while she fumbled with the buttons on the television. I was having an out-of-body experience. Right at that very moment, my body was sitting on the couch beside Ackerley, but I wasn't there. I was still sitting in the rocking chair on the front porch, still trying to blink away the confusion, still unable to comprehend what she said, still unable to accept the truth of who he was.

A faint trace of a fingertip on the back of my hand brought me back into the here and now. The television flickered to life with a blue glow, and I could see a sly smile pulling at the corners of Ackerley's mouth while he unwaveringly stared straight ahead. Rhi pressed the play button on the DVD player, and then she took a sit on my other side as the slideshow started.

A church organ struck up the tune of a familiar hymn, and then the postcard-picturesque sign reading, "Welcome to Sulfur Springs," filled the screen. Its cheerful paint and richly cultivated flower beds screamed the promise of a small town where nothing could ever, would ever go wrong.

Rhi had taken pictures of our small town, capturing all the pretenses of who people were trying to be. Pictures of fake people carrying on their fake lives with fake intentions crossed the screen. No one would've been able to guess the two-faced nature of the two-faced town of charm. Perfection was on every corner. There were those quaint houses with their lush gardens. There was the high school fit for a television show. There was the park with the greener than green, green grass. There was the church with people dressed in their Sunday best. The church....

My head tinged with a nagging ache. The revelation that had been dropped on me what felt like moments ago had made my brain stop functioning. It refused entry to the fact he was a person—a real person—and all thought on the matter. Ungodly feelings ricocheted through me as the soundtrack's piano keys were struck.

The picture faded to black as the words etched across the screen as if written by an invisible hand:

First impressions never matter.

A picture of Martha Gibson and her fellow church hens, including my grandmother, flashed across the screen. They were dressed to the nines for Sunday service. Their hair was expertly coiffed underneath ridiculous hats. High Horse Lola had her eyes closed, and one hand was clutching a Bible while the other was outstretched in a "Praise Him" gesture. Then, the picture faded.

The same group of women appeared on the screen seated outside the church during the picnic, but they weren't the same as before. Their expertly coiffed hair was dripping with sweat, and their perfectly made-up faces were looking rough. The picture had been candidly taken while an unknown figure with a wisp of blonde hair exited the frame. The church hens were caught with sourpussed expressions on their face as they watched with obvious disdain. High Horse Lola's eyes were daggers. Her head was cocked with her mouth slightly agape. She had been caught gossiping.

Picture by picture, the slideshow presented the truth of the small town of Sulfur Springs. Rhi had spared no one in her pursuit. Ackerley and his mother flashed across the screen. She was standing behind him with her arms wrapped around his shoulders. They were both smiling *that* smile. Then, the picture faded. A family portrait of Emma Arnold, her new husband, and their kids appeared. Ackerley was barely visible in the background—a shadow.

I cautiously cut my eyes over to him. He didn't say anything or look my way or show the least bit of concern. Still, he stared straight ahead without emotion.

The next picture showed Rhi's parents. They were withdrawn from the photo like they weren't present. Both of their eyes were tired, somber, and defeated. Then, the picture faded. Sandra Moreno was holding Stephen in her arms. Alex was standing beside her. Both of them were smiling with that spark of life ablaze in their eyes.

Stephen…Rhi's little brother who had passed away. The little boy whose mother wanted to switch places. The little boy who never got a chance to live. The little boy who was happy with chubby cheeks and an outstretched hand. The little boy who was innocent. The little boy who I used to be.

The deafening roar of stunned silence was louder than ever. Like a thousand voices all talking at once. "That man was nobody," one voice said. "He wasn't a real person," said another. "He never mattered to anyone!" declared a third. "All of you are wrong," softly whispered the dreamlike voice of familiarity that had been lurking on the edges of suspicion.

I wanted to pretend to let it go. I wanted to be able to speak and change the subject altogether. I wanted to push it to the recesses of my mind. However, something inside me wouldn't let go or change the subject or allow it to go ignored.

The whispering voice...I knew that voice. I—wait...why was I looking at myself? The current picture on the slideshow was of the party Raleigh had dragged me to at the beginning of summer vacation. There stood Terri drunk off her ass, and there I was with a look of horror caught in mid-spasm.

Memories surfaced of a camera happy photographer and blaring music. The picture had been taken right after Terri had invaded my personal space. I remembered the harsh, intrusive flash going off in my face. I remembered the elephant sitting on my chest. I remembered the feeling of suffocation, anxiety, fear.

The picture faded to the next.

The weather had been perfect that day. I could remember the soft breeze that kept the smothering heat at bay. We were just two kindred spirits taking on the world together. We were just a big brother and a kid sister who had the playground to themselves.

We were both caught in mid-run. Memphis's hand was clasped in mine, pulling me along. Her face was looking away from the camera, but mine...mine was looking right at it. Like I knew Rhi had been taking the picture right at that very moment. The most astonishing thing was the expression on my face. I was smiling, actually smiling. It was a smile of childhood, of innocence, of happiness.

The picture faded to nothingness.

I waited for either of them to say something. I waited on Ackerley to comment on the oddity of that out-of-place smile. I waited for Rhi to say that it had been someone else, not me. Neither one of them said anything about it. Nothing.

What exactly had I just seen? Had I imagined it? Why were they not alarmed? Was...was that the me they have been seeing this whole time?

I wasn't present in my own body. I wasn't present when I congratulated Rhi on her work. I wasn't present when we walked up the basement stairs. I wasn't present as we said our goodbyes. I wasn't present as my feet carried me down the sidewalk.

"Hold up a minute," Ackerley called, his shoes slapping the pavement.

He was galloping up the sidewalk like a dog returning from fetching a stick. There was that goofy smile that promised all was right in the world. That was the same smile in the last picture of the slideshow. I wasn't present, but he was.

My face felt weird, strange even. I lifted my hand to my mouth, and there it was—the smile from the picture. It was uncharted land, and I was Columbus. Like I had just discovered my world wasn't flat but round.

"What?" I asked when he caught up to me on the corner.

"I, uh," he stammered, gasping for breath. "Damn, you're a fast walker."

"I guess." I had made it halfway around the block. We were on the corner of 3rd Street and Dogwood Lane. "What's up?" I asked with an awkward laugh.

"You seemed like you had a lot on your mind. Are you okay?"

"I'm just sleepy. I've had a long day."

It really was a long day. There had been the job interview, the talk with Mrs. Thomas, the time spent trying to wrap my mind around the fact that he was a person too, and then Rhi's presentation. Damn it. Was everybody able to sense when I was having an internal meltdown?

"So...how's life?" he asked, falling into step beside me as we walked toward my house.

"Eh, the usual." I was in my usual state of confusion. There was the usual unsettling information. There was the usual disturbing feeling of having no future. "You?"

"It's the last weekend of summer vacation," he said with a sigh. "I start my senior year of high school this upcoming Wednesday."

His senior year of high school? I never really thought about our two places in the world, but I guessed everything was different during the summer. The heat had melted away all the technicalities and details that had conformed each of us. If he was a senior in high school when summer was over, then what was I going to be? I didn't know, and I was scared of not knowing.

"I will miss seeing you bag groceries on Thursdays," I said, nudging him with my elbow.

"You'll just have to come a different day then, won't you?" He nudged me back. "You know, there are other places we could see each other...."

Summer changed everything. People went into it without any second thoughts, but they were left with more thoughts than they could deal with after it was over. Who was expecting that I would make friends stuck in the hell hole that was Sulfur Springs? Not me, that's who.

"That is if you wanted to," he added, looking down. He knew summer was reaching its end and that things always changed once it was over.

Just because some things changed when the heat was over with and done didn't mean everything had to.

I would still be here in this small town, but it was going to be okay. I had to believe it would be okay. "Yeah. I'd like that."

"Really?"

"We're friends." *And we're going to stay friends no matter what*, I mentally added.

"Oh...we're just friends then?"

Were we just friends? After everything we knew about each other, how could we be *just* friends? We would never be *just* friends.

"Ackerley—"

"It's okay," he interjected, turning to face me as we reached the walkway in front of my house.

It wasn't okay. I wasn't just a college graduate. He wasn't just a senior in high school. We were more than that. Right then and there, I could see it in his eyes. It wasn't only me who had needed a friend, someone to rely on. It wasn't just me who had felt alone all this time. Maybe we both were in that proverbial baseball game of life, waiting to see if we were going to strike out.

Despite the nagging headache, the confusion, the events of the day—despite everything, I wasn't that guy in the first picture, not anymore. I didn't know what it meant or what would happen, but I found myself wanting.

I wanted to embrace him. I wanted to show him I cared. I wanted to be close to him.

No, I didn't care about the rules of attraction. No, I didn't care about the repercussions of what it might mean. No, I just didn't care about any of it. Why? Because after everything that had happened to me, I was able to be close to someone without that haunting fear to which I had grown accustomed. It was me. It was just me without the events of the past having any effect. That had to mean something, right?

For the first time in my life, I did what I wanted. The atmosphere gave a breathless sigh as we sank into one another. Both of us had been waiting to hear the same thing all these years, but there was no need to discuss it. We knew what our words couldn't say: *everything is going to be okay.*

He was Ackerley, and he was my first, *real* friend. His stride was confident as he made his was down the sidewalk. His smile was full of sincerity as he looked back over his shoulder. I didn't know what our friendship meant, and I was okay with that. The territory was uncharted, but only time could map it out.

The front door closed behind me, and then I was alone with the buzz of lurking thoughts. When you were alone you were never actually alone. There were always those second thoughts, worries, shortcomings, and doubt. Sometimes, you just had to let go of everything plaguing your sense of sanity. It was tough to loosen your grip, but I was trying at least.

I walked from the foyer into the living room. Memphis and Jackson were sprawled out on the floor and playing a board game. Something was off. Raleigh was lying on the couch with the remote in hand as she flipped through the television channels. It was out of character for her to be home on a Friday night, especially the last Friday before school started back.

"What is it with you and not answering your phone?" she asked demandingly.

"I left it upstairs," I said, pointing up for emphasis. "Why?"

She looked over at our siblings, and then she motioned for me to follow her up the stairs. Once we were out of earshot, she said, "Some major shit went down this evening."

"Like what?"

"I overheard mom and dad arguing when I got home from practicing with Terri. Mom was making a big deal out of everything because of the news about grandma."

"Wait. What news?"

"From what I could hear, the doctor found a lump and they think it's cancer"

"Oh."

"Then, mom said that dad didn't care about it. They were talking about the family reunion, and I...I heard your name a few times. I don't know. They...they were talking about it...you know, the thing that happened to you. Dad was scary. He wasn't yelling or anything. He said he couldn't live this way any longer. It...it was the calm in his voice that made everything sound final."

It was more food for thought, and I was losing my appetite. My dad had finally done it. He had broken free from those restraints. Everything was happening. Too much was happening. Would I ever be free of the past? Would Terrance Covington always impact life as I knew it?

"Mom is over at grandma's, and dad has been out in the garage ever since. I tried calling you. I...I just didn't know what to do, Phoenix. Jackson and Memphis still don't know. I told them I was babysitting and let them order a pizza."

"You did the right thing, Ral," I said. I wanted to comfort her and tell her everything would be okay, but I knew nothing would be *okay*. "It's a lot to process. Just keep doing what you're doing, and I'll be down in a minute."

She nodded her head a few times, and then she retreated down the stairs. My head was pounding with each heartbeat. I was having an information overload. I wanted to go check on my dad, but that would have to wait. Too much was happening. I just wanted to lie down and rest my eyes for a minute.

Maybe just five minutes and everything would be manageable. I shrugged my shoes off and collapsed onto the bed. What else was going to happen before the day was over with? I tried to get comfortable, but something was digging into my chest. It was my cellphone.

There were five missed calls, four of which were from Raleigh. The fifth was an unknown number, and I had a new voicemail.

Message (1) from caller: UNKNOWN

Phoenix Harper, this is Ms. Wetherell. I was calling to inform you that the job position you interviewed for this morning has been filled by another candidate; however, we have had an unexpected opening come up. I know it is a last minute's notice, but I'd like to extend the offer to you. Come in Monday morning for teacher workday, and we'll get you set up as the senior English teacher at Sulfur Springs High School. See you then, Mr. Harper.

END OF ALL NEW MESSAGES

I had finally had too much to process. I didn't want to think about what it all meant. I didn't want deal with anything. I just wanted to close my eyes. I just wanted to sleep. I just wanted to disappear.

I am engulfed in flames.

Trees. Sky. Houses. Church. Eyes. Hand. Fear.

The world was lopsided, tilting above me. The words. The words rang out. The words were deafening. The words took my breath. The words choked me. The words hurt me. The words sliced through me. The words.

"I won't hurt you. I promise," Terrance Covington said.

Pain ricocheted through my body, racing alongside the speeding heartbeat. My knees cracked against the concrete. It hurt. It really hurt. I wanted my momma. I wanted her to make everything better.

Red—warm, wet, sticky red. Blood trickled down my legs. It was on my hands. It was everywhere. Make it stop. Make the bleeding stop.

Then, there was the voice. The voice was new. The voice was familiar. The voice was male. The voice was coming from behind me. The voice came with hands. The voice's hands picked me up.

"I've got you. I promise you're going to be okay."

The voice had a face. The voice had a smile. The voice I knew.

The dream flickered. I changed places.

It was my voice. It was my hands. It was me.

"I'm not going to let anything bad happen to you," I said to my ten-year-old-self.

I held him close and whispered into his ear those three little words that we both had been longing to hear.

"I love you."

—

I hadn't awoken with a start. My eyes had simply opened with ease. I hadn't gasped for breath. My breaths had been slow and steady. I hadn't been lost in disorientation. My mind had reacted with purpose—I had known what I needed to do.

The night air was peacefully saturated with coolness. A full moon casted light upon a world still fast asleep, but I was very much awake. In the isolated quietness, I sat cross-legged on the hard earth dried out by summer's heat. All was dead in Sulfur Springs Cemetery, but I was very much alive.

My eyes stared fixedly at the gravestone in front of me. In my palm, I held the stem of the single, lone flower that I'd found lying underneath the engraved name. I didn't know why I had come, only that I had to. Like some unknown force had called out to me, beckoning for me to bid farewell.

After all this time, I was finally confronting him.

He stole my childhood. He murdered my innocence. He raped my youth.

He was the reason why my life turned out the way it had. He was the reason why I wasted my life trying to forget. He was the cause of my repression. He was to blame for everything—for who I was.

Years of hatred coursed through my veins. Anger washed over me. I wanted to destroy his grave. I wanted to bash down the granite headstone. I wanted to stand up and piss on the dry grass above his rotting corpse. I wanted to pour my frustration out, but I couldn't. I wouldn't let myself fall victim to him again.

Out of all the malicious and spiteful things I had always dreamt of saying, I couldn't bring myself to say any of them. It felt pointless to curse him to the fiery pits of Hell where I hoped he suffered the worst pain imaginable. What would it leave me with besides a temporary high of satisfaction? Nothing. It wouldn't take away the memories. They would still be there, pinning grievances to my heart and soul.

"Everything would've turned out differently if you hadn't gone off to war."

The words escaped from out of my mouth in a barely audible whisper of trepidation. I had said the only thing that had come to mind. I had said the only thing that would've made everything go away.

The strong scent of the daylily ensnarled my senses. It wouldn't have been my life that he robbed, no. Would Amelia still have had the life she'd had if he hadn't gone to war? Would she still have known true love? Would she still have had a daughter? Would she still have had all her years filled with happiness?

"You really hurt her, but it worked out for the best though."

I sat up straighter, peering over the top of the tombstone. Across the cemetery, I could see the bouquet of daylilies resting on a matching plot with one side empty. Like the rocking chairs. There was a place saved by his side for when her time on this earth had reached its end, for when she went home, for when she was reunited with her husband.

"Jimmy gave her the life she deserved—a life filled with love and happiness."

My words fell silent in the predawn hours. The night vibrated with anticipation. Like the buildup of loathsome bitterness had swelled and spewed and burst forth, leaking into the summer night. I could feel it rippling against me as I pulled my knees into my chest and stared straight into the smoothly carved letters of his name.

"She told me all about her childhood friend, all about your life—everything. I never wanted to know you. I never wanted to admit you were a person. I never wanted to know you were a little boy once. Like me. Like I was."

I let out a morose laugh, and it slithered silently into the night.

"In a way, I'm glad she did though. I'm glad I know you now. In my head, you were a cartoon villain, somebody who wasn't real. I had forced myself to make you cease to exist. I thought it was the only way I would get rid of you, but I was wrong."

An indefinable feeling was building inside me.

"You were still there. You were still lurking everywhere I went. You were the shade tree with branches I couldn't reach, couldn't climb to see the light. You were the sky above me, always out of reach but always there. You were house where no one lived, where that little boy was trapped. You were the church of grief, of lost religion."

A hush fell all around me as I focused on the engraved letters of his name. I held my hand in a gun gesture and brought it to the side of my head. "Bang," I shot, breaking the silence that had grown between us.

"So you took the easy way out. What? Couldn't live with the guilt over the things you'd done? I don't know what happened to you, what warped your mind, what messed your life up. Even if I did, it wouldn't make it right. It wouldn't justify your actions. It wouldn't make things better."

The feeling was raging and roaring in the pit of my stomach.

"Did you really think a bullet to the head would erase everything you had done? You did what you did. There's no way you can take it back. There's nothing in the world that could make up for your actions. You know what you could've done though? Pulled the trigger a whole lot sooner and spared me the sorrow."

My words were level and even. Anger wasn't laced around them, tying them together in a hateful rant. I had spoken matter-of-factly. I knew I'd probably cry later when I came to terms with the collision of the past, present, and future. There would be sad tears and angry tears and maybe one or two happy tears lost somewhere in-between.

"How was your funeral? Did people grieve for you? Was that little boy whose innocence you murdered waiting for you on the other side? Did you see him? What did you say to him? Did you apologize for what you did?"

There were no answers from beyond. Nothing aside from the soft whimper of the night as rays cut through the dark. The sky was starting to bleed. The air was full of tension. The feeling was raging, roaring, escalating with too much pressure.

"You deprived me of my life—my identity. You were the blinding darkness in which I lived, but my eyes are finally adjusting," I said with conviction, grasping onto the flower. "The world is a place for survivors, for veterans of the internal battles we have to fight every single day. You were the cruelest of warfare, but not anymore. It's over. It's done. It's time."

Something inside cracked.

Something inside fractured.

Something inside shattered.

I was no longer trapped inside the house where no one called home. I was no longer burning from the heat. I was no longer suffering from the past. The restraints were no more. I had finally broken free from the ties that bind.

With assurance, I rose to my feet and stood my ground. "I've spent too much time searching for my place, and acceptance was where I least suspected it. There was no need to run away for all the answers. They were right here in this small town all along."

The resounding dawn of a new day made its way across the sky. The sun breached the horizon, shining with all its glorious light of redemption. Morning had chased away the darkness of night. At last, my dawn had finally arrived. I lifted my face and let sunlight wash over me. A steady breath rattled through my lungs as if it were my first.

"That little boy isn't lost. Not anymore. I've finally found him."

I smelled the flower once more, and then I laid it on top of the buried earth. Slowly, I turned to face the east. The little boy held my hand, and we were as one as we walked toward the light.

I am new.
I am soaring.
I am weightless.

acknowledgements

Thank you:

<insert your name here> for reading

Mom and Dad for being loving and supportive parents

Meagan for being my rock, encouraging me, and editing my grammar mistakes while I was writing

Zach for being such a talented graphic designer and giving *I AM* a "face" with his book cover design

Whitney for being my Wise Girl

Addison and Alicia for your larger-than-life personalities and delightful shenanigans

Shay and Draven for advising and offering insight

Sagan for helping to inspire the short story "Subterfuge Grocery" that was the basis for this novel

All the haters in the literary world for rejecting me and declaring that I'm not good enough to write; you've helped me to realize I am one hell of a writer who has the power to write, write, write, write, write. Write you off.

about the author

Matthew Hubbard grew up in Alabama, and he knows more than he is willing to admit about small towns. Ask him what he wants to be when he grows up, and he will say the catcher in the rye. His goal in life is to give back and make a difference. He believes in shooting stars, four-leaf clovers, and eyelash wishes. He talks to himself in different accents. He is rather strange.

Visit his website if you desire to know more: www.matthewdalehubbard.com